Cee in the MIRROR

A Novel

GREG CARSON

ILLUMIFY
MEDIA.COM

CONTENTS

ACKNOWLEDGMENTS

I want to thank my precious wife, Vivian, for all she did to assist me in completing this novel. She proofread my manuscript and provided feedback from beginning to end. She also graciously accepted that the work would take me away from her for hours at a time. Her continuous support helped me to the finish line, for which I'm eternally grateful.

INTRODUCTION

Fourteen-year-old Cara Corrigan, displaced from her comfortable life in Texas, battles bitterness and an imagination she can't explain. Her father's promotion uprooted the family, sending the family to the Denver area. Cara couldn't fight the move that separated her from her closest friends. She despises her new surroundings, and the resentment she feels is controlling her life. Her parents are perplexed at their daughter's anger but don't know what to do.

When Cara's father brings an antique mirror to her bedroom, Cara's world is rocked. But is it only her mind running wild again? Cara turns to her best friend, Gracie, for clarity.

Cara is plagued at night by horrible dreams and during the day she experiences bullying that others deny even happens. When Cara overhears her patents' private conversation, she spirals further down a dark path, constantly talking to herself for reassurance.

Her dreams and imaginations continue while family relationships deteriorate, drawing her closer to the girl in the mirror, who is also facing dire circumstances. Cara must help her but doesn't know how or if she has the courage to do so.

A much-needed relationship blossoms when Cara meets Davey—a young man she trusts. With his and Gracie's help, she regains her senses enough to find the courage to do the right thing. They support her, but Gracie and Davey don't believe Cara's claims about the mirror. When Aunt Anna comes for a visit, her revelations rock the family to the core.

As Christmas approaches, the family looks forward to grandma's visit. She has valuable information needed to make critical decisions. And as they ponder those decisions, danger forces Cara to muster the courage she's never had. But can she make the sacrifice? And if she does, what will become of her?

1
IT BEGINS

"I guess I'm an enigma. I'll try to explain if I can. It started a long time ago, but I'll begin last May when Brent Corrigan got the break of a lifetime, the one he always hoped for."

"What break?"

"He accepted a promotion that moved our family from Texas to Colorado, Dr. Symons."

"That was a problem?"

"Not for him. It fulfilled his dreams, gave him the prestige that he always wanted. Now he had the house and car that said, 'Look at me, everyone, I've made it!'"

"How did that affect you?"

"It ruined my life. I was comfortable in Texas; it's all I knew. But now, there were no more sleepovers with the eighty-sixers, no sharing the secrets of fourteen-year-old girls and holding hands through tough times. I felt powerless—full of fear—and didn't know how to cope with the move. I begged him not to do it, but there was no changing his mind. I never experienced such hurt and betrayal. It must sound odd that it affected me that way, but I went into a deep depression. And it got worse after our move to the Denver area in September. I was slipping away."

"I'm afraid you've lost me. A fourteen-year-old American girl, a move from Texas, I'm confused."

"Of course you are, Doctor Symons. I'll try to explain as I relate the events from the diary and my memory."

October 14, 1982, 6:05 p.m.

"Bring the milk while you're in there."

"Anything else?"

"That's all."

Dad's sitting at the dining room table with the milk in one hand and his bottle of Coors in the other. Mom's looking down, as usual, with that sullen look on her face. Ahh, better go in, Cara, so they don't think you're spying on them.

"Where's Danny?"

"Your brother's staying at Luke's tonight."

"He's been doing that a lot, Mom."

Father's coolly tapping his fingers on the modern dining room table with square corners. He's staring at the wall behind me, the three round mirrors against gold-flecked wallpaper. It's a stylish, large dining room; everyone says so. Maybe, but I loved the cozy nook next to the kitchen in Texas—small and homey.

"Your plate's in the oven, Cara—been there for twenty minutes. I called you three times."

Meatloaf, mashed potatoes, and peas. Yuk! Father's still avoiding my stare as he tips his bottle of beer. Mother's finally raising her head and looking at me from a great distance. The large table makes me feel like I'm on first base, Mom's at home, and Dad's on third.

"Can't you try to replace that frown with a smile? For the ump-teenth time, Cara, when are you going to get through whatever this is and accept your new life here?"

No, Mom, I'll just keep rolling these peas around on my plate, saying nothing.

"Dammit, Cara, stop that! Eat your supper."

Sure, Father. I'm forcing down a few bites, but now Mother's starting in again.

"Your father and I are at our wit's end. This hiding out and feeling sorry for yourself has to end. Trust that we're making the best decisions we can for the family."

She's hardly coming up for air, a repeat performance for the third time this week. "I see that you got the mirror out of storage."

"Have you decided if you want it in your bedroom?"

"I guess I'll take it, Mom."

"I'll bring it up later."

"Wait till after seven, Dad."

7:40 p.m.

"It's heavier than it looks. Where do you want it, Cara?"

"Hmm, here, by my bed, next to the closet."

"Kinda awkward there; not much room."

"I wanna see myself when I sit on the bed. That's good, right there. I still have room to get in the closet. And I can see the window in the mirror."

"Whatever you want. Would make more sense by your dresser where there's more room."

This mirror is clunky. I hope it'll be useful. But I'll never like the room. It's larger and has more stuff, but I miss my comfy bedroom in Texas.

"What the . . . what was that?"

"What, Cara?"

"The mirror sparked or something. You didn't see it?"

"I didn't see anything. I swear, Cara, I'm more than a little concerned about you. What next?"

Storming out of the room again—saying nothing—so what's new? Oh, the phone, it's 7:45. Gracie's weekly call.

"Gee."

"No, Potsy Webber."

"Don't barf me out with Potsy. I laughed at that once, not again. I'm still not in the mood for it, Gee."

"Come on, Cee. Knock, knock."

"No jokes, Gracie! I wanna cry not laugh."

"Cara, you're sense of humor's slipping away. How can I help? You've been my bestie for years. Tell me what you need."

"Just listen to me ramble; help me through it. That's all."

"I'll try, Cee. Any news this week?" *What should I say? Look at this room, the window.*

"Cee, are you still there?"

"Ah, sure. What did you say?"

"Anything new in your life?"

"The mirror father brought from storage. I'm not sure if I like it. Mother says it's an antique. Could be valuable."

"What's it look like, Cara? Where'd it come from?"

"Full length, kinda oval. Mother said it's French provincial. Gotta cool edge. She said it's gilded gold, swirls, and that sort of thing. They had it in storage. I guess my grandma got it from Germany. It's by the bed, so I can see myself in it and next to the closet to check out my clothes."

"You told me already but tell me again where everything is."

"Well, my full-sized bed's on the north wall, facing south. It has two bedside tables with the mirror and closet to the left. On the south wall, to the east, is my new dresser. Across from the bed is my new vanity. Next to it, on the west, is that old chest of drawers. You remember it. There's a stuffed chair next to it, the one that was in our den. The cedar chest and seat are under my window to the west."

"Sounds like the bomb to me."

"I guess. It just doesn't matter. I mean, it's nice, but I don't care. But something happened tonight that threw me, Gee. The mirror sparked or flashed. It was weird."

"Spooky. Does light shine through your window?"

"No, it wasn't from the window."

"Had to be something like that, Cara; what else could it be?"

"Only in my head, I guess. Father was standing close by but didn't see it. I wonder if I'm losing it."

"Don't say that! Gives me the willies. Anything else going on?"

"Uh-huh, that same boy at school. Freaks me out, Gracie. He doesn't say a word; he stares at me. It's daggers, and I don't understand why. I've never done anything to him."

"I don't like it at all. Have you told anyone?"

"What would I say? He hasn't done anything except psych me out."

"I have to go. Be careful, Cee.

"Yeah. I'll call at this time next week. Bye, Gee."

2
DANGEROUS

October 19, 1982, 3:12 p.m.

"Oh, why's he doing it? Leave me alone. Stop staring at me! I don't understand; I've never done anything to him. Stop talking to yourself, Cara; that man's looking at you." *Dear God, I'm so rattled. I hate this walk home; twelve blocks of endless houses and people. And all of them are happier than me. Why not? They have no problems and live in nice homes with beautiful yards and trees shedding their leaves. I'm surprised that you noticed, Cara, you usually walk through life's scenes seeing little or no detail. Face it, bitterness has turned you inward, causing you to miss any beauty around you. Why can't Mom or Dad pick me up? Get a hold of yourself, Cara—get a grip now. I'm not sure what's what anymore. Am I imagining it? Chill, maybe he's staring into space, drugged out or something. That girl in history class said his name is Albert Hobbins. Dumbass name.*

No! Why's he coming across the street toward me? Stay . . . stay cool. Ahh . . . no one around. Run for it! No, no, walk slowly and keep your eyes ahead, don't look back. Are you imagining it? "Ow, get your hands off me! What are you doing?"

"Stop! I've been yelling at you to stop."

"Why? You've hurt my arm, Albert. Let me go!"

"Damn you. Why ya saying those things about me?"

"I've never said anything about you. I don't know you. Ow! That hurt—stop, please!"

"Stop crying. Tell me what's going on. Take that, ugly bitch! Get up; you're not hurt."

He hit me. I can't believe he hit me. "Help, help!" *Thank God, a police car.* "Stop! Stop!"

"What in hell are you doing, young lady? We almost ran you over."

"I'm sorry, officer. I had to stop you; he's attacking me."

"Who's attacking you? What's going on?"

"Him, Albert Hobbins, over there!"

"Which one, young lady? There's two boys with two girls."

"What? Where did they come from?"

"Which one was it?"

"That one, Albert Hobbins."

"Okay, young man, what do you have to say?"

"She attacked me for no reason."

"What? I never attacked you!"

"She sure did, officer."

"And what's your name, young lady?"

"Andrea Wicks. We were walking down the street when she ran across from the other side. She was yelling at Al. Kept saying, 'Why do you keep staring at me?'"

"That's a lie, officer! Albert came up from behind—punched me and threw me to the ground. He kept saying, 'Why are you saying those things about me?'"

"No, no, that's not it. After yelling at Al, she grabbed his jacket and scratched his face. See the blood on his cheek."

"What's your name, son?"

"David Elliot."

"That is quite a scratch, Albert. She did it?"

"Yeah, she's nuts."

"He's a damn liar; I never touched him!"

"Well, that's not what they're all saying. I see the scratch on Albert's face, and I don't see any dirt or grass stains on your skirt or jacket. What's your name, young lady?"

"Cara Corrigan."

"You better come with me, Miss Corrigan. Wipe your eyes and get in the squad car. I'll drive you home. The rest of you can leave unless you want to press charges."

"I don't. Just keep the crazy away from me."

3:28 p.m.

"Ahh, this is your house?"

"Yes."

"Nice. I always liked a two-story with dormers. Is your mother home?"

"She should be."

"Okay, I'll ring the bell and we'll have a talk with her."

I'm getting sick. What's she gonna say when the door opens? She has to believe me, but she might not. Stop crying, get ahold of yourself, Cara. Oh, she's opening the door.

"What . . . what's happened, Cara?"

"An altercation with a boy coming home from school, ma'am. I'm Officer Smith."

At least mother's taking me in her arms and trying to comfort me. If I don't calm down, I'm going to lose it.

"That doesn't sound like Cara."

"Well, they had different accounts as to what happened. But there were four of them who said your daughter's story was false. Apparently, she attacked a boy and scratched his face deep enough for it to bleed. She was so upset that I felt it best to bring her home."

"It's not true, Mom! The boy attacked me for no reason. They all lied."

"I believe you, Cara. Are you going to take any action, officer?"

"No, the boy's not pressing charges. But your daughter should stay clear of him to avoid further trouble."

"I understand. Thanks for bringing Cara home."

"Sure. Have a good day, ma'am."

"Um, Cara, Cara. Go up and wash your face. Lie down for a while and settle yourself."

"You don't believe me, do you?"

"I never said that. It's just everything going on with you, and now this. What do I do? Why would that boy attack you, Cara?"

"I don't know, and that's the truth."

"Go upstairs now; I need to think about it; your father won't be happy."

8:23 p.m.

"What's he doing here, Danny?"

"Dude, your sister needs to chill."

"Yeah, good luck with that, Luke. He's staying over tonight, Sis."

"Mm, why? I don't want him in here. This is my room; no visitors—get it?"

"Bitchn' room, though. How'd she get it, Sherlock, and you got the dink room? Thought you were the oldest, bro."

"Doesn't matter to me. You know, it's that thing I told you about."

"The thing is me, Danny. You've already told him; why cover it over now. They gave me the room to stop my moaning, Ace. To soothe me—shut me up. Understand?"

"Don't rag on him, Cara. He doesn't mean anything by it. Anyway, you're in enough trouble without borrowing more. Dad's ticked at you about what happened today. And you didn't help yourself by zipping it at the dinner table. What really happened?"

"Um, Albert Hobbins happened."

"That sucks, dude. Tell your sister to stay clear; he's bad news—dangerous!"

"Duh, I speak English; you can talk directly to me, Luke."

"I would if you'd stay in one place instead of pacing back and forth like a caged tiger. What did Hobbins do to you anyway?"

"Attacked me and threw me to the ground. Then when a cop showed up, they lied and said I started the fight. No one believed me because he had a big scratch on his face."

"Who was with him, Sis?"

"Two girls."

"He's always got toadies with him, bro. I'd say totally stay away from them, girl. Righteous stuff: bed, vanity, and that mirror—whoa!"

"Who said you could walk around my room and pick up stuff?"

"No harm meant. High bed. Lots of room to hide under it. Big closet. I bet there's plenty of room to hide in there too. Nice window; three people could hide behind those drapes."

"What's he saying, Danny? Sounds threatening to me."

"He's harmless, Sis. Let's book, Luke; we've got more important things to do."

October 21, 7:55 p.m.

"Cee?"

"Sorry, I'm late. It's been an awful week, Gracie."

"I was starting to worry; you're usually on time. What's going on now?"

"What I dreaded, Gee. The boy I told you about attacked me on Tuesday."

"Attacked you . . . dear Lord, how did that happen?"

"I was walking home from school. I saw Albert Hobbins following me. He had three boys and two girls with him. They rushed me, and he started cussing at me. He walloped me, Gee, knocked me down."

"My God, kid, he hit you?"

"Hard. But I got up. I was mad as hell and started flailing my arms. I must have hit him; he had a big scratch on his face that bled."

"Good for you! That's the spirited Cee I know."

"But they all lied—said I started the fight. If the police hadn't shown up, I don't know what would have happened. But no one believes me, Gee. You do . . . don't you?"

"Of course, don't cry, Cara."

"Huhu, I need to put the phone down for a sec—get some Kleenex. . . . ."

"Where were you, Cee? It takes three minutes to get Kleenex?"

"Something happened. Hmm, I might be losing it, Gracie. When I went to the vanity, I saw a shadow in the drapes."

"Yeah, isn't there light shining in that throws shadows?"

"No, you don't understand. It was a person's shadow; at least, I think so."

"You're sure?"

"Not exactly; I'm starting to think I can't tell what's real and what isn't. It scared me stiff to walk to the window. I was shaking when I pulled back the drapes, and no one was there. How did I get so screwed up? My anger and fear have turned me inward. I think only of myself. I walk through each day seeing little of life's detail around me. I wish I could go back to when life was sweet. Remember when we were eight? Our lives were simple, so good. School was even fun."

"And we enjoyed church and Sunday school."

"I miss that too, Gee. We sang happy songs, learned about God, went on picnics. Even made commitments and promises to God."

"Yeah, sad, it's only a memory now."

"Hmm, my father again. I can't remember what caused it, Gracie. The pastor said something that ticked him off. No one ever told me what it was, but we were out the church door and never came back."

"Then our family left a month later. Do you ever think about what we learned, Cara? Do you believe it—still believe in God?"

"I guess. I don't practice it, but I pray sometimes; lately, a lot. I think I've been mad at my father from the day we stopped going to church. I'm always asking myself why I can't have a father who loves me the way he should."

"Ahh, he must, Cee. It's probably hard for him to show it."

"I don't know but remember how they taught us in Sunday school about our loving heavenly Father. I want my father to have that kind of love for me. He could at least try, but he won't. Everything's for his career, trying to pretend it's about taking care of us. I see through it. You know that I can't remember when dad said he loved me, let alone took me in his arms and comforted me. And lately, Mom's been distant too."

"I focused more on Jesus' love for us, Cara, how he died for miserable people. I don't understand why, but I believe He did."

"I have a hard time believing; I want to. Hmm, I remember one Bible verse about the greatest thing you could do is lay down your life for a friend. But I know I could never do that, Gee. I failed as a Christian and can't find the faith that better days are ahead."

"I struggle with it, too, so don't be so hard on yourself. Anything else? I don't want your time to run over and get you in even more trouble with your parents."

"Well, I shouldn't tell you, but the mirror sparked again last night. Now you'll think I've gone over the edge for sure."

"Of course not, but what's going on with the mirror?"

"Maybe it's haunted—has a spell on it."

"Be careful, Cee, that's scary. I better go."

"I wish you could talk longer—keep me company. I could listen to your cute Texas drawl all night."

"And don't lose that hint of a drawl up north. Cara, always know that I love you."

"Uh-huh, love you too, Gracie—bye."

"Bye."

3
DESCENDING

October 26, 1982, 3:22 p.m.

"Mother, where are you?" *She's already ten minutes late—she should be here! Most of the kids are long gone. I hate these ugly stairs and pipe handrails.* "Andrea Wicks." *She's staring at me. God, why won't they leave me alone? Why is she still here? Walk normally to the curb, Cara; don't let on that you see her.*

"Ouch! My books are all over the place."

"So sorry—didn't see you."

Don't say anything, Cara; just pick up your stuff and get out of here. You bitch, Andrea! Shove the papers back in your notebook, no time to straighten them. Keep your head down; move—quick. Thank God, there's Mom. Run!

"Fasten your seat belt, Cara."

"Where were you, Mother? Being late put me through another terrible experience. Did you see what happened? Watch out!"

"Aah, I almost hit that boy! They don't even watch where they're going."

"Get us out of here, Mom."

"I will; calm down. I'm sorry about being late, Cara; I got tied up at the store. What happened now?"

"Andrea Wicks knocked my books out of my hands on purpose. Papers were all over, and she pretended like it was an accident."

"She's not one of the girls—

"She is one of the girls who lied about me. If you'd only been on time, Mom!"

"Oh, dear, are you okay?"

"No! I wanna go home; forget all about it if I can. Crap! She messed up the corner on my library book."

"Cara! Watch your language; that's no reason to be vulgar. Library book, what are you reading?"

"*The Diary of Anne Frank.*"

"Huh, why that book? I mean, I read it at your age; I even liked the movie. But it's a downer—depressing. Do you want to take all that in now?"

"We've been studying about Europe during World War Two in history class. Miss Walters said it might give us a new perspective on things that happened. So far, I like it. I know it's sad, but I like how her father loved her and she loved him. That makes me feel good."

"Hmm, I'm surprised that that would catch your attention with all that's going on in the story."

"To be honest, Mother, you don't know why?"

"I hope you're not talking about your father again. How many times do I have to tell you that he's looking out for our best interests and loves you."

"Do you remember the last time he said it? When he comforted me? I don't."

"Your father's not demonstrative; you know that, Cara. It's the same with Danny and me. He's trying his best to take care of us, but he isn't a perfect man—he's made his share of mistakes. Mistakes I can't go into now; maybe when you're older."

"I don't care about all of that. I only want a father who'll put his arms around me and make me feel secure and loved. A father like Otto Frank."

"Darnit! Please get out, dear, and move Danny's bike out of the driveway. I swear, how's that boy ever going to be responsible for driving a car."

Sure, Mom, thanks for laying more baggage on me about Dad.

October 27, 1982, 9:54 p.m.

"Ow! Darn mirror, that hurt!" *Clumsy, watch where you're going, or wear shoes, Cara. This mirror has to go.* "You're sparking. Not again!" *What's this mirror trying to tell me? Spooky—definitely has to go tomorrow.*

10:03 p.m.

I'm so exhausted. I have to sleep tonight. What did Mom mean about Dad? Is it what I think? What else could it be? Just get it out of your mind, Cara. Lord, help me to sleep, please! Don't stub your toe again; be careful getting to the window. "Ahh, no, not again!" *It can't be a person; you're losing it. But the shadow looks like a person. Stop shaking. Get ahold of yourself, Cara; it can't be real. Go slowly, step by step. Here goes; pull back the drapes quickly.* "Whew, thank God no one's there." *Okay, time for bed. Pull the covers over your head and pray for sleep.*

11:58 p.m.

"What's that? Something, someone's under the bed. Oh no, what should I do? Ahh, a hand! What? Who? Albert Hobbins! Get off me, what'd ya doing? Help! Help! Someone help me!"

"Cara, Cara, wake up, Cara! You're having another nightmare; wake up!"

"Mom! Oh, it was a horrible dream. I'm out of breath."

"What happened? Another dream?"

"Yes, Danny, your sister's had another nightmare."

"Fifth time, at least, since we moved. What is it, Mom? She never had any in Texas."

"Probably everything piling up on her, Son. I'll hold her for a minute and hopefully she'll be able to go back to sleep. In fact, you should sleep with me tonight, Cara."

"Thanks, Mom, but Dad won't always be out of town. I'm old enough to face a bad dream and not fall apart. Maybe you could sit with me until I go to sleep, Danny."

"Sure, Sis, I'll sit in the stuffed chair till you get back to sleep."

October 28, 1982, 2:49 a.m.

"Ahh, Danny, Danny! Are you there, Danny?" *Turn on the lamp. He must have gone back to bed. My head's spinning. Sit up for a minute. Um, feeling strange.* "Look at yourself in the mirror." *Not good at all, Mirrors don't lie, but you're looking weird. You're not seeing right. What's going on? Your face is blurred—distorted. It's the mirror; it has to go.*

"Is someone there? Hello, hello."

"What? God, now you're losing it badly, Cara; hearing a voice in the mirror."

"I can faintly hear you; who's there?" *Turn off the light and bury yourself under the covers. Dear God, what is it? Am I really losing my mind? I must be since I'm hearing whispers coming from a mirror. I'll never sleep now.*

7:42 p.m.

"Call Gracie. You need to tell her what happened. Thank God. Gee?"

"Not Potsy. You sound out of breath."

"I have a lot to tell you. Nothing good, Gee."

"I've got news, too, but tell me yours first."

"I'm losing it, Gracie. It's been one thing after the other, all week. Yesterday was the worst. Albert Hobbins's toady, Andrea, knocked the books out of my hand on purpose. Later I thought I saw someone hiding behind the drapes."

"Again!"

"Yeah, but like before, no one was there. I must be going crazy. Later I had an awful dream; Albert was hiding under the bed, then he jumped me. He had rape in mind. I screamed loud enough to wake up Mom and Danny. But the worst came later. I woke up in a fog. Then the strangest thing happened. The spooky mirror went off again. I had a distorted, blurry face, Gracie—couldn't recognize myself. Then I heard a faint voice calling out to me. I swear I heard it, but how could that happen?"

"Umm, wish I knew. Do you need help, Cee?"

"What kind? Like a shrink? I'm almost to the point where I don't know—maybe. But now I need to get it out of my mind. So what's your news, Gracie; hope it's better than mine."

"Only a little. Bee's moving away in January. Her mother's sister has a ranch in California. They think it would be a good change for both of them."

"Oh, I've only talked to Belle twice since we moved; I miss her a lot."

"We've drifted apart, Cee—don't know why. And Tanya's hot on a new boy. I see her at school, but she doesn't come over anymore."

"A boy taking her away was going to happen sooner or later. She's the beauty. The three of us did well in never being jealous of Tee."

"But it's not like we're dogs. I think you're cute, Cee. So did Joey Aston. He might have been your first real boyfriend if you hadn't moved away."

"I don't know; could have been, I guess. Everything's changing too quickly. Except for you and me, it looks like the eighty-sixers are no more."

"That brings me to the bad news; I hate to tell you."

"You're scaring me now, Gracie; I don't need more bad news. So what is it?"

"Did you tell your mother about the mirror talking to you?"

"Ahh, yes, this morning."

"You know she talks with my mom sometimes."

"I guess it slipped my mind; I didn't know it was a big deal, Gee. Are you saying my mom called her?"

"She did and told her about all the things going on with you, including the mirror."

"My God, why would she blab it all over?"

"According to my mom, she's concerned about you, Cee. She even mentioned psych help. They both think it's to the point where help is needed."

"What?"

"That's what I dread telling you, Cara. Mother thinks your issues will drag me down. I don't think so, but she does."

"I'd never hurt you, Gee."

"Of course, you wouldn't. I know that. But I've worried about you a lot. It's depressing to see my bestie go through this crap."

"Oh, Gracie, I'm sorry."

"I'll come straight out with it. They don't want us to call each other for a while. I hate it, Cee."

"You've got to be kidding—not that!"

"I'm hurting too. I look forward to our weekly calls. But it's temporary; keep that in mind. Mom said if you start getting through this stuff, we can start calling each other again."

"That sounds like forever. How do they think taking away the best thing in my life will help?"

"They don't, Cee. They're protecting me, even though I don't want it. Now you have me crying."

"I can't help myself. I'll cry all night. So this time, it's really goodbye."

"Not forever—remember that."

"I'll try. Bye, Gee."

9:12 p.m.

You can't cry anymore. Stop it, Cara! Sit here on the bed and calm down. Get ahold of yourself; it's temporary like Gee said. Darnit, now your eyes'll be all puffy and red. Look at 'em. Oh, I can't see them. My face is blurry. It's happening again; I can't make myself out in the mirror. Forget it. Turn the lamp off and get under the covers.

"Wait . . . I can see something. Is anyone there?"

"What!" *Ahh, did I really hear that? It couldn't be, could it?* "Who is it? What do you want?"

"You do hear me. I can barely make out your form and only hear you faintly."

"You can see me?"

"I see your form in the mirror. I see your hair, but your face is hard to make out."

"Mirror, you're looking in a mirror?"

"Yes."

"Your voice is stronger now. You have an accent."

"So do you; I can hear you clearly now. Your face is coming into focus. I see your brown hair and brown eyes."

"Um, do you see my face where yours should be?"

"I do." *This can't be, Cara; slap yourself, do anything to snap out of it. But I clearly see her face now; brown hair, blue eyes, perfect nose, and mouth—so beautiful.*

"Are you still there?"

"I am. I'm just doubting what I see. You can't be real."

"I'm sure that I am."

"Who are you? Where are you? How can I see you in my mirror?"

"Well, I have no idea about what's happening. But I'm sure of who I am. I'm Britta Schumann, and I live in Stuttgart."

"I don't know where that is—haven't heard of it."

"You haven't heard of Stuttgart? Where in the world are you?"

"West of Denver, in Colorado."

"In America!"

"In America, of course, where else would I be?"

"In Germany, like me. This is quite confusing. How can I be seeing someone all the way across the ocean?"

"I'm totally psyched out."

"I've never heard such a funny phrase. English always baffles me."

"Wait a minute. You say you're German, but you clearly speak English. What's up with that?"

"I speak three languages: German, French, and English. My father's a language professor, and he taught me."

"Oh, I barely get by with English."

"Cara, who are you talking to?"

"What are you doing, Mother? You just can't barge into my room. Were you listening at the door?"

"No, I was walking by and heard you talking. I'm sorry, but I didn't hear any other voices. I thought you were talking to Gracie again."

"No! Darnit, now she's gone. I mean, forget it, Mom."

"You're looking at the mirror, Cara. Please tell me that's not it. You're not talking to that foolish mirror, are you?"

"So what if I am? Maybe I'm going bonkers."

"That's it! I've had it up to here with this business, Cara. We're going to do something about it and soon. We can't put up with it anymore!"

"What, Mom, what are you going to do?"

"I don't know but something. Now get to bed!"

October 29, 1982, 3:08 p.m.

Don't look around, Cara; keep your eyes down. Danny, Danny—come' on! Thank God. "Where were you? You know I don't like standing around after school."

"Chill, Sis! I said I'd walk you home since Mom can't pick you up."

"Damnit, it's too late now, Danny!"

"Where'd ya think you're going, Danny boy?"

"We're going home, Hobbins. Please move; we don't want any trouble."

"Ha, ha, please; he's making nice, Andrea. I've heard about you, Corrigan. You think you're the bad dude in school now. Maybe we'll take it outside and see."

"Stop shoving my brother; leave him alone! He never said anything like that." *My God, Hobbins is pushing two-hundred pounds, and Danny is barely one-fifty—he'd get killed.*

"Shush, Cara! No, we're not going outside. We're going home."

"Chickie, chickie, chickie."

"Oh, shut up, Andrea! I'm going home; get out of my way. Come on, Danny."

"Maybe not today, but your time's coming—both of you, right, Andrea?"

"You don't have to run, Sis. We're two blocks away from school, and no one's following us. Thanks for sticking up for me, but I can take care of myself."

"He's a monster, Danny; he'd really hurt you. I couldn't take that; it'd be my fault. They're after me; you shouldn't have to pay."

"But what would it look like if I didn't stick up for my sister?"

"Thanks. Where's Luke?"

"His father wanted him home early, something to do with the church."

"Isn't he kind of out there, Danny? How'd you ever get involved with him? I mean, he isn't your type—not like your friends in Texas."

"Yeah, he kinda latched on to me."

"Umm, how's that?"

"Well, he just came up to me one day and started talking. We seemed to have the same interests, and he complimented me a lot. It went from there, and now he wants to be around all the time."

"That's weird, Danny. Don't you think?"

"A little—haven't thought that much about it. Kinda strange, though. He's gotta problem with his father and thinks the people in their church are hypocrites. He goes when he has to but doesn't believe in religion."

"Huh, does he take anything seriously?"

"Not most of the time. But he lost it once—went ballistic. He got furious with me instantly for no reason. In a minute he was okay again, apologizing all over the place."

"Something about him I don't like, Danny. I don't know what but be careful."

"Is it going any better for you trying to make friends?"

"I've given up. Twice I thought a girl was warming up to me. Remember, Allison, who came over to the house?"

"Yeah, why did she stop coming over?"

"I don't know, Danny. I thought about it a lot, but no answers—the same with Mary Ahern. When we started to get close, she stopped talking to me just like Allison."

"Umm, like someone told them to?"

"That's what I thought. Thanks for walking me home, for being there when those asses showed up."

10:11 p.m.

The ceiling's spinning. Put the book down, Cara. Close your eyes. It must be eye strain. Or could it be something else? Lord, I don't know anymore. I can't concentrate on what I'm reading, anyway. How did Anne go through hell like that? Where did she get the courage? I'd die right away. Moving to another state totally frazzled me. But at least she had the love of her father. That's it! That's what got her through. He takes her in his arms and comforts her; what a special father. I'd make it to if I had a father like that. The room stopped spinning. Get up. It's time for bed. You're quiet tonight, mirror, I guess you can't spark with my coat over you.

No, they're fighting again. Stop yelling! What is it this time? You shouldn't, Cara, but let's see. Tiptoe be still. Watch the table. Don't get any closer to their door; you can hear them from here.

"Quiet down, Sarah! You'll have the kids in here again."

"I don't care anymore; they're old enough to know the truth, anyway!"

"Yeah, your truth, of course."

"We're not doing this, Brent. I screwed up, and I've paid for it ever since. I'm not blaming you again. You know your part, what you did to me."

"Let it go then; let's get some sleep."

"No, not yet. I'm too upset about Cara. I need clarity on what to do for her. I need your help—your support."

"I'm as baffled as you, Sarah."

"Help me, Brent. Should I tell Cara about her great-grandmother? I've sheltered her and Danny from it all their lives. Maybe it's time."

"Why?"

"They're old enough now; it's only fair they know the danger they may face."

"You're treading on thin ice, Sarah. Cara's already out of control. Knowing her great-grandmother committed suicide in an insane asylum with a mental illness that's hereditary won't help."

"Umm, I suppose you're right. The doctors say it might skip generations. We don't know when or if it'll strike again. It could hit me and skip Cara."

"So, it serves no purpose to tell the kids when we don't know what'll happen."

"Okay, Brent, you're right; we'll leave it alone for now."

I'm done! Don't start crying here, Cara; get back to your room. Oh, God, I am going crazy, and I don't believe it's my fault. It's not fair! What now? What will I do? What can I do? Now a crazy relative from the past's going to ruin my life. Hang on, don't lose it now. Wait! What about the fight before they dropped the bomb on me? What did Mom mean when she said, "I screwed up?" And what did she mean before when she said that Father wasn't a perfect man? It can't be what I'm thinking—can it? Get to bed and forget about what you heard, if you can.

"What! Not again, please, God." *Get your coat off the mirror before it burns.* "Stop it, stop sparking!"

"Are you there?"

"Ahh, Britta? Of course, it is; who else could it be?"

"Yes. I see and hear you much clearer than before. You know my name, but I didn't get yours."

"Cara Corrigan."

"A pleasant, melodic name for a sweet girl. I don't know why, but I feel close to you, Cara."

"Sweet couldn't describe me now, Britta. I feel sour inside."

"Oh, why?"

"What my father did. I resent it so much. He took my life away, and I'll never forgive him."

"What did he do to you, Cara?"

"He took a job promotion, and we moved from Texas to Colorado. I had to leave my close friends and the only life I knew. And now I can't get past it."

"But you're safe, not in danger, right?"

"Well, yes."

"Aren't you thankful for what you have? I treasure my few possessions and try not to dwell on what I lack."

"I'm not that strong. It must sound like I'm spoiled and unthankful; I guess I am. But I can't get past it, Britta. And with the mirror and you—and what I learned tonight—I think I'm going nuts."

"What happened tonight?"

"I don't want to go into it now. It's my parents . . . marital problems, that's all I want to say. I could trade both of them in about now."

"That's sad, Cara. I loved my mother, and father's my rock. His love is special."

"Is your mother gone?"

"Yes, cancer three years ago. Father's my only protector. But he makes me feel secure in a world that isn't."

"Oh, I could only dream of a father like that; you're blessed, Britta."

"Yes, I am. I was wondering, how old are you, Cara?"

"I'll be fifteen in three months. How about you?"

"Sixteen in four months. I thought you looked about my age. And I can't tell you how glad I am to have someone to talk with, even though it's all so strange. I'm in my second year of what I think you would call high school."

"I'm a freshman, first year."

"What are you studying in school? What do you enjoy doing? I like to read and treasure the books father brings me."

"In world history, we're studying about your country. And it's a coincidence that I'm reading *The Diary of Anne Frank*. Go figure."

"I don't understand; who's Anne Frank?"

"What! Now I'm confused. You live in Germany and don't know about Anne Frank. The story of her life's classic. Everyone here knows about her."

"Oh, I'm sorry, but I haven't heard the story."

"Huh, they were German Jews hiding in a secret compartment in Amsterdam. Someone turned them in, and they went to a Nazi concentration camp where Anne died. It's inspiring but sad. It all happened back in World War Two, what we're studying in history class."

"What do you mean, Cara, back in World War Two?"

"It's history. It happened forty years ago."

"What! What year is it?"

"That's a silly question, 1982, of course."

"Oh my, maybe we're both losing our minds, Cara. You won't like this, but the date is September 9, 1943, at least in my world."

"Ah, I don't know what to say. This whole thing gets weirder all the time. You're totally real to me, and I like you a lot, Britta, and I need a true friend now. But I know it can't be real. I'm definitely going insane; the past has caught up with me."

"No, no, you're not. I can't explain it, but what we're experiencing is real. It has to be. We each need a special friend, and I know we've already formed a strong bond."

"I feel it too. Where are you, Britta? I only see a bare wall behind you."

"I don't know how to tell you, though I'm starting to see why this is happening. My father and I are hiding from the Gestapo. Just like in the book you're reading, we live in a room behind a secret entrance in a closet."

"Not even! It's impossible that all of a sudden, I see a girl in a mirror who's living the same life as a character in the book I'm reading. Talk about crazy. Doesn't it show that I am, Britta?"

"It would, but I'm experiencing it too, and I think I'm totally sane."

"But why are you there, and who's with you?"

"Just me and my father. The Gestapo arrested him for transporting Jews to Switzerland. Somehow he escaped, and we went on the run for weeks. Then four months ago, a friend of the underground agreed to hide us. The secret room we live in was already in their house."

"Wow, it must be small."

"Only a small bed, a stuffed wooden chair, a small table, and a lamp. And, of course, this full-length antique mirror that they didn't want the Nazis to find. I think it has value. I hate it here. The air is dank, the light dim, and it's cramped. But I'm here day and night, only leaving to go to the bathroom three or four times a day and bathe once in a while. The food they bring is sparse and not appealing. I'm lonely, and now I have someone. Real or imaginary, I treasure you, Cara."

"I don't understand it, but I need you, Britta. We can help each other through whatever we have to face. What time is it there, anyway?"

"About six in the morning."

"That's early. When do you sleep?"

"Any time I want. I don't have a schedule. My father brings me books to read and notebooks to write in, and chocolate sometimes. So I spend my days reading and writing. I only sleep when I get sleepy."

"In a way, it's nice to be free to do what you want when you want. But I get it that doing the same thing, in the same place, day in and day out, is hard to take. I'm feeling a little ashamed, Britta, that I can't cope with my problems. They're minor compared to what you're facing."

"Don't be. I understand."

"What do you write in your notebooks?"

"Of course, I write about what's happening daily, though it isn't exciting. I also write poems and short stories, anything that comes to mind to keep occupied."

"Can we meet in the mirror every day, Britta?"

"I'll always be here, waiting to see you. I'm not going anyplace soon. But I am getting sleepy now; same time tomorrow?"

"Yes. Bye, Britta."

4
THE DECISION

October 30, 1982, 6:12 p.m.

I can't believe all four of us are here for dinner on a Saturday night, definitely unusual. Mom and Dad are still brooding over their fight last night—wish I'd stayed in my room. Dad's gone half the time; maybe he'll find a way to be gone longer. He looks tense, tapping his fingers on the table as usual. Why's Danny so quiet? It seems like he's ready to slide under the table and disappear. They're all halfway to disappearing anyway—so far away. I hate this room, this table.

"Since we're all here, there's something we need to talk about as a family."

Let me guess what it is, Mom.

"Cara, I've discussed this with your father and talked to Danny concerning something you told me. The long and short of it is, Amy Logan knows a reputable psychologist. And, well, I've made an appointment for you to see him next Tuesday."

"But I—"

"Let me finish. We're all concerned about you, Cara. I think this is the best way to help you. We can't let this continue—the imaginations and the mirror. Doctor Reyna's the best way to get through this."

"Do I have a choice?"

"No, it's decided; you'll see the doctor for as long as it takes. And another thing; the mirror has to go. We're putting an ad in the paper to see if we can get something for it. Your father will take it to the basement."

"No! Please don't take it away. You took Gracie away, and now you want to take Britta too."

"My God, Cara, that's precisely why; imaginary friends in a mirror can't help you. It'll only make things worse."

"Umm, I guess, Father, but I need her now, and no one else understands. And why do you have to put me down in front of Danny? He has no part in it."

"He does, Cara. I've talked to Danny and both the boys' and girls' dean at school. As your mother, I had to verify your stories. Albert Hobbins told Dean Borelli that he didn't instigate the incident while you were walking home. He also said that he never shoved or threatened Danny. Dean Hanson said that Andrea Wicks backed up both accounts. She also said that she never purposely bumped into you or pulled your books from your hands."

"Wait, Mom, Danny was there and knows that Albert shoved and threatened him."

"That's not the case; Danny told me that Albert and Andrea were messing around, but that's all."

"Danny! Why did you say that? It's not true. Why are you doing this?"

"I'm sorry, Sis! Stop crying, please. Ahh, I've got to get out of here."

Danny, I don't understand. Now you run away.

"Finish your dinner, Cara; it's getting cold."

"It can freeze, Mom; I'm done!"

"Then go to your room, but you will see Doctor Reyna Tuesday. That's settled; we have to end this craziness!"

7:10 p.m.

"Where are you, Britta? Why can't I see you?" *Oh, God, I haven't lost her, have I? First, it's Gracie and now Britta. I need someone to talk to who understands. Come back, please. Stop crying, Cara; it won't help. Lean over and put your face in your hands, get ahold of yourself. My hands are ice cold. What's wrong with you?* "Help, please!"

"I hear you. Were you calling for help, Cara?"

"Thank God, I thought you left me. Where were you, Britta? I needed you. My family's turned against me. They're lying, and I don't know what to do. And now I have to see a counselor on Tuesday."

"Why would they lie?"

"I don't know—don't know anything now. I think you're real, Britta, but maybe I'm mentally ill, and I only imagine you."

"If you are, I am too. I can't explain it, but our connection is real, Cara."

"I hope so. You scared me; where were you?"

"My father returned from a three-day trip. I worry every minute until he gets back. He brought me chocolate and two notebooks. I sat in his lap for an hour while he held me and said everything would be okay."

"I'm happy for you, Britta. I only wish my father would do that once. I think I could forgive him if he did."

"Forgiveness is powerful, Cara; maybe it's the answer to break your anger."

"I wish I could forgive, but I hate what he did."

"My father's waking. I need to go before he hears me talking to the mirror. I won't be able to meet you for a few days. Goodbye, Cara."

"Bye, Britta." *I hope this isn't the last time I see you. I have to keep the mirror.*

October 31, 1982, 5:07 p.m.

"I'm taking your father to the airport in a few minutes. I want both of you to share passing out candy to the trick-or-treaters. And stop your bickering; do you hear me!"

"Then make him tell why he lied about me, Mom. He clams up—won't say a word."

"Tell her to chill, Mom; I want her to stop bugging me. I can't say any more."

"Then screw you, Danny, I'm going to my room, and you can take care of the kiddies!"

"Cara, Cara! Get back down here now."

"Not happening, Mom."

I could wring his neck! Why would he lie? He's never done anything to hurt me like this. Think, Cara, what could it be? Or maybe who could it be is the question. Luke Glover's the likely one. But why? He's a dweeb hipster but seems harmless. Danny doesn't know anyone else, though, and it's not like him to stab me in the back. You have to figure it out, Cara.

Maybe I'll read more about Anne. No, I wonder if Britta's in the mirror. "Britta, are you there? Britta!" *That's right. She said she wouldn't be able to talk for a few days. I miss seeing her already. Oh, might as well read. What, uh, oh—the closet!* "Who's there? Who's in the closet? Come out!" *Crap, not again, Cara. I see people behind the drapes; now this. Run! Get Danny. No, no, it's nothing. Slide the closet door slowly.* "Ahh!" *Get out of here and down the stairs!*

"What the hell, Cara? You almost knocked me down! Why are you running down the stairs? Why'd you scream?"

"My closet, my closet, Danny—a monster!"

"What? A monster. Come on, have you gone off the rails again?"

"No, no, come see. Be careful!"

"Okay, follow me, Cara. Be quiet, slow, slow. Who's in there? Dammit, there's no one in your closet! What's wrong with you, Sis? You really need a shrink."

"Huh, someone, something was there, Danny. I swear it!"

"Then where'd they go?"

"I don't know. Maybe it was someone wearing a Halloween costume, a monster, or a space creature. I'm not crazy, Danny. I saw it. Tell me where Luke Glover is now."

"His father made him work the Halloween party at their church; why?"

"I don't trust Luke. Could've been him."

"Really, Sis, are you kidding?"

"Okay, but someone was in my closet. You better get downstairs and cover the front door. I'm still ticked at you, though."

5
DOCTOR REYNA

November 2, 1982, 4:32 p.m.

Ahh, I hate this. You don't know if it'll help or hurt, Mom. Umm, no one else here. I guess Mom got the last appointment of the day. What can this guy do to help—maybe he'll screw me up even more. This waiting room's the pits. Yuck, pea-green walls, worn gold shag carpet, old chairs with faded fabric. How does this give me confidence in the doctor behind the door? The door's opening. I guess I'll find out soon enough.

"Can I speak to you for a minute, Mrs. Corrigan?"

"Of course."

"Mom!"

"It's okay, Cara; the doctor will see you in a minute."

Why does he want to talk with Mom first? She'll give him the skinny—tell him all about how crazy I am. No, she won't do that, will she? Maybe fill him in, so he knows what to ask me, how to help. Come on, Mom, I don't want to be here. Maybe I'll leave and walk home. No, they'd just make me come back. Get it over with, Cara. Why won't she come out? Mom, Mom, what are you doing? Finally, it's about time!

"You can go in now, Cara."

"Hello, Cara; I'm Doctor Phillip Reyna. Have a seat over here."

"Ahh, not the couch?"

"No, no, we'll chat over here; get to know each other. Relax and get comfortable. I don't want you to feel threatened in any way."

"How should I feel, knowing what mother probably told you?"

"She only gave me more information related to her concerns for you, Cara. She cares for you a lot and only wants to help."

"So, how does this work?"

"We'll talk, and I'll get to know you. Nothing heavy today. Then we'll see where we go in our next session."

"Oh, next session, how many will it take?"

"That depends on how productive our time together is. It might take a few appointments, or it could take many. Do you understand why?"

"I guess."

"Good, then tell me about yourself, Cara."

"Not much to tell. I'm nervous about what to say, how to do this."

"Relax and be open and honest—that's all. I'm here to help, so I want you to tell me everything happening in your life. You can trust me. Nothing you say goes outside this room. Okay?"

"Yeah." *Settle down, Cara. Don't show him that you're shaking. Gracie would say he's choice, even hot with the wavy black hair and dark eyes and complexion, over six feet with a lean bod. Wonder what Mom thought? No, don't go there—not sure where that came from. Boy, this office is nothing like the waiting room: expensive leather couch and chairs, large mahogany desk, cool paneling, and plush blue carpet. Easy to see where all the money goes.*

"Cara, Cara, are you still with me?"

"Oh, sorry, guess my mind drifted. What did you say?"

"What's going on in your life?"

"Umm, honestly, nothing's right in my life. I'm angry—angry that I'm not in Texas, mad at my father, upset with my brother, even my mother. I want to be with the eighty-sixers in Texas, where I belong. Oh, I'm sorry I blurted that all out without thinking."

"No, it's quite alright, Cara. That's the interaction I'm looking for. Tell me who the eighty-sixers are."

"My besties, ahh, my best friends in Texas. The four of us are tight—at least we were—and now it's over. We all graduate in '86. That's where the eighty-sixers comes from."

"Clever. So, your move to Colorado ended the group?"

"Yeah. I guess it was starting to crumble anyway, except for Gracie. She's my best friend in the world. And now I'm cut off from talking to her. I hate it, but there's nothing I can do."

"Change is hard for everyone. But how about new friends here?"

"Can I have a glass of water, please?"

"Certainly. The water cooler and paper cups are in the corner. I'll be right back."

"Umm, thanks, Doctor Reyna."

"What about new friends, Cara?"

"Zero. Oh, several girls at school seemed to like me; wanted to be friends, I thought. Then, for reasons I'm not sure of, they dropped me like the plague."

"How does that make you feel, Cara?"

"Ahh, angry and mad as hell at my father!"

"Oh! Tell me why."

"He had a perfect job in Texas. We had everything we needed. But he had to ruin it; his pride, I guess—had to get ahead and show everyone he was making it big time."

"And that's why you're angry?"

"Of course! Wouldn't you be angry at someone who pulled the rug out from under you, trashing everything you loved?"

"Anger's a valid emotion, Cara. Next time we'll explore the reasons for it. Perhaps talk about your new friend, Britta. But I do have a prior engagement, so I have to cut our session short. Your next appointment is at the same time on the ninth."

God, I need to get out of here.

"Can you show yourself out, Cara?"

"Yeah."

"So, how did it go?"

"Let's talk in the car; I need to get out of here, Mom."

5:37 p.m.

"Well, Cara, what do you think of Doctor Reyna?"

Stupid question, Mom. What am I supposed to think of a man who's trying to see if I'm nuts?

"I guess he's okay."

"Just wondering how it went."

"What did you expect, Mom? We didn't spend much time together; we only talked about my anger. That's about it."

"Next week, he said he'd have more time for you.

"Where you going, Mom?"

"Down Kipling. It's on our way, and I need to stop at the meat market."

"Slow down, Mom!"

"Why?"

"I saw Luke going into the drugstore."

"Luke Glover? So why does that matter?"

"I'm pretty sure Andrea Wicks was with him. Doesn't jive, but I'm almost positive."

"I thought he warned you and Danny to stay clear of that crowd. It makes no sense that they'd be together. Besides, we're going forty; would be hard for you to get more than a glimpse."

"Forget it, let's get to the market."

November 3, 1982, 6:12 p.m.

"What's he doing here?"

"Sit down, Cara; you're late again."

Get over it, Dad. Luke Glover's eating with us now—think I'm going to barf. This is your chance, Cara, but be cool with it. "So, Luke, I saw you going into the Rexall on Kipling last evening."

"Yeah, picked up my mom's prescription."

"It looked like you weren't alone. Did I see a girl with you?"

"No, no one with me."

"Cara, please."

Duh, Mom, he can hear you whisper. Don't worry; I won't push it, at least not now.

"Danny tells me that your father pastors the Nazarene church up the street."

"That's right, Mr. Corrigan."

"I've heard being a pastor's kid can be hard. One of my best friends growing up was a PK. At times, he had serious problems with it."

"I'm down with it. Dad and I are cool. I mean, we don't square up on everything, but we get along."

"The Nazarene church has a bunch of dos and don'ts—"

"Cara!"

"It's cool, Mrs. Corrigan. All churches have too many rules; I don't follow all of them. My father's not down with it, but we get by."

Yeah, you don't follow all the rules. What's your deal, anyway?

"Thanks for dinner, Mom. We're out of here."

"Where are you boys off to, Danny?"

"Joe Brogan's house. He has some great new records, Dad."

"Be home by nine, Danny. Drive carefully, Luke."

"For sure, Mrs. Corrigan."

6
THE BASEMENT

November 3, 1982, 7:29 p.m.

Why did they put it back in the storeroom? Why'd they finish only half the basement? It didn't take long to clutter up this room, and the light's too dim. There it is, over by the box springs and mattresses—thanks a lot, Dad. Had to cover it with a blanket; they're afraid of it. At least they put the mirror across from our old couch. Scoot it up a little closer. There, put the blanket on the sofa—gross-out dirty. No sparking. Wonder if it'll work down here? Will I see Britta again?

"Britta, Britta, are you there, Britta?" *Nothing. Oh well, I'll sit here for a while and see what happens. I could read Anne Frank, but the light's pitiful. She's in a prison camp now. Sometimes I feel like I'm in my own prison. But she really was, and you're not, Cara. How does a person do that, take the abuse, and deal with the fear? I couldn't. I can't handle everyday disappointments. No one's threatening my life; you're just a baby. Look what Anne went through and what Britta's facing. Are you really sane, Cara, or—*

"Are you there, Cara?"

"Yes, Britta, thank God you're back!"

"I'm sad."

"About what? Has your father left again?"

"He left several hours ago. Two families—nine Jews—are meeting him and Aaron Gabel. Three of them are small children, and the trip will be dangerous. I can't stop worrying about my father, Cara."

"How long will he be gone? Who's Aaron?"

"With the children, they'll take a longer, safer route to Switzerland. He might not get back for a week. I've never met Aaron Gabel. He's eighteen; the Gestapo killed his father last summer. Father says he's well trained, sharp, and uses good judgment."

"Sounds like a good guy. Umm, I've been sitting here thinking about you and Anne Frank, the book I'm reading. I feel terrible about you. I've never felt so bad about anyone, Britta. You know, I'm selfish and spoiled."

"I see your heart, Cara. You're going through a lot, but you're a good person who's become special to me."

"Ahh, I don't feel special. Most of the time, I'm angry, depressed, and wonder if I'm in my right mind."

"I think you are."

"So, you don't think the pressure you're under is why you're seeing a girl in the mirror?"

"As I said before, no, I don't."

"Can I tell you about what's happening in my life, Britta? I need to talk with someone, and I can't talk to Gracie anymore or my family, and certainly not the doctor, at least not yet."

"Go ahead, Cara. What happened?"

"My appointment with the shrink was okay, I guess. It was a get-to-know-you session. But that's not what I need help with. It's my brother, Danny, and his friend, Luke Glover. Also, something about my parents."

"Oh, you think I can help?"

"See what you think. I need to unload. I don't feel right about Luke; I don't know what it is, but something is off. He threatened me in a kidding way, but I got his drift. I also saw him with Andrea Wicks, the girl who's bugging me. She's buddies with Albert Hobbins, the turd who attacked me. At dinner, Luke denied he was with Andrea—lied to my whole family, and I don't know why."

"So he's hiding something, Cara, but what is the question."

"Yeah, and I can't come up with the answer."

"Whatever he's hiding must be illegal. But I'm struggling for ideas living at a different time. What would a boy his age do that he'd want to keep secret?"

"You're on to something, Britta. Several things come to mind. I'll think about how I can find out. Thanks."

"I'm worried too, Cara. You might be able to help me with a problem. I have no experience with boys and how they treat girls."

"I'll do what I can, but boys baffle me, so I'm not sure how much help I'll be."

"I'm afraid!"

"Afraid, what is it?"

"The problem's Ernst Keller. We're staying at his parents' house. Albert and Inge are good people, but Ernst isn't."

"What has he done, Britta?"

"Last month, when father was gone, he came in and kissed me by surprise. He had his arms around me before I knew what happened. I didn't like it and shoved him away. He got angry. He cursed and threatened me."

"What did he say? How old is this loser?"

"He's eighteen. Ernst said no girl has ever refused him, and I certainly wasn't in any position to deny what he wants. Then he called me several names and said, 'next time, you better be nicer to me.'"

"Oh, has he tried again?"

"Twice. Each time I shoved Ernst away and told him to get out. He left both times after cursing me. He raised his fist, the last time, and threatened me."

"I'm sorry, Britta, have you told your father?"

"No, not yet. I don't think Albert and Inge know what their son is like. They might not believe me. And father would be upset and tell them what happened. I fear it could make such a problem that the Kellers would ask us to leave."

"I get it, Britta. It puts you in a tight spot, though."

"I'll fight him off as long as I can. But there's something else about Ernst that might be more dangerous to father and me. A few weeks ago, I overheard my father talking to Herr Keller. The Kellers are concerned about Ernst's new friends. They're in the Hitler Youth, and it appears their propaganda influences Ernst."

"Oh, your father must think that's a big problem."

"He says we need to be careful. And we might have to leave if he starts threatening us."

"No! Oh, I'm sorry, Britta—always thinking of myself. If he threatens your safety, of course, you'll have to boogie."

"Boogie, what does that mean?"

"I'm sorry for the slang. It means to leave now. We certainly do come from different worlds."

"We do. I'm curious, would you tell me about your world in 1982?"

"I'll try, Britta."

"Thanks, listen, Cara; it would break my heart if we had to leave, and I lost you as my friend."

"Hmm, I can't burden you anymore, Britta; you've got problems which I can't imagine. Mine are petty compared to yours. It's just that you're now my besty, the only one I can talk to."

"Maybe it won't happen, I hope not. But we have to face it, Cara; the day might come when we'll have to say goodbye for good."

"I know—it kills me to think about it. Oh, Snuggles, how did you get down here? I guess I left the basement door open."

"Is someone there?"

"It's our Maltese, Snuggles. Can you see him?"

"No, it's too dark."

"With all that's going on, I've neglected my little friend. I'm sorry, Snuggles. That's right, sit on my lap and let me love on you."

"We had a poodle before the war. Topper was a beautiful dog; he's gone now."

"Oh, too sad. I hate to leave you on a downer, Britta, but I need to finish my homework. Tomorrow night?"

"Yes. And thanks again for giving me a detailed picture of your life in 1982. I can envision your room, home, and neighborhood. I almost see Danny's bicycle in the driveway. And with your descriptions, I feel like I know your family, Gracie, even Bee and Tee. Goodnight, Cara."

"Bye, Britta. Okay, Snuggles, let's go up to my room. You can help me solve math problems—ha-ha."

8:37 p.m.

"Jump up, Snuggles. Where were you? You were going to help me solve math problems. Lie down next to me. Math is such a drag." *Rest your eyes, Cara. Love stroking my little sweetie.*

"Danny and Luke, what are they up to now? Well, let's see." *Tiptoe. Danny's door is open a crack. No closer, you can hear them from here.*

"Come on, Bro, don't wimp out now."

"Sneaking out of the house is too hard, Luke. How would I explain it if my parents caught me at midnight?"

"Have some guts, Corrigan; this is you and Andrea's initiation night."

What! Danny and Andrea together. What the hell's going on?

"I'm not sure, Luke. Not sure about this initiation thing. Maybe you should go ahead without me. It scares me a little."

"Dude, it's totally righteous. Don't be a nerd."

Don't do it, Danny, whatever it is. Tell him to go to hell!

"No, count me out, Luke; I'm not into it like you are. It's strange and spooky—not my bag."

"Crap, Danny, you have the down-low and can't walk away now! You know things and can't say no; it's too late."

You can say no to whatever it is, Danny. Do it! Get the SOB out of here.

"No, I'm not going to your church—only on a night when my dad isn't home. Go ahead with Andrea. I need to think about this more."

At Luke's church, what are they talking about? What could they do that has Danny frazzled?

"If that's the way it's going down, but keep your mouth shut, Corrigan, or else!"

Damn, he's threatening my brother; what can I do? Better get back to your room—sounds like Luke's leaving.

"Catch you on the flip side—be cool, Bro, real cool."

Hurry, hurry, quiet, get on the bed. There he goes. Move over, Snuggles. What could they be doing at Luke's church at midnight? It'll drive me crazier than I already am if I don't find out. Oh crap, Cara, can you sneak downstairs and out the front door without anyone hearing you? So what if they catch me? They think I'm nuts anyway. I'll do it—I have to.

Are you really going to do this? Yes! Got my coat and gloves. Watch the table. Second step down creaks, skip it. There. Well, you made it downstairs, now the door. Easy with the lock. Good, now open it slowly. Close it gently. Okay, you have ten minutes to get to the church—hurry!

Whew, almost midnight. Be careful, Cara; this is deep stuff, and stop shaking. Good, the door's open; no lights on. But there's light over to the left; must be stairs to the basement. Oh crap, you should turn around and leave now. God, I can't stop shaking. If you're there, help me. Hope these stairs don't creak. It's dark down here. Give your eyes a minute to adjust. Yes, that's better; go slow and watch your step. Oh no, voices coming from the far side of the room. I see light; a door's not quite closed. Easy, watch your step. I can't chance looking in, but I can hear them. Sounds like singing. No, it's more like chanting. Like from movies I've seen. My God, what're they up to? Get back, don't let them see you, Cara; this is dangerous.

"And now I'll turn the ceremony over to our Grand Warlock for the initiation of Andrea Wicks. Your Honorable Holiness."

"Thank you, Warlock, Luke. Luke said the other candidate backed out, but he brought someone else, so we have a coven."

Oh crap, get your breath, Cara, stop panting; they'll hear you.

"The blood initiation will now commence. The candidate will drink the fresh blood of a white dog—as she recites her vows—according to the sacred rules of initiation. Do you have the animal and a sharp knife, Luke?"

"Yes, master."

Ahh, couldn't be, could it? Don't, Cara—gotta look! "No, my God, no! Come here, Snuggles, hurry!"

"Grab the dog! Grab that girl!"

"Yes, master. Get 'em now!"

I've got you, Snuggles. Run, Cara. Crap, that hurt, damned desk. They're coming; you can't outrun them, find a hiding place. That door; looks like a crawl space under the stairs. Get in, quick! Dark, go back as far as you can—quiet, Snuggles. Please, God, protect us. Don't look in here. They're going up the stairs shouting, thank God. Aww! stay here for now; calm down, stop shaking! Oh no, please, a breath on my neck. I'm going to faint or die. No, no, a clammy hand's squeezing my arm!

"Now you're mine forever."

"No, please, not the knife! Ow! God no, my throat—blood flowing down my coat! Help, help, help!"

"Wake up, Cara, you're having another nightmare!"

"What, what? Oh, my throat, my throat, they cut my throat."

"It was only a dream, Sis. When are they going to stop?"

"Go get a damp, cold washcloth, Danny, she's burning up, and the bed is wet with sweat. Oh, dear, what are we going to do with you?"

"Hold me tight, Mom. It was real—like I was there. I've never had such a horrible dream. I can't be alone. Can I sleep with you, Mom?"

"Of course. Does the cold washcloth feel good?"

"I'm still hot, but it does, thanks. A peck on the cheek for you. Thanks, Mom."

"Hmm . . . your kiss warms my heart. I know you'll get through this. Danny, help your sister to my room. I'll bring your PJ's; you can change there, Cara."

"I don't know if I can sleep, Mom."

7
AUNT ANNA

November 4, 1982, 3:42 p.m.

"Where are you going, Cara?"

"Ah, I left my sweater downstairs, Mom."

"No, I don't think so. You're going down to talk to that mirror. Oh, what am I to do with you? Come with me, Cara, let's sit and talk."

"Yeah, sure."

"Pull your chair close to mine. I'll bring you a glass of milk while I sip my tea."

"Ahh, can we not talk about the mirror and Doctor Reyna, or any of that stuff? I'm still upset about the dream and don't want to deal with anything else. It was real, Mom! The detail and fear—like I was there."

"I've had dreams that I swore were real. They're hard to get over. But what I wanted to tell you is that Aunt Anna is coming for Thanksgiving after all."

"Oh, I thought she decided not to."

"She did, but it turns out that Beth and Rick changed their minds; both are staying at Northwestern for the weekend."

"Well, I'm glad Aunt Anna's coming. Did she call earlier?"

"Around 2:30. That's why I wanted to talk—to give you the good news. My sister's always had a soft spot for you, Cara."

"Yeah, she gets me, Mom."

"I'm aware of that. Though, I've never figured out what bonds you two."

"A lot of things, I guess. She isn't afraid to tell it like it is. She's real all the time, even if it hurts. And Aunt Anna's always had my back, no matter what. Plus, she's funny, a real hoot."

"Yeah, a real hoot."

"I've never asked, Mom, maybe I shouldn't, but why have I always sensed tension between you and Anna? Seems like you're on the outs a lot."

"Sadly, you're right. Our age has a lot to do with it, Cara. Being nine years younger, I felt like she looked down on me. Oh, it's hard to explain, but when I was young, she paid little attention to me. Then Anna went off to college, and we had no time to get close. We never bonded like the two of you have. And that's why it's puzzling to me; why I'm a little envious."

"I guess I never understood. I'm sorry it hurts you, Mom. You've never been so honest about something personal. Thanks, Mom."

"I love your kisses, and you are right. I haven't been very personal, at least with you, or maybe everyone. But you're almost fifteen, and I need to treat you as an adult—need to be honest with you. I do wish we could bond like you and Anna."

"I'd like that too. Maybe when I get past all this stuff. But now I better go upstairs and get some homework done before dinner."

"Thanks, dear."

November 8, 1982, 3:17 p.m.

Cara, you have to walk home from school today—just get over it! It's not Mom's fault her bridge club meets on Monday afternoons. Ahh, I hate this school already. It sucks; look at these scratched-up lockers, dim lights, like the dim bulbs that go here. Like, get out of here and get home.

Halfway home. Chill, Cara, stop twisting your neck, looking around. Wait! It's Andrea Wicks and Luke. She's behind Luke like she might be following him. So what, Cara? The drugstore, I saw them together there. I wonder if they are up to something. I'm not up to the tension, but if I don't follow them, I'll never find out what's going on with Luke Glover. He could hurt Danny; he's done something to him already. I don't want to do it. Go for it but be careful.

They're headed for Youngsfield street. Wonder why they didn't want anyone to see them together at school? Hold it! They're stopping in front of the beer joint. But they're not old enough to go in. I bet I can sneak across the street and hide behind the beer truck in the alley. Damn, the cars zoom by so fast. I'll crawl up by the front bumper where I can peek around just enough to see them. Wonder who those two guys are. Sheesh, Andrea's as tall as both of them. She must be five nine and 140 pounds, but she is not fat. Crap, she must have thirty pounds on me. She'd kill me if it ever came to blows. She has a pretty face, though. What does Andrea see in Luke Glover? They can't be an item. It has to be something else, something shady. Wait! What is Luke giving him? Are they dealing drugs; I should have guessed it. That's enough, Cara. Don't screw up now— boogie!

"What are you doing there, Babe?"

Oh crap! Turn slowly and play dumb. "Just dropped a quarter; it rolled under the truck."

"Yeah, right. Hey, Luke, look who I found hiding behind the beer truck."

"Stop, you're hurting me!"

"Well, well, well, look who's been following us, Andrea."

"Uh-huh, I sensed someone was tailing us. Bring her back in the alley, Andy, where no one can see us."

"Get your hands off me! I was only heading to the drugstore for a malt. I wasn't following you. Stop hurting me!"

"She's yours, Andrea. Teach the bitch a lesson."

"My pleasure, Luke."

"Leave me alone, Andrea. I'm, I'm telling Danny, the police, and everyone else that you're drug dealers." *Umph, that hurt. I can't take much more of her blows.*

"You bitch, I'll kick your skinny ass to the ground."

"Ow!" *Is that her knee in my back. Damn she has my arm in a hammerlock. Lord, what can I do?* "Stop it! Let me up, Andrea; you're hurting me!"

"That's the idea. Just a warning to leave us alone. Stay out of our business or else. The next time you won't get off this easy."

"Get up, Cara."

"You're in trouble, Luke. Everyone's going to hear about this."

"Yeah, going to hear from crazy Cara? Haven't you figured out that no one believes nutso Cara's stories? Isn't that right, Andrea?"

"Right on, Luke, I wasn't even at school today. I was home sick, so get out of here, crazy Cara. Spread your fantasies; see how well that works for you."

Run while you have a chance, Cara. No, just walk quickly. Gotta get home. Just make it to my house. Oh, finally home. Just get to the bathroom before anyone sees you. Gotta clean up. Oh, my arm! It doesn't look like Mom's home yet. Where's Danny? Who should I tell? What should I say? Are they right? Am I crazy, Cara, who no one believes?

8:12 p.m.

"I'm glad you called, Cee. Sorry I wasn't there for your first two calls. Mother wondered about the hang-ups."

"I hated doing that but had to take a chance. I'm sorry for dropping all my drama on you before you could say a word."

"It's okay. What's your father going to say when he sees the three long-distance charges on the phone bill when they told you not to call anymore?"

"It'll tick him off, Gee, but I don't care. I needed to talk to you. Mom caught me again at the basement door. She'll do anything to keep me away from the mirror."

"Oh, your friend in the mirror again?"

"I know I can't convince you; I won't try. To tell the truth, Gee, I'm not sure what's up or down now. What I told you earlier about this afternoon was horrible. I know it happened, but will anyone believe me?"

"I want to, Cee."

"Mom seemed to believe me, but I know she has her doubts—the questions, the stares. She's taking me to the police station tomorrow afternoon, before my appointment with Doctor Reyna."

"Did you tell anyone else?"

"No, I couldn't tell Danny, and Father's away. But because of everything that's happened, Gracie, I decided to start keeping a diary, like Anne Frank."

"You kept saying you'd start one someday."

"Anne made me see how important diaries are. I need to put down what's happening to keep it all straight in my mind—what's left of it. I started it with father telling us that we'd be moving to Colorado. I put in something about moving into our house and my first days at school. I also entered details about my room, the house, and our neighborhood. But the daily record begins the day father brought the mirror to my bedroom. Anne wrote to an invisible friend, Kitty. I'm only entering the date."

"It's a good idea, Cara, but I'm still worried about you: those thugs, the mirror, everything."

"Yeah, but Danny worries me the most—his lie about Albert Hobbins and how he's mixed up with all those losers. It's not like him to go against me like that."

"He always seemed like a good guy to me. What are you going to do?"

"Keep my eyes and ears open, maybe get a chance to spy on him and Luke—hear what they're talking about. It fries me, so let's drop it for now. Oh! My mother told me Grandma's not coming for Thanksgiving this year."

"Huh, she always has since your granddad passed."

"Something came up. Mom said a long-lost friend from Germany asked her to come over there as soon as possible. I don't know what it's all about, but I guess my grandparents knew this woman when grand-dad was stationed in Germany way back in the forties."

"She's up for that kind of trip?"

"Yeah, Grandma's a spry old gal for seventy. She usually runs cir-cles around Mom."

"Maybe it's for the best."

"Probably, but I'm sure she'll be here for Christmas. I'll have to hear a few go-rounds then. Mom and Grandma don't click, and I've never figured out why."

"Yeah, we've talked about it before—puzzling. I've seen pictures of your grandma when she was young, a real babe. Do you think it bothers your mother?

"Maybe, something does. Did I ever tell you Grandma suggested Cara for my name?"

"No, that's strange. Whoops, Mom's in the dining room, and I don't want her to overhear. I'm worried about you, Cee. Take care, and maybe I'll try to sneak a call to you next week."

"Be careful, Gee. Bye."

8
THE FOG IS CLEARING

November 9, 1982, 2:48 p.m.

"We're running late, Cara, are you almost finished?"

"Chill, Mom, I'm about done with my statement. We have forty minutes before my appointment, and it's not that far away."

"Aw, just hurry up."

I hope I remember this right. They gotta believe me. It's so busy in here; are all these people victims? Must be twenty hard chairs—lined across the room—filled with people and their clipboards. The smoke gags me out—filthy habit. It's too depressing here, a scary place for sure.

"Are you Cara Corrigan?"

"Yes, sir, and this is my mother."

"I'm Sergeant Sullivan; come with me, please. Your mother can wait for you here."

Mom will be on pins and needles the whole time, wondering what I'll say and how I'll hold up. What a small cubicle; doesn't rate an office, I guess.

"Have a seat, young lady. Have you finished your statement?"

"Ah, one more sentence."

"Take your time and get all the details down."

"Okay, I'm finished. I hope I remembered everything correctly."

"Relax and give me a few minutes to look it over."

"Yes, sir." *Hmm, wouldn't want to meet this guy in a dark alley. Kinda mean looking; big and scary too. Must be fifty, though—*

"Okay, so you know two of these characters and not the other three? How do you know this Luke and Andrea?"

"Well, Luke's my brother, Danny's, best friend. And I know Andrea from school."

"They ever do anything to you before?"

"Not Luke, at least not anything I'm sure of. But Andrea's always rattling my cage—pulled books out of my hand at school, lied about me, plus what I said in my statement."

"Ever see them with drugs before or hear anything about them being dealers?"

"No, nothing."

"Do you think your brother's involved? Is that why you were suspicious?"

"I hope he isn't, but, yes, that's what kept bugging me. Danny's never been mixed up with anything like that; he's never broken the law."

"Huh, any other details? Even minor details are important."

"Well, I can't think of any."

"This is serious business, Miss Corrigan. We know there's drug activity around most schools. We'll investigate and get to the bottom of it. Meanwhile, I'd stay away from these characters. I'll be in touch if I need additional information."

"Thanks, sir."

Glad that's over, and I'm out of that smoke-filled cubicle. Umm, are you sure you didn't miss something?

"Hurry up, Cara; we've got to get to your appointment."

4:10 p.m.

The ceiling tiles are turning yellow and the air's musty, but at least this couch is relaxing. At least for my body—my mind's still frazzled. Come on, Reyna, how long does it take to review your notes after I spilled my guts for thirty minutes? I've had enough for today.

"Good session, Cara. I'm glad you opened up and talked freely about what's going on in your life. I know it's difficult, and you must be uneasy, if not frightened."

I wish he'd back up his chair; he's right in my face. Don't you know about Listerine or something? Horrible breath! "I'm scared, afraid I'm losing it. Does that happen, you know, with the people who lie on this couch?"

"All the time, Cara. I don't see many fearless patients. It's normal; just try to relax as best you can. Let's talk more about what you've told me."

"I'm tired. Can it wait till our next session?"

"I understand, dear, but we must probe a little deeper while everything is fresh in our minds. Are you up for it?"

"Ahh, I guess."

"Good. Let's talk more about Danny and Luke and the other ones at school. Why do you think they lied about what happened to you?"

"I can't figure it out, Doctor Reyna. Danny's never lied to me. He's not a liar."

"But he did lie. At least that's what you're telling me. So if he's not a liar—never has been—then maybe there's something else to consider."

"Something else? Are you saying he didn't lie?"

"I'm only asking you to consider it. Think about the incident at school, the quarrel with Albert Hobbins. You said you were extraordinarily distressed and fearful when you saw Albert and Andrea coming your way. Maybe what you saw and heard was only teenagers fooling around—horseplay. Is it possible that you misinterpreted what happened? Think about it, Cara; you don't need to give me an answer now."

"I'm getting confused. I guess. Like I told Gee, I don't know if I can tell up from down anymore."

"Hmm, before our time is up, I'd like to talk more about the mirror."

"Can we not talk about it? You must think I'm off my rocker."

"No, Cara, I don't. There's a reason for your experiences with the mirror. Will you consider what I have to say and see if it makes sense?"

"Yeah, I'll try, doctor; I need answers."

"First, let's talk about your father. I think you love him but have issues about what he did. Is there more to it than the move?"

"Yeah, I guess there is. I love my father, but sometimes I hate him too."

"Hmm, why is that, Cara?"

"It's hard to explain; maybe I've never straightened it out in my mind. He takes good care of us—gives us what money can buy. But I can't remember when he put his arm around me or told me that he loved me, and it hurts a lot!"

"Does he treat your mother and brother the same way?"

"Ahh, maybe I see things wrong, but no, he doesn't. When Danny made the basketball team, dad hugged him and said, 'Congratulations, son! I love you.' I'm ashamed to say it hurt like hell to see and hear that. Just one time, I wanted it to be me that he cuddled and said those words to. For once, I wanted him in my corner—wanted to feel his love."

"Of course, dear, it's understandable."

"But why, Doctor Reyna, why doesn't he do what most fathers do?"

"I can't answer that question, Cara. But try to put what you've told me in context with what's going on with the mirror."

"I, I guess I don't understand."

"What kind of father did Anne Frank have?"

"A father that loved her and told her so. He hugged her, made her feel safe when they weren't. I'd die for that."

"And Britta, what's her father like?"

"Like Anne's father. She says he takes her in his arms and holds her until the troubles of the world go away. That's all I want."

"Of course, you do. Every daughter expects that of her father. But do you see what I see, Cara?"

"I guess, but maybe I'm a little fuzzy on it."

"Isn't it more than coincidental that both Anne and Britta have the father you want? And isn't it strange that Britta's leading the same life as Anne?"

"Well, I guess. That never came to mind, but you must be right, Doctor. I think I see it."

"Sometimes, Cara, people under intense stress seek shelter in a safe place where the world is as they want it to be. It's what we call a defense mechanism. Do you understand what I'm saying?"

"I guess I do but am I off my rocker?"

"Not necessarily. We'll work on it in future sessions. But do you know that people can't live in mirrors? It's impossible."

"I think so, but why will it kill me to say goodbye to Britta?"

"Hmm, well, she's vital to you. As we work through why, though, your need for her will diminish. Our time is up for today, Cara, but we're making progress. I'm proud of the work you're doing."

"I want it to go away, Doctor Reyna, that's all."

November 11, 1982, 6:10 p.m.

You shouldn't go to the basement just because mother's on the way to the airport to pick up dad. Don't kid yourself, Cara; you know you're going to do it. I have an hour before they're back. Watch the third step; father needs to replace it. "Oh, Snuggles, come on down, come boy. Now jump on the couch with me."

"What should I do, Snuggles? Doctor Reyna's right, I'm sure. I mean, really, people don't live in mirrors—it's impossible, like he said." *So why are you down here, Cara? If it's all in your mind, you don't want to fool around with it; it'll only confuse you more. But Britta needs me. I'm the only one she can talk to when her father's away. And I like her so much. It's only a mind game—or is it? Ahh, I don't know. I'll sit here and chill for a while; love on Snuggles. Crap, the door; they can't be home already.*

"Cara! Are you down there?"

"Yes. What do you want, Danny?"

"You know you're not supposed to be down here. It'll tick them off if they find out."

"I guess you'll tell them."

"I should, but I won't. I'm mad as hell at you! What's wrong with you, Cara? Are you trying to get both of us killed?"

"What are you babbling about, Danny?"

"You know damned well. The fantasy you had Monday, then going to the police with Mom. Why are you doing this to us? You need to see the shrink every day—sick, sick!"

"It's no fantasy, I'm sure of it, and Mom insisted I go to the police."

"Well, they questioned Luke and Andrea today. Luke chewed my butt up one side and down the other. He threatened me, Sis, do you understand?"

"Why? You did nothing wrong, and neither did—"

"No, shut up and listen! They denied everything, and Luke said they'll never find evidence that the incident happened. Look, Cara, I don't know if you're telling the truth or in a crazy dream world. But the thing is, you don't know who you're messing with. I can't say more except be careful for all our sakes."

"But it's true! How can they get away with it, Danny? And why don't you protect me like a big brother should?"

"Crap, it's bigger than all of us, Cara. I can't say more. Stay away from them, and keep your mouth shut. Just do it! I'm done. Turn the light off when you are done."

How could the police believe that pack of liars? What am I supposed to do, let them beat me without saying a word? No, no, I won't! Danny's right, though; you have to avoid them. "Oh, I need help, Snuggles." *Let's get this blanket off and see what Britta thinks.*

"Britta, are you there? Nothing Snuggles." *Let's wait a few minutes.* "Britta, Britta, where are you. I need to talk to you; need your help." *It's been fifteen minutes; she must be gone, gone for good. It tears me up. I miss her—need her. But if she's gone, am I getting better? I hope so.* "Let's go upstairs, Snuggles. Might as well put the blanket back on the mirror for good. Bye Britta."

9
DAVEY

November 12, 1982, 3:08 p.m.

Okay, Mom, be on time today. Don't make me wait at school again, please! None of the thugs are around; I haven't seen them all day. Hopefully, they arrested them. Chill out, Cara; mom will be here—

"Hold up! You dropped your pen."

"Oh, I can get it."

"Got it—here you go."

"Thanks. Aren't you in my history class?"

"That's right. I sit two rows over and one seat up."

"Ahh, I never counted. You know a lot about history and ask more questions than anyone else."

"Well, I don't know if I'm that up on it, but history fascinates me. I probably raise my hand too much; I should let someone else have a chance."

"History isn't my favorite subject. But the Second World War is interesting."

"No doubt, it's exciting and important."

"What do you think about Germany; what Hitler did, the Jews and all the stuff that happened?"

"It's hard to imagine what went on."

"Yeah. I'm reading the *Diary of Anne Frank*. Have you read it?"

"Last year. It was too sad. I'm not sure how they lived with the constant fear."

"It's getting to me, but I love her. And her father's special." *I can't believe you're talking to a boy, Cara. And he's friendly and cute. No boy's paid attention to me since we moved. Be cool, don't blow it—he's nice.*

"Let me get the door."

"Thanks. I'm Cara Corrigan."

"I know; I've heard the teacher call on you. I'm David Windly. You've probably heard my name in class too."

"Yeah, I did."

"Everyone calls me Davey. I saw you and your brother in the front yard the other day. You live only two blocks from me."

"Oh, my mother's picking me up. Would you like a ride home?" *Cara! Why'd you do that? Stupid—hope it doesn't scare him off.*

"Sure. It's too cold for a long walk."

"She usually picks me up over there, but sometimes she's late. I've been going to school here for a couple of months; we moved from Texas. You probably guessed that from my accent, though my friends say it isn't heavy." *Don't babble on, Cara. Let him talk.*

"You have a slight accent; I couldn't tell from where, though. It's nice—I like it. We moved from Colorado Springs in July, so I'm also new. It's hard making new friends."

"Tell me about it. I thought two girls were becoming my friends; then, for no reason, they stopped talking to me." *Okay, be cool, Cara. Where's Mom?*

"Did your father get a new job here?"

"Yeah, I hated to move. All my friends are in Texas. I'd rather not talk about that, Davey."

"Sure, I didn't care much for moving either."

"Here's Mom—finally! We can both ride in the front seat; I'll get in first. Mother, this is Davey Windly. He's in my history class and lives a couple of blocks from us. Is it okay if we drop him off?"

"Of course, glad to meet you, Davey."

"You too, Mrs. Corrigan."

Silence, I hate silence. What should I say? Don't say anything stupid. Mom, don't embarrass me, please. I have to say something. "Davey's a history buff. He knows more about it than anyone else in class." *Dumb, Cara, dumb!*

"Thanks, Cara."

"I'm glad to see that you've made a new friend, Cara. How long have you known each other?"

Please, Mom, don't go there, don't—

"We've seen each other in class, Mrs. Corrigan, but we officially met for the first time a few minutes ago. A pen fell out of Cara's notebook, and I picked it up for her."

"That's sweet of you, Davey. Isn't it, Cara?"

No, Mom. What am I supposed to say now? "It was." *That's all you can say, Cara?*

"Thanks, Cara. Turn left at the next corner; it's the third house on the right. Thanks, Mrs. Corrigan. Thanks, Cara; see you at school Monday."

"See you in third period, Davey."

"He's a nice boy, Cara. I'm glad you're making friends with good kids. It'll make a difference, you know, in everything."

"Yeah, I get your drift, Mom."

November 13, 1982, 10:42 a.m.

"Sorry, we couldn't find you a new coat, Cara. At least you found new boots, Danny.

"I thought for sure Wards or Sears would have a better selection. Oh well, my old coat's a little thin, but it'll do for now." *Wait! Is that Davey walking down our street?*

"Isn't that your new friend, Cara?"

"New friend, who is he?"

"Just a boy I met at school, Danny." *Wonder why he's walking over here? He'll be at our driveway by the time I get out of the car. What should I say? I can't avoid him—don't want to.* "Hi, Davey, what brings you over this way?"

"Kinda bored, thought I'd take a walk since it's so nice out."

"This is my brother, Danny; he's a junior. This is Davey Windly from school."

"Hey."

"If you're not doing anything, would you like to walk with me, Cara?"

"Sure, I'm not doing anything else."

"Do you walk the neighborhood, Cara?"

"Not usually, I'm not much of a walker, I guess. It would be good for me; just don't take the time."

"Oh, our family walks and hikes a lot."

"Why'd you decide to walk down my street?"

"I usually walk the other way. But to be honest, I hoped I'd see you."

He likes me—I can't believe it! What do I say? Don't blow it now. "Ahh, that's sweet of you, Davey." *Dumb, dumb, why'd you say that, Cara?*

"Listen, Cara, I know we just met, but I was wondering if we could be friends. We're both new here, and you said you were having trouble making friends, just like me."

"I'd like that." *Wow! He's hot, but what does he see in me?*

"Good. We both need someone to talk to—share our feelings with."

"Yeah, my parents cut me off from my closest friend in Texas. I miss her a lot."

"I've only seen my closest friend from Colorado Springs twice since we moved."

"It sucks, Davey, moving away from where you're comfortable. I blame my father. I shouldn't tell you that, but it's true. He didn't have to move us."

"I'm sorry that it hurt you. But I'm not sorry that it allowed me to meet you, Cara."

"But I'm ordinary, with baggage." *Crap, Cara, now you've done it; baggage—really!*

"Hmm, I don't know about baggage; I think we all have it. But I do know that you're sweet and nice to be around, and pretty too."

I can't believe he'd think that let alone say it. What do I say now? Please don't mess up, Cara. "I'm not sure about that, Davey."

"You should be. You have a lot to offer, and I'm looking forward to knowing all about you."

"I don't know, I'm afraid you won't think so when you know about all that's happening in my life. It'll be hard to share those things, but I think I might need to at some point. Not today, though, Davey."

"Someday, I hope you will. Well, back to your driveway. Thanks for walking with me, Cara. See you in history class."

"See you Monday, Davey, bye." *Oh my, Cara, you might have your first boyfriend if you don't screw it up. But you'll need to be careful about what you say. Don't drive him off with all your drama. I need to tell someone, Gee and Britta.*

3:53 p.m.

Finally, they're gone. Mom and Dad should be at the movie and dinner till seven. Not sure if Danny's in his room or not. Call Gracie now; hope she's home, and her parents don't answer.

"Where are you, Gee?" *I have to tell someone about Davey. No, don't think about it, Cara. You're getting better, and Davey's part of it. You can't talk to Britta again; can't go back to that anymore. But I need to talk about it, tell someone who'll understand. Go ahead, see if she's there.*

"Come on, Snuggles, jump up." *Let me get this blanket off the mirror.* "Britta, are you there? Nothing, Snuggles. Britta, Britta, Britta." *She's gone! That's a good thing, Cara. Like Doctor Reyna said, "People can't live in mirrors; it's impossible." Yes, you're getting better. Thanks, Doctor Reyna, thanks, Davey.* "Let's put the blanket back on the mirror, Snuggles, and go upstairs. Wait! Is that the basement door?" *Crap, Mom and Dad came home early. Turn the light off, Cara, hurry! Footsteps on the stairs; we have to hide, Snuggles—behind the mirror. Get down, be quiet.*

"Are you down here, bitch? I know you are."

No, it's Luke. Why's he here, and where's Danny? Stop shaking and gasping. Oh, God, help us!

"Must be hiding in here. Let's turn the light on and see. When I find you, Cara, my hands will squeeze your throat until you're dead. Damned cluttered room, full of crap. Umm, not over here, how bout over there. No, what about behind the couch or under it. No, where are you, bitch?"

Stay quiet. He's walking around out there looking for me. God, don't let him come in here—please! Wait, wait, that's his footsteps going back upstairs. Keep down until you're sure he won't come back. My God, Cara, he wants to kill you! You've got to tell mom and dad right away. You should call the police first. Why in the world is Danny mixed up with him? Okay, Snuggles, let's sneak upstairs and see if he's gone. "Careful, Snuggles. Oh, now you've pulled the blanket off the mirror. It's okay, little one, we'll cover it again."

"Are you there, are you there, Cara?"

"Oh! Ahh, I'm here, Britta. I can hardly hear you, and your face is blurred."

"You sound far away, Cara. I can barely see your face. What's wrong? Are you alright?"

"No, not at all. Danny's friend, Luke Glover, just threatened to kill me. We hid behind the mirror. He said he would choke me to death if he found me. I'm still shaking, Britta."

"Did I hear you correctly, he tried to kill you?"

"Yes, he's crazy, and Danny's not stopping it! I don't know where his head is, probably up his butt. A lot's happened since the last time we talked. I can't believe it was ten days ago."

"Now, you're coming into focus, and I can hear you. What's happened, Cara?"

"Yeah, I can see and hear you better, too." *I'm not sure that's a good thing, though. I thought you and the mirror were fading, and I was getting better.* "I saw Luke and Andrea Wicks dealing drugs. They caught me watching and roughed me up. My mom took me to the police station, and I gave them my statement. They're investigating it, but they all lied and said I didn't know what I was talking about. I'm not sure if anyone will believe me or if anything will happen to them, Britta. But that must be why Luke wants to kill me."

"Dear God, we're both in danger."

"A lot of other stuff has happened since we last talked. I don't want to dredge it all up now. You said, dear God, Britta. I should have asked before, are you religious?"

"My parents were religious, so naturally, I was too. But with all that's happened, I'm not sure anymore. I believe in God, though, and pray to Him all the time. What about you, Cara? Do you trust in God?"

"Ahh, I don't think so. It's hard for me to trust anyone except Gracie. I love the idea of having you as my friend, too, but I can't trust that you're real, Britta. I'd like to, but Doctor Reyna says it's impossible; that I imagine you to help me with the baggage I'm carrying."

"That hurts, but I understand."

"Oh, I'm sorry. You know, I'd like to go back to the years when we went to church; when I was closer to God. I could trust him. It's distant now. I do believe that Jesus died for us, though. But I don't pretend to understand that kind of sacrifice. When I think about it, it reminds me of the scripture that the greatest love anyone can have is to lay down his life for his friends. I've talked to Gracie about it before. I know I could never do that, Britta. It's not like I wouldn't want to; I just don't have courage—I'm not that good a person."

"You are that good, Cara. And you have a lot more courage than you think. I would trust you with my life."

"I hate this; it tears me up. But I have to let Doctor Reyna help me get better. Now that I have Davey, I can do it."

"Davey, who's Davey?"

"He's a boy at school I met. It sounds crazy, but I think we're going to be a couple. Maybe God sent him to help me recover."

"I hope He did. I'm happy for you, Cara."

"But it's not good for you, Britta. I'm thinking Davey's here to replace you; I know he's real."

"It's okay, whatever's best for you. I'll be here alone."

"Huh, hu, now you have me crying too. But I have to go—need to face reality. And I have to figure out what to do about Luke Glover and his band of thugs. Bye, Britta."

"Goodbye, Cara."

She's gone. I'll never see her again, and I don't know when I'll stop crying about it, when I'll stop thinking about her. Now, what to do about Luke? We have to go to the police as soon as Mom and Dad get home, not call them now. But first, I need to see who's in the house. Has Luke left? Is Danny home? "Come on, Snuggles, let's sneak upstairs."

7:58 p.m.

"Cara! What are you doing on the carpet? Why are you crying? What happened?"

"It's, it's Luke. Aww, help me up." *Stop crying, Cara, tell them!* "Luke tried to kill me!"

"What! What do you mean, tried to kill you?"

"I was downstairs, Dad, and he came looking for me; said he'd choke me to death."

"Downstairs, it happened downstairs?"

"Ahh, yes, Mom."

"What were you doing, Cara? You know you're forbidden to go down there. But, he attacked you, really?"

"Well, he would have, Mom, but I hid, and he didn't find me."

"Damnit! Nothing good happens when you go to the basement. What are we going to do with you, Cara?"

"He was going to kill me, Dad! Are you listening?"

"We're listening, Cara, but, well, we need to sort this out. Are you sure? That damned mirror; you need to get it out of the house, Brent!"

"It's gone tomorrow; a couple's coming over to look at it."

"The mirror be damned, Dad. What about me, and what Luke did? You're not hearing me!"

"It's hard to know what's real with you, Cara. When did this happen? How long have you been crying on the floor?"

My God, they don't believe me. What else can I say? "I'm not sure; since four, I guess."

"Since four? *The Man from Snowy River* started at 4:10. Danny and Luke sat three rows in front of us for the entire movie. How could that be, Cara?"

"No, it couldn't be, Dad! It had to be someone else with Danny; Luke was here—I'm positive!"

"No, it was Luke, dear. There's no way he could have been here at four and in the theater ten minutes later. It's the mirror, Cara; it does something to you every time you're around it."

"No, no, no, it's not the mirror; please, God, someone believe me! Well, I wanna go to the police station and tell them what happened."

"My God, Cara, we've been discussing how we'd tell you, but now we have to come right out with it."

"Come out with what, Dad?"

"Sergeant Sullivan called your mother earlier. Tell her what he said, Sarah."

"Luke and Andrea both said that you made up the story; that for some reason, you've been out to get them."

"What! Someone else had to see them."

"The sergeant said they checked with people in the area, and no one saw a thing. He also checked with the school. Andrea's mother called them and said she was sick. She wasn't at school that day, Cara. So how could she have been with Luke at school when you started to follow them?"

"She was, Mom, please! My God—will no one ever believe me?"

"Do you see why we're hesitant to take you back to the police station? I'm not sure they'll believe you or even take another report. Do you want that humiliation?"

"I understand, but it happened, and I still want to tell the police."

"Aww, I can't do this again, Brent; you take her."

"Crap! Okay, Cara, put your coat on, and let's get this over with."

November 15, 1982, 3:21 p.m.

"Thanks for walking me home, Davey. I feel safe."

"Don't worry, Cara. No one will bother you, will they?"

"That's just it; they might. Remember the other day when I said I couldn't tell you everything, that I had baggage?"

"Ah, now that you mention it, I do."

"Well, part of that baggage is Luke Glover, Andrea Wicks, and Albert Hobbins. They all go to our school. Do you know any of them?"

"No, at least not by name. Why?"

"They've attacked me. Albert assaulted me several weeks ago. Andrea threw me to the ground last week when I followed them. They're dealing drugs, Davey!"

"Dear God, I had no idea. Did you report them?"

"To the police, each time. But they lied, said I was making it up or out of my mind. It was their word against mine. That's the problem, Davey; nobody believes me."

"What about your parents and brother?"

"They want to believe me, but I don't think they do. The police investigated each incident, but no one backs me up. And for some reason, Danny's been against me the whole time."

"Huh, how many times have they come after you, Cara?"

"Four. Saturday night was the final straw. I was in the basement, and Luke came looking for me. I hid, and he didn't find me. But he threatened to choke me to death; he was so angry."

"Wow! You did report it?"

"My father took me to the police station for the fourth time. And again, the thugs lied, and no one backed my story. Now the police and my family have doubts about anything I say. I'm afraid they'll never believe me again, Davey."

"Well, I do. Why would you ever lie about something like that?"

"I wouldn't, I didn't. But there's more I need to tell you. I have so much baggage. I, I hope it won't change how you feel about me."

"It won't, Cara. Tell me what else is going on."

"I'm seeing a shrink, a psych counselor. Part of it relates to what I told you, but there are other things too. I'm having the worst nightmares, and then there's the mirror."

"The mirror?"

"Oh, I hate this, telling you about the mirror. You'll think I am crazy, but I need to be honest with you, Davey."

"Go ahead; I won't think less of you, no matter what it is."

"I see and talk to a girl in my mirror. She's my age and lives in Germany during the Second World War. She's in trouble, and so am I. And for now, that's all I'll say about it."

"Ahh, it's the book you're reading about Anne Frank. Is it affecting you?"

"You're too sharp. My counselor thinks so. Davey, do you need this—getting involved with a girl who's way out there?"

"Listen, Cara, I like you; this won't scare me off."

"Thanks. I like you a lot." *How could any boy like you, Cara? Boys aren't looking for girlfriends that might end up in the loony bin. He's not saying anything, mulling over what I've said, probably deciding if he wants to leave me behind and never look back. You can't say anything more. Leave it alone and let him decide. At least I feel safer with him walking me home. I wish Mom would drop the Monday afternoon bridge club. It's a beautiful day for a pleasant walk home. I like him so much and only hope it doesn't end before it begins.*

"Cara, wait up!"

Oh, crap! What're they doing here? "What do you want, Luke? Why are you following us?"

"We're not following you, only walking faster. I'm on the way to your house to meet Danny. Albert and Andrea are going over to Youngsfield."

"Well, leave us alone."

"What do you mean, Cara? Of course, we'll leave you alone. You've met a boy. Glad to meet you; I'm Luke Glover. I've seen you at school."

"I'm Davey Windly."

"These are my friends, Albert Hobbins and Andrea Wicks."

Really, your friends, Luke! What in hell are they doing? Playing nice, trying to fool Davey. Don't let them sucker you.

"Nice to meet you, Davey. I've also seen you around school."

"I've noticed you too, Andrea."

"My father, and the church, are praying for you, Cara. We understand what you're going through and don't blame you. We only want you to get better."

You've got to be kidding me! Don't believe a word of it, Davey.
"Sure, Luke."

"You both have a pleasant day; nice to meet you, Davey."

"You too, Luke . . . that was strange."

"Ahh, completely. I don't know what they're pulling, but that's not the real Luke, Albert, or Andrea. It's a load of crap. You have to believe me, Davey."

"I do."

Does he, though? Or is he thinking twice about me—about having anything to do with me? You've laid too much garbage on him all at once. I wouldn't blame him if he walked away and ended whatever it is we have.

"Cara."

"Oh, sorry, my mind was drifting. Well, this is my corner. Thanks for walking me home. I'm sorry about everything."

"It's okay, we'll sort it all out. See you tomorrow, Cara."

"Bye, Davey." *Please, God, don't let me lose him. I need someone real, someone here, someone to believe me.*

10
TWO POINTS OF VIEW

November 16, 1982, 5:05 p.m.

"Well, that was a good session, Cara. We're making headway as you open up and honestly look at yourself."

"Ahh, I guess, but, I'm not sure."

"Committing to putting the mirror behind you is a big step. Now we can work through the issues with your father without complicating them."

"Oh, I haven't been totally honest, Doctor Reyna. I didn't meet Britta in the mirror, but I couldn't let those people take it away."

"What do you mean, dear?"

"A couple interested in buying the mirror came over Sunday to look at it. When they showed up, I came downstairs; Mom and Dad didn't want me to. The woman said she was superstitious. You know, breaking a mirror brings seven years of bad luck."

"So, I'm guessing you interceded, Cara."

"Yeah, like I said, I couldn't let the mirror go. After the woman said she was superstitious, I blurted out that it's haunted. Dad was ticked, told me to get back upstairs. He wanted to get the hundred bucks more than getting rid of the mirror, like Mom.

"So, it still has a hold on you. What happened next?"

"The woman freaked out when I said I saw people in the mirror. She said she wouldn't have it in her house. Then her husband got mad at her. He's the one who wanted it. He knew he could make a profit. Anyway, Dad blew up, and Mom left the room. Then the couple left, upset with all of us. Aww, what a mess. I can't help it, but I'm glad the mirror is still in our basement."

"You should think about why, Cara, and the consequences. We'll delve into it again next session. We also need to look at the run-ins you keep having with Luke and the others."

"Can I ask a question before we finish, Doctor?"

"Go ahead."

"Can mental illness be passed down from your grandma or great-grandma, you know, is it hereditary?"

"Umm, strange that you should ask that. Well, without being technical, most experts think that certain maladies have hereditary components. But I'm curious as to why you're bringing it up."

"Well, I'll have to be honest about this too. I overheard my parents talking about it. Mom said that her grandmother went insane and committed suicide. When she learned that it might be hereditary, she worried a lot about it. But now—with everything going on with me—she thinks I inherited great-Grandma's mental illness."

"Do your parents know that you overheard them?"

"No. I snuck down the hall when they were in bed and listened near their door. I, I shouldn't have."

"Maybe it's for the best that you did. To be honest with you, Cara, your mother spoke to me about it—her concern that you've inherited what's causing your problems."

"So, I guess I'm crazy because of my great-grandma?"

"That's two questions, and I never care for the word *crazy*. The truth is, though, I don't have conclusive answers. Could mental illness be passed down to you? It's possible, but the odds are against it. Are you mentally ill? Only to a certain degree by clinical definition. To what degree and its remedy are what we'll work on in future sessions."

"Why would God let that happen? Have such a thing passed down to me."

"I'm a doctor, a man of science; I don't know anything about God's involvement."

"You don't believe in God."

"I didn't say that. I really don't know. The world would classify me as an agnostic who believes in facts and evidence. It's hard for me to find either in God. But you apparently do, Cara."

"I have as many questions as you, Doctor Reyna. I believed in the past, but it's faded away. It's my fault; I walked away."

"Why is that?"

"Well, we all went to church when I was younger. I liked it; I even made commitments. But then something happened, and my parents suddenly stopped going to church. I missed it—the sweet feelings. Now it's a distant memory. It was hard to be a Christian with no one to help me. I guess it makes no sense to you."

"No, I understand what you're expressing, Cara. I even had some of those feelings when I was a child. But now I live with the cold facts of reality."

"But isn't psychology based on theories instead of hard facts?"

"Well, dear, you got me there. I have to laugh about that. But for now, we'll have to end our philosophical discussion as I have a dinner engagement in twenty minutes. If you don't mind showing yourself out, Cara, we'll see you next Tuesday."

November 18, 1982, 4:28 p.m.

"I have to keep this on the down-low, Cee; Mom's lurking in the dining room. Did your phone bill come?"

"It's not here yet. But it'll fry Dad if this call's on it. I don't care, Gracie; I need to talk with you."

"I miss you, Cara. If, if only we could go back to the time we talked about everything till three in the morning. I'm thrilled that you found a nice boy; it sounds promising. Maybe it's one good thing that'll come out of your move."

"I think it is . . . probably the only thing."

"I remember our disappointments with the few boys who might have become boyfriends. There weren't many, but each turned out to be a bust. Maybe it was our fault, I don't know, Cee."

"We didn't know what to do—how to act. I'm not sure if I do now. But I like Davey more than any boy I've ever met. He's good and loyal, and it doesn't hurt that he's cute. But I'm afraid I'll blow it, Gracie—mess up and lose him."

"You sell yourself short, Cara. You're quite a catch, and he'll see that. Plus, you're cute; don't forget it."

"I'm not sure he believes me with all the crap I've laid on him. Dear God, I told him how awful Luke and all the cruds were. Then two minutes later, they come along and are super friendly to us—fake as hell. I told him that, but he might not accept it. I'm afraid!"

"Yeah, I know, Cee. But there must be a way to get those jerks off your back. Can you think of anything?"

"Well, I've tossed around a few ideas but nothing that makes sense. Do you have any thoughts, Gracie?"

"It seems to me that Luke is at the center of your problems, except for the mirror. Is there anything you can do to take him out, so to speak? What about his father? Didn't you say he's a pastor?"

"Yeah, at the Nazarene church not far from here. What are you driving at, Gee?"

"As a pastor, he must be a decent man, right? Maybe if you talk to him, he'll clue you in about Luke. I don't know; you have to do something, and soon. You can't have a maniac running around threatening to kill you."

"I don't know. I guess it wouldn't hurt—nothing to lose."

"That's my girl. Let me know how it pans out. But now I've got to run; Mom's calling for me to set the table. Be careful, Cara."

"Yeah. Bye, Gee."

November 20, 1982, 6:07 p.m.

What're Dad and Danny doing here? I thought Dad stayed over in Wyoming and Danny had his first JV game tonight. Keep your mouth shut, Cara. Don't open up a can of worms. Whoops! What's Dad pulling out?

"I'm looking at the telephone bill, Cara. What's this call to Gracie when we told you not to call her again?"

"I, I needed to call her."

"Speak up, young lady, that call cost over five dollars. I'm taking it out of your allowance, and you'll do Danny's chores along with yours for the next three weeks—got it!"

"Oh, Brent, don't be so hard on her. We took her best friend away; can't you show some understanding?"

"Butt-out, Sarah, this is my decision! The girl needs to learn a lesson—take responsibility."

Crap, I didn't have to say a word, and the war is on. Take your medicine—you deserve it—and lay low.

"No, I won't butt out. We make decisions together, and the children need to know it. Our daughter's going through a tough time, Brent; please show a little compassion."

"After last weekend, no, I can't! I took your daughter to the police station Saturday night, knowing she was hallucinating again. Hell, the cops don't believe her anymore; they hate to see her coming. Then, Sunday, we have the mirror sold for a hundred bucks until she sticks her nose in and blows the deal."

"Settle down, the kids!"

"I won't; I'm mad as hell! If you don't straighten up, Cara, and pull yourself together, you're going to the funny farm!"

"Don't threaten my daughter!"

"Face it, Sarah, the rest of you too; something has to change around here. I've had it up to here with this craziness!"

"Don't, Dad, it's not all her fault. You don't know that she isn't telling the truth."

"Then why don't her stories check out, Danny? And what about that God-forsaken mirror? It has nothing to do with telling the truth. It's pure fantasy."

They're tearing themselves apart because of me. Maybe I should go away, go to an institution. They'd all be better off. Dad's probably right; I'm sick and need help. What do I say? "I'm sorry, Dad. Please don't fight anymore. Maybe I should go away; find a way to get better."

"See what you've done, Brent! You're not going away, Cara. Doctor Reyna doesn't think it's necessary yet."

"But, Mom, what about your grandma?"

"What, what about her, Cara? What do you mean?"

"Well, I told Doctor Reyna and thought he probably told you. I'm sorry, Mom, I overheard you and dad talking about your grandma, how she was insane and committed suicide. How that—with everything going on—you were afraid I inherited her illness."

"What's that all about, Mom?"

"Not now, Danny. Did you eavesdrop, Cara? Why would you do such a thing?"

"Dammit, we deserve more respect than that, girl! When we talk privately, the conversation's private, not to be invaded by you or anyone else. It's disgusting!"

"I'm sorry, Dad. But is it true, did I inherit great-Grandma's mental illness? Am I going to end up like her?"

"Oh, Doctor Reyna isn't sure, dear. But he thinks you probably haven't inherited whatever's going on with you. He must have told you that more sessions are needed to make that determination. But, no, you're not going to end up taking your life like Grandma."

"Yeah, but maybe I need to go away for everyone's good."

"Dammit, Brent, why couldn't you leave it alone? I've had it! Let's drop the whole subject. Anna's coming Tuesday, and I don't want her involved in this. It's none of her business. I didn't say anything before, but Anna wanted to bring us a puppy. A friend gave her one, and they're looking for a home for the other one. I told her no."

"What kind of dog, Mom?"

"Oh, I'm not sure, Danny, a spaniel, I think. But we don't need another dog now."

"Why not? It's been two years since we lost Snuggles. I think we're all over it and ready to have another dog, at least I am."

"Maybe you are, Danny, but I doubt if Cara is. I know you're still dealing with the pain, dear. But anyone could have left the gate open. You didn't know Snuggles was in the backyard. And you can't blame yourself that he got out and got hit by a car."

"But I still do, Mom! I hate myself for it; what I did to Snuggles."

"Okay, I'm done. Luke will be here anytime."

"Keep him out of our house! Mom, you said he couldn't come here anymore."

"We banned him from our home, Danny. And that goes for our yard too. If you must continue seeing him, meet him somewhere else. But for your sister's sake, I hope you end that friendship."

"Yeah, wish it was that simple."

"Can I be excused, too, Mom? I want to go to my room."

November 21, 1982, 1:22 p.m.

"Mrs. Windly?"

"Yes. You must be Davey's new friend Cara?"

"I am."

"He's told us all about you. My husband, John, and I would love to meet you sometime."

"Oh, okay. Is Davey home?"

"I'll call him."

"Hi, Cara. What's up?"

"I need to talk with you. I can't call Gracie anymore. And Britta, well, I can't go into that. Anyway, we had a blowup at dinner last night."

"Oh, sorry, what happened?"

"I knew it would happen, Davey, just a matter of time. But I didn't expect my father to blow his lid completely. It was the long-distance call to Gracie after they told me not to do it. He went ballistic, and now I have to do Danny's chores for three weeks and have five dollars taken out of my allowance."

"He didn't ground you, though?"

"No, but he probably will when he gets next month's bill and sees that I called Gracie again. But it was worth it, Davey."

"I know, from what you've told me how tight the two of you are."

"That's only part of what happened. I didn't want to, but I told them that I knew about my great-Grandma going nuts and committing suicide."

"What?"

"I know, something else I didn't tell you. I eavesdropped on my parents and overheard them talking about my great-Grandma's insanity. It's haunted me ever since, thinking I inherited the mess I'm in."

"That's a heavy burden for you to carry, Cara."

"Yeah, I guess that's why I need you, Davey. But if you don't want to have anything more to do with me I wouldn't blame you."

"I'm not going anywhere. So, I guess your father blew up again."

"Did he ever. Mom surprised me, though. She stood up for me and told my dad to shut up. That was a first. I mean, she was upset too but tore into Dad when he got out of hand."

"It surprised you that she would?"

"Well, we don't see eye to eye on many things. And she usually doesn't defend me. But last night, it's almost like she was a lioness protecting her cub. I loved it."

"It helps to have support, but where does that leave you, Cara?"

"I wish I knew. I can't stop my head from spinning long enough to figure it out—the mirror, Snuggles, everything that's happened. Half the time, I don't know what's real and what isn't. And I hate dragging you into this mess, Davey. It's not fair. Please always remember that I treasure you, even if I have to go away."

"No, you won't have to, Cara. You'll be okay. I'll see to it."

"Umm, I know you'll try, and I'll try to hang on for you. Would you give me your opinion about something, Davey? It's what Gracie and I mulled over. We've both scratched our heads about Luke and Danny. We know Luke is evil, but we're puzzled about Danny and why he's protecting him. Gracie figured I might learn something if I talked to Luke's father. He's the pastor at the nearby Nazarene church. He must be a decent man and might shed some light on what's up with Luke."

"Pastor Glover, right?"

"Yeah, do you know about him?"

"It's a coincidence, but my father recently updated the insurance policy for Pastor Glover's church. Dad said he was friendly and outgoing—a nice guy."

"Oh, that does it, then! It has to be a sign that I should talk to him, don't you think?"

"Sounds like it to me; might as well try it, Cara."

"Good, I will tomorrow."

November 22, 1982, 3:17 p.m.

"Mom, drop me off at the next corner. I'll walk the rest of the way home."

"Are you sure, dear?"

"Yeah, I'll be home in a while."

Okay, only a block and a half to the church. Take your time, Cara. Think about what you're going to say. Aw, if I only knew.

Here goes. Beautiful doors—look new. Be quiet. No one's in the foyer. Check out the sanctuary. Not a soul in here. Maybe Pastor Glover isn't here. Wait! There's a stairway over there. Huh, it's like in my dream. Should I? No, no, don't do it, Cara. He might be downstairs; it won't hurt to check. This is way spooky—go back. The stairs, the room, and the door on the far side are the same as my nightmare. "Anyone down here?" *No one. Oh, there's a door for storage under the stairs. Run! No, just settle down, stop shaking, Cara. Stroll over to the door and see if Pastor Glover's in the room,* "Ahh!"

"Can I help you, young lady?"

"Y-you . . . scared . . . me h-half to death."

"I'm sorry; it wasn't my intention. But I usually don't find strangers wandering around the church, especially in the basement. Are you looking for someone?"

"Well, yes, are you Pastor Glover?"

"I am. Do you want to speak to me?"

"Yeah. Is your office down here?"

"No, it's upstairs, follow me. Right in here. Have a seat. What's your name, young lady, and how can I help you?"

"I'm Cara Corrigan, and—"

"Oh, the girl that's harassed my son."

"Well, that's why I wanted to talk with you. I hoped you'd be able to help me understand."

"Understand, understand what? I know the police have hounded Luke because of you. Maybe I'm the one who needs to understand why you're harassing Luke and spreading lies about him."

"I'm not, Pastor. I know he's your son, but I'm not lying. Everything I said happened."

"Luke's far from perfect, but he and his friends swear that your accusations are only in your mind—they didn't happen. And I've talked to them all. Your reputation precedes you. No one trusts what you say, Miss Corrigan."

"Yeah, I know my rep is shot. So, now, how do I make you or anyone else believe me?"

"You probably won't. Why did you think I would help you? I'm puzzled."

"I guess it was a mistake. I thought you could shed light on why Luke's trying to destroy my life and how he's got a hold on my brother Danny. But I can see you'll never believe me—never take my word over his. I shouldn't have come here. I'm sorry I bothered you."

"I'm sorry, too, Miss. But I do hope you get the help you're seeking. Under the circumstances, though, I'm not the one who can do that. I'd never share personal information with a stranger. I don't know where you stand spiritually, but God is the one who can best help you."

"I don't know Him anymore. I did at one time, but it's faded, and now I'm lost."

"You made a commitment to the Lord?"

"In a Baptist church, when I was younger. I don't know what your church believes, but they said I'd never be lost. I feel that way, though, and don't think I'll ever find my way back."

"You and your family don't go to church?"

"Not for a long time. I don't know why; my father blew up over something, and we never returned. But I loved being there, the feeling, the peace."

"Maybe you should return. I think you're old enough to make that decision. It might be awkward, but you're welcome here."

"Thanks, pastor, probably not. I do know God's the answer, though. I wish I had the courage."

"Courage for what, Cara?"

"I don't know; it's hard to explain. One of my friends is going through hell. She's scared but has incredible courage. It's the kind of courage I want and will never have. How do you get it, pastor?"

"Faith and hope are the ground that brings forth courage."

"Oh, I never thought of it that way. How did Jesus have the courage to take our sins and die for us? I know He's God, but still, I could never lay down my life for another person, let alone the whole world."

"It's the most admirable deed that we'd all find hard to do."

"Yeah, I guess. I'm sorry for wasting your time, Pastor Glover. I only wanted to understand. I'll probably never figure it out but thanks. I need to get home now."

"I hope it works out for you, Cara."

10:14 p.m.

Quiet, Cara. Watch your step; don't trip in the dim light. Open and close the door slowly; watch out going down the stairs. Good, no one heard me, but I'll catch hell if anyone checks my room. I have to do it; Britta's the only one I can talk to this late. I need to tell someone how frazzled I am. Will she be there? Get the blanket off; it won't take long to find out. "Britta, Britta, are you there?"

"Cara, are you there? Please be; I need you!"

"I'm here, Britta; I need you too. It must be early in the morning there."

"Yes, after four. My father's sleeping, so I have to whisper. Can you hear me?"

"I can if I get up close. Did something happen?"

"Ernst attacked me again. It was horrible, Cara! He went insane, ripping my blouse off. I, I had nothing to wear under it. He tried to touch me, but I kicked him in the shin and ran for the door. I was too slow, and he threw me on the bed and tried to jump on me. He was screaming at me—filthy threats! I yelled until Frau Keller ran in."

"My God, Britta, what did she do?"

"She screamed at Ernst and told him to get out. Herr Keller came up later to make sure I was alright. The Kellers are good people."

"I can tell you're not alright, Britta. Did he physically hurt you?"

"Well, I twisted my back. It's the fear, though; I can't take it anymore, Cara! Herr Keller told my father when he returned from Switzerland last night. The Kellers said they could no longer influence Ernst; he's too involved with the Hitler Youth. I'm afraid he'll report us to the Gestapo."

"Umm, what are you going to do?"

"My father and Herr Keller will talk with members of the underground today. We'll probably leave our hideout in a few days. We have to go, Cara, but I can't stand not seeing you again. I, I don't understand how, but I've grown to love you like the sister I never had."

"Oh, damn! I know you have to go, Britta; you have to be safe. I don't know what I'll do without you, though. I love you too and wish I had a sister like you by my side all the time. Where will you go?"

"We don't know yet, perhaps Switzerland. It's a dangerous journey. Maybe we'll find another safe house. Oh, I have to get my mind off it. What happened to you, Cara?"

"It's lame compared to what you're going through, Britta, not worth mentioning. I need to suck it up—grow up and get over it."

"Please tell me."

"Only more of the same. It's my family, the police, and the people at school. It angers me that no one believes what I say, and I can't make them, Britta."

"But Davey and Gracie do, me too."

"Thank God for that. But I need to be smarter. Gracie and Davey thought I might learn more about why Luke's after me if I talked to his father. He's a pastor and a good man, but it was a bust. I should have known he wouldn't share anything personal with a stranger."

"I'm sorry."

"Thanks, Britta, but enough about me. I'm worried about you. What can I do to help?"

"Be close, listen and encourage me. What else can you do?"

"Well, can I touch you? That's it! Put the palm of your right hand against the mirror. There, I see it clearly. Now I'll put my palm on the mirror where yours is. Oh, it's tingling, almost burning. Pull your hand away. Did you feel it, Britta?"

"Oh, yes! I heard the mirror crackle, and my palm burned. I can't explain it, but—

"Did you feel my pain? I felt your dread, the confusion of not knowing what to do."

"I did feel your pain. Somehow, we connected; touched each other down deep."

"Wow! Did we ever? I felt I was part of you—still do. And now I know I can help you, Britta. And my courage is building to do it."

"But what about your doctor and everyone telling you that I'm only in your mind?"

"They're wrong, and I don't care about that anymore. I love you and have to help! I guess I'll only know how in time."

"If you only could help me, Cara. Are we in our right minds? Often I daydream about living where you do in 1982. It helps pass the time to picture it. With the details you've shared about your family and home, I imagine a safe world free of the horrors of war. I think about living your life instead of mine. I know you understand why."

"Of course, knowing where you are and when. I think about your life all the time, Britta."

"I better go now; touching you in the mirror knocked me out. I need to sleep before father wakes."

"Yeah, I'm totally wiped. I don't know what happened, but we'll never be the same. Bye for now, Britta—love you."

11
THE COMING STORM

November 23, 1982, 12:14 p.m.

"Cara, what are you doing in the lunchroom? You have second lunch. Won't you get in trouble for skipping fourth period?"

"I hope not, Davey; it's only study hall. I'll tell them I needed to eat early; my stomach was growling or something. But I need to talk with you."

"You're still going to your appointment after school?"

"No, that's one of the things I have to tell you. Doctor Reyna canceled my appointment. Mom said one of his friends passed away, and he's on a plane heading back East."

"Oh, too bad. Are you okay with missing the session?"

"Well, there were things I wanted to tell him, but I guess they'll have to wait till next week."

"I think you like him, Cara. Are you starting to trust he can help you with all you're working through?"

"Yeah, I do trust him, and he's putting some pieces together for me. But, Davey, something's happening beyond Reyna's understanding. And that's the other thing I have to tell you."

"Okay. Am I going to like this?"

"Maybe not; it might send you packing—running away from me for good."

"Well, go ahead, or maybe you shouldn't tell me."

"I have to. It's clear in my mind that Britta's real. She's not a figment of my imagination who only lives in a mirror. Doctor Reyna will never understand, so I'll dance around the subject when it comes up. And I'll only tell you and Gracie what I believe. Before you say something, Davey, don't try to talk me out of it because it won't do any good."

"Umm, I know, so I won't."

"Thanks, Davey. I have three friends in the world who understand. And I love each of you. Don't be shocked. I'm not hiding anymore. I have to be real to get through it all."

"I, I love you too, Cara. I wouldn't have believed it a few days ago and never dreamed I would say it to you. It might be a wild ride, but I'm not getting off."

"Oh, thanks. Your love, and Gracie's and Britta's, is what I need. For a while, I've thought I might go away to get better. I don't believe that anymore. But the weird thing is, Davey, I know I'll be going somewhere. I never want to leave you, but I have to help Britta. I don't know how, but I believe I can if I find the courage. It's muddled in my mind, and I can't expect you to understand."

"I only want to be with you, Cara, to help in any way I can. Understanding isn't important now."

"Dear Lord, you're something else. Hold my hand under the table." *Aw, so sweet. I wish he could hold me now—even kiss me. Calm down, Cara, it'll all happen, don't rush it.*

"Cara, are you still with me?"

"Yeah, just enjoying my hand in yours. Oh, I almost forgot to tell you; my Aunt Anna's coming for Thanksgiving. Mother's picking her up at Stapleton in an hour. I hope you can meet her; she'll be here till Sunday afternoon."

"You said she's a real card, a lot of fun."

"She is; you'll like her. And she's always in my corner. Well, I think I've had enough of this mystery meat. Do you always bring a sack lunch, Davey?"

"Most of the time. Bologna and cheese are my lunch staple."

"And your mother sends a piece of cake and a banana too?"

"Yeah, I like them and don't even mind bologna."

"She must bake a lot of cakes. Oh, looks like we only have ten minutes till history class. I'm off to the restroom. I'll see you in class."

6:17 p.m.

Good, mom has me sitting beside Aunt Anna. Now I don't feel so distant. I wish they'd take the leaf out of the table; make it cozier. I'd hate the table anyway; it puts us far apart. Yeah, I guess that's because we are. But you'll like this meal with Anna. Put all the junk away for the night, enjoy her.

"Did you get your homework done, Cara?"

"Knocked it all off, Anna. I'm looking forward to a long talk with you later, catching up."

"What are you two cooking up?"

"Oh, nothing, Sarah, nothing to concern you. Only girl talk."

"Yeah, girl talk between forty and fourteen-year-olds."

"I hope it doesn't get your shorts in a knot, Brent."

"You don't have to be snotty about it, Anna. And stop that laughing, Cara. You too, Danny—it's not funny."

"It's no biggie, Mom, and it—

"Quiet, Danny!"

"Okay, Mom. And moving on, how was your flight, Anna?"

"Good, except for the whopper sitting next to me. Thanks for asking, Danny."

"Whopper, that's funny; what do you mean?"

"A four-hundred-pound doofus, Cara. How'd you like fat hanging so far over the seat arm that it was all over your hip and thigh?"

"Shush, don't encourage her, kids, and stop laughing."

"Hu-hu, you're biting your tongue, so you don't laugh, Mom."

"Yeah, loosen up, Sis. It's okay to laugh. But the funniest thing happened when they brought lunch. The guy was woofing it down like it was his last meal. When the little girl in front of him put her seat back, well, food and drink covered his pants—what a mess. I busted out laughing. I don't know why, but he didn't appreciate that."

"That's hilarious, Auntie; I can picture the scene."

"It's not that damned funny, Cara."

"Come on, Dad. So, what happened; was the guy ticked?"

"He went ballistic. The girl's mother apologized profusely, but it did little good. The stewardess brought towels and asked if there was anything else she could do. I asked her if they had any spare tents on the plane. In hindsight, that didn't help the situation, either."

"Ha-ha-ha! Now you did it, Anna, even got Mom and Dad laughing."

"Mission accomplished, Cara—finally. Speaking of food, the fried chicken is excellent, Sarah. You are quite the cook, the whole meal's delicious. With the kids in college, I don't bother much with cooking; way too many TV dinners."

"Thanks, Anna. I need to say it politely but so you understand. When you and Cara have your little confab later, nothing about what we talked about on the way home from the airport. Okay? What I said is private."

"What do you mean, Mom?"

"Not your concern, Danny. Nor anyone else's either."

"Sarah, being in my forties, I'm old enough to determine what I'll talk about, with whom, and when."

"Just keep your nose out of our business, Anna!"

"Thanks, but don't butt in, Brent. I can handle this."

"But Mom, you know Aunt Anna and I talk about everything. That's what buds do. Anyway, you've put your spin on things; let me have a chance."

"Oh God, why do we have to go through this every year. At least mother's not here to muddy the waters further. I'm done—gonna bring in dessert."

"Well, we're off to a flying start, but thanks for the laughs, Anna."

"Of course, Cara, I mean to please but don't always, I guess. We'll cover everything in our cozy chat later."

7:24 p.m.

"So, this is your new bedroom?"

"Come in, Anna, have a seat in the soft chair."

"It's big, much larger than your Texas bedroom. I like it, Cara. New bed; looks comfy. Nice vanity and a walk-in closet to boot. Everything a girl needs, huh?"

"I guess."

"Not a very enthusiastic response, sweetie. Is there something I'm missing?"

"It would be great if everything else was as good as the room."

"Still not going well with your parents?"

"I've hated this move since the moment I heard about it and still do. Plus, Mom and I have our differences. And why can't Dad put me first at least once in his life? But, oh no, he has to uproot us for the sake of his career. I don't understand it, Auntie. He never says he loves me, and I can't remember when he comforted me in his arms. It's not normal, is it?"

"Not for a father, it isn't, sweetheart. Dammit, anyway!"

"Oh, I didn't know you were that ticked at him. I know you've never cared for my dad, but has something happened?"

"Cara, dear . . . no, forget it; I need to keep my mouth shut."

"About what, Auntie?"

"Suffice it to say, it's not my business."

"Now I'm puzzled—what's new? I guess Mom told you about what's going on with me."

"She filled my ear on the way home from the airport. But I learned long ago to take what she says with a grain of salt. She mentioned before that you were having mental issues—her words, not mine. Now she says you're in therapy."

"Doctor Reyna."

"Yeah, I don't like 'em, Cara, never have. When did this start?"

"Ahh . . . a few weeks ago. I think today would have been my fourth session if Reyna hadn't canceled."

"Sarah said you had run-ins with kids at school. What happened, dear?"

"I can guess what Mom said. Well, they attacked me twice and did other things. No one believes me, though. I filed police complaints, but the thugs always lied, and the cops found no one to back me up. Mom and Dad think I'm losing it, that I imagined everything."

"I believe you're sincere, sweetie. Do you have a clue as to why or what they're up to?"

"For some reason, they hate my guts—don't know why."

"Maybe I can help before I leave Sunday. I don't know how, but I'm in your corner, Cara."

"Thanks, Anna, but what can you do?"

"Well, we'll see. What about the mirror your mom mentioned? She said you're talking to a girl in it. What's going on with that?"

"I doubt you'll be with me on this one. Mom told you the truth, Anna; I've been talking to a German girl in the mirror. The mirror they took from my room to the basement."

"You know that's crap, Cara; people don't live in mirrors!"

"No, no, I don't know that. No one believes me, but it's alright; I know I'm not imagining it. And I don't want to talk about it anymore."

"Okay, we'll drop it for now."

"Mom and Dad think I inherited your grandma's insanity. They're sure it's behind my problems."

"That's bull crap, Cara! How'd you know about that, anyway?"

"Well, I eavesdropped, heard them talking about it. Mom was worried that I inherited her grandma's illness—maybe that I'd kill myself, too."

"Okay, it's gotta end, sweetie; this cover-up has gone too far. Damn, I can't believe it!"

"What is it, Auntie? Cover-up, what do you mean?"

"I need to think this over, dear. It might be time—high time."

"You lost me a while back."

"I'm sorry, Cara. I won't say anything more now but brace yourself. I might drop a bomb or two tomorrow. This deception has to end, for all your sakes. What you're going through isn't right. But now I'm worn out from the trip; we'll talk more tomorrow."

"Sure. Have a good night's sleep, Anna."

She's in my corner; I know that. I didn't expect she'd be keen on the mirror; that's okay. But what is she talking about? I'm confused.

November 24, 1982, 3:05 p.m.

"You're sure they won't mind me riding home with you?"

"Why would they, Davey? Besides, I told Aunt Anna that I had a boyfriend, and I want her to meet you."

"Boyfriend? Then I guess I have a girlfriend."

"You're stuck, Davey. Are you cool with it?"

"Totally. What did you tell her about me? And why would she ride with your mom to pick us up?"

"One question at a time, please. I didn't have time to say much about you, only that we met recently and liked each other. And you're smart and cute."

"Oh, hope I don't disappoint."

"Don't worry, you won't. There's Mom's Olds." *Darn, Anna's not with her; wonder why? She said she would come.* "Aunt Anna decided not to come with you, Mom?"

"I think the altitude's bothering her. She wanted to lie down—had something to think over."

"Umm, did she say what?"

"No, but she's been on edge all day—not sure what's going on, Cara. Do you know what's bothering her?"

"Well, I can't think of anything. Drop me off on Davey's corner. He's going to Colorado Springs for the weekend, and I want to tell him something."

"Private, huh?"

"Mother! No, it's not private. I want to say goodbye, you know."

"Well, here's the corner; sorry for embarrassing you. Enjoy your Thanksgiving weekend in the Springs, Davey."

"Thanks, Mrs. Corrigan; have a nice Thanksgiving too. Okay, what else did you need to tell me, Cara?"

"It's about Aunt Anna and what she said last night. She came down hard on my case about the mirror; I knew she would. But she believes me about the attacks."

"Did she hurt your feelings?"

"No. Anna's in my corner—like she always is—but she's no-nonsense and doesn't hesitate to tell me when I'm wrong. Something she said bothers me, though. I'm having trouble figuring out what she means."

"And you need to tell me."

"No, I don't need to, but I thought you might help me with it. I'm scared, Davey, afraid there might be big trouble tonight."

"I'm sorry."

Thanks, Davey. Being in your arms makes me feel safe. I wish you weren't going away. I want to kiss you, maybe when we say goodbye.

"So, what did she say?"

"She said this cover-up and deception has to end. It's high time for all our sakes or something like that."

"Wow! What do you make of it, Cara?"

"I think it's about my issues and great-Grandma, but I'm not sure. Whatever it is, she said she'd need to think it over. I think that's what she's doing today before she drops the bombs—why she didn't come with mom to pick us up."

"Bombs! What do you mean?"

"She said she might be dropping a couple bombs tonight. That's what worries me, Davey."

"Yeah, well, I'll call you Friday to see what happened. I wish I could help now."

"There's nothing you can do. Maybe say a prayer if you do that. Now I need to get going, face whatever's going down. Would you kiss me?"

"Ah, of course!"

Umm, umm, better than I ever dreamed. Press harder, Cara. Hug him tight, soak it up. "That was wonderful, Davey; should last me till Sunday. Be safe; I'll look forward to your call Friday."

"You'll be in my prayers, Cara."

November 24, 1982, 6:21 p.m.

So far, so good. I can't get this queasiness out of my stomach, though. Too much tension. When is Auntie going to drop the bombs? Wonder what she was talking about? Whatever it is, I hope she forgets it, and we can have a peaceful dinner.

"Are cold cuts and soup alright? I had too much preparation for tomorrow to put a big meal on the table tonight."

"Sandwiches and soup always work for me, Mom. Besides, I need to eat and run—got a date."

"Not Andrea Wicks, I hope."

"Duh, are you kidding, Cara? I stay clear of her."

"Well, you better, Son. I wish you'd stay clear of Luke and the rest of them too."

"Yeah, Mom."

"Who's the girl, Danny?"

"Someone from school, Sis. You don't know her. I hate to eat and run, but I'm meeting Diane at quarter till. I'll be home by ten; see you tomorrow, Aunt Anna."

"Take care of yourself, Danny."

Sure, Dad, give your son a love pat on the backside as he passes. Of course, you'd never think of doing the same for me. I need to leave the table, too, but I'm afraid of what might happen if I do. Better just lay low.

"After we've cleaned up the dishes, I'd like to talk some more, Cara."

"What about?"

"Last night, we left a few things unfinished, Sarah."

"No, I don't like you and Cara having private conversations. I know what you're talking about, anyway. And as her parents, we're responsible for her well-being. So anything you have to say to her, say it now in front of us all."

No, Mom, you don't want that—please! She's getting upset, and Dad's tapping on the tablet. Ahh, leave it alone. Anna's been so quiet. I'm not sure if she's not feeling well or ready to explode. Please, Aunt Anna, no bombs tonight. Dear God, let there be peace. I only want to be alone with Davey, away from here.

"Are you sure, Sarah?"

"I know it's about Cara's issues. But it's none of your business, and what can you possibly add to help her? You should just butt out!"

"I should, but I can't for Cara's sake and yours too."

"I don't understand, Anna; how could anything you say help both Cara and me? It makes no sense."

"The last thing I want to do is hurt you, Sarah; I do love you. But it's high time the deception ends, and you all know the truth about Cara's illness. It'll cut you deep, Sarah, but it has to be."

Oh no, here it comes, but what in the world is it? Cut Mom deep; I don't understand. God take me out of here; something bad's about to happen, and I don't want Mom hurt.

"Cut me? Just say it, Anna!"

"Please, no interruptions till I get it all out. Well, Sarah, I'll start with Mom's trip to Germany. She told us that a friend needed her help right away. But I grilled her further to find out what was really going on. It wasn't a friend she was going to see, but a woman out of her past. You know the army sent Father to Germany in 1946. We spent fifteen months there. The woman who summoned—"

"I'm sorry for interrupting, but what does this have to do with Cara and her problems?"

"Please, Sarah, I'm getting to it. Anyway, the woman who sent for Mother wanted to give her a heads-up about a potential problem. Mother only casually knew this woman who worked at the local orphanage."

I can't stop shaking. Cara, chill. It can't be that bad, can it?

"Oh, Sarah, Dad wanted the truth to come out years ago. He tried to say something in hospice before he died, but Mom made him swear not to. I never understood why she wanted to hold onto it. I was nine in 1947 when it happened. From what I overheard, the woman at the orphanage knew a young girl with a two-month-old baby. The girl was destitute and couldn't possibly raise the child. So the orphanage finalized the adoption in February. I remember that day well, the day Mom and Dad brought the baby home—brought you home, Sarah."

Oh, God, no! Now, mom's bawling and even Dad had a tear running down his cheek. I've never seen him cry. At least Anna's trying to comfort Mom. Wow! What can be said, the shock of it all, the sadness of tears?

"Calm yourself; let it soak in, Sarah. I'm sorry for being the one to tell you."

"But, why didn't she want to tell me, Anna? Damnit! She should have—I'm mad as hell at her! I can't believe it; are you positive?"

"Remember when you said, more than once, how you felt like an outsider. How many times did you tell me that you wanted to look like Mom and didn't understand why you didn't? Do you remember all the times that it came up, Sarah?"

"Yeah, I do. Maybe I suspected it all along but squelched the thoughts. I don't know; I'm dizzy with it all; it'll take time to digest and sort out."

"Umm, a long time, sweetie. I had to tell you, though, for Cara's sake, and yours too. I couldn't have you and Cara go on believing that she inherited whatever's going on with her. I know it hurts like hell, Sarah, but try to understand why."

"I hate it but understand. Please hold me, Brent, help me."

I hope he can, Mom. Dear God, I didn't inherit my problem! Thank you, Lord, maybe I'm not sick at all. Mom will never be the same. I hope she'll be better off for it in time—please, for her sake. What a bomb, but Anna said she might drop a couple. Ahh, is there more?

"That's half the story, Sarah. It's not the ideal time, but we have to clean the slate, take everything out of the shadows. She'll be fifteen soon and deserves to know as much as you did. Cara, I'm sorry."

"No, damn you, Anna; keep your nose out of our business; it's not your place!"

"You're wrong, Brent, and you share the blame for it."

"Oh, please don't, Anna, it'll take time for me to get over the shock of this. I can't stand the humiliation and shame of that too. Not tonight, as my sister, I beg you—no!"

"What's Anna talking about, Mom? Humiliation and shame, what do you mean?"

"We've already said too much, Sarah; tell her, or I will."

God, what in the world's happening! Mom's bawling again, and Dad's pale as a sheet. "Tell me, Mom; I want to know."

"Umm, how do I begin, Cara? I don't want to hurt you—make you feel like I do now. Oh, hell, I hate this! You know your father and I have had a strained relationship for as long as you can remember. We've talked about it before, skimmed over the surface."

"Yeah, I know, but most marriages have tough times, don't they, Mom?"

"I suppose, dear, but this is more, much more. I need to come right out with it, Cara. Remember when we left the Baptist church that you liked, maybe six or seven years ago?"

"Of course, I was upset and didn't understand why."

"An eight-year-old couldn't understand. Rumors spread through the church—ugly accusations. One of the deacons threatened—"

"No! Stop, Sarah, don't—"

"Shut up, Brent, it's too late! One of the deacons threatened to reveal our secret if we didn't immediately leave the church, so we did. Adultery snared me, Cara."

"Oh, what are you saying, Mom?"

"I wish that were the whole story, darling. I hate throwing your world further out of kilter. Aww, let me gather myself for a second—stop crying. It only happened twice, Cara, but fate was against me—I was pregnant. Brent was furious, of course, and wanted to abort the baby, but I flatly refused. Damn him! He cheated on me three times that I know of."

No, she's not saying that! Davey, please come and take me away.

"He fought it all the way, but I had that beautiful baby girl, you, Cara."

I'm so numb; what am I supposed to think or say? "Why couldn't you tell me, Mom?"

"We wanted to protect you, dear, that's all. Now both of us face hard times ahead, being dumped on the way we were. If we do it together, maybe it'll help."

"I can't believe you spilled it all. What purpose will it serve? Damn! I'm out of here!"

"Fine, Brent; we don't need you here."

"Oh, shut your dammed mouth, Anna! You caused all of this. You should be the one packing your bags and getting the hell out of our house and never returning!"

"Please leave, Brent."

"I'll deal with you later, Sarah."

This is too much I need to be alone. "Huh, huh, I need to go-go to my bedroom now."

"You should go with her, Sarah; she shouldn't be alone."

"Ahh, would you go, Anna? I'm washed out and have nothing left to give. I've gotta work things out in my mind.

"Sure, Sis. Can I go with you, Cara? We can talk things out, and I'll try to answer any questions."

"I'd like that, Auntie. Oh, can I take your arm? I'm dizzy."

"Be careful, Cara, slowly take one step on the stairs at a time. Now take your shoes off and lie down; I'll lie next to you for a while."

"Thanks, Auntie; I think the crying jag is over."

"It'll be alright, sweetie. Time will be your friend, you'll see. Here, let me fluff up your pillow and pull the comforter up."

"Was I too young? You know, before now."

"Probably, Cara, who knows for sure. It was a hard thing for your mother to admit—to anyone. But at least you know the truth at fourteen. It'll be harder for your mother at her age."

"I guess. I feel bad for her, Anna, and don't blame her for not telling me. At least Mom and I can be thankful that we'll never inherit great-Grandma's mental illness."

"That should bring a semblance of peace to both of you."

"Oh, it just came to mind; it all makes sense now."

"What's that, sweetie?"

"Why Dad—do I still call him Dad?"

"Of course, he raised you and is your father in every way except biologically."

"But it explains why he never takes me in his arms, hardly ever comforts me, why he doesn't put mom or me ahead of what he wants. Does he love me at all, Anna?"

"Probably, in his own way. I've never cared much for Brent, but maybe we both have to put ourselves in his shoes, Cara. For a long time—I'm sure—when he looked at you, he saw the fruit of what his wife did. And I know he must have also felt guilty about his share of the blame in the whole mess. Can you begin to understand that, sweetheart?"

"Yeah, I think I do, but it doesn't help. I need a father like Britta's, one who'll protect me, cuddle, and comfort me. It's not too much to expect, is it, Anna?"

"It isn't, dear, but you'll only disappoint yourself if you expect it. I don't think it'll ever happen. It broke Brent, and I don't think he'll ever recover. Focus for now on taking care of yourself—getting your mind straight. Your parents made their bed at a high cost; now they'll have to deal with it in their way."

"I guess I don't have a choice. Why does life have to be so complicated?"

"It shouldn't be, especially for a young lady who should be enjoying life. Hell, I don't have half the answers, Cara. But know this, I'm with you every step of the way."

"I know that, Auntie, thanks. Will Mom recover? Will she ever speak to Grandma again?"

"Well, she might not be coming for Christmas. Time will work it out, though. If you're okay, sweetie, I'm going to check on your mother."

"Go ahead; I'm frazzled and feel like I could go to sleep."

"I'll check in on you later."

November 28, 1982, 3:39 p.m.

"Brr, it's too cold and windy to stay out here much longer, Cara."

"Yeah, but just a while longer. Hold me tighter, Davey, I'll be okay. I like this park even though the grass is brown, and the trees have lost their leaves. I-I get a sense of peace here. The cold wind revives me—helps me shake the funk I've been in since Wednesday night."

"I get it; it's hard to believe what happened."

"It's all I think about. I wish it'd go away, but it won't. Does this change my life forever, Davey, or will I return to normalcy someday?"

"You will, and I'll be there all the way."

"Well, now you know what happened Wednesday, and Thanksgiving wasn't any better."

"How could that be?"

"Dad didn't come home till three in the morning. He was soused. I heard them yelling; it woke me from a bad dream. He looked like hell when he showed his face for Thanksgiving dinner. Poor mother slaved all morning, preparing a feast that she knew no one would enjoy. Anna pitched in and spent the morning comforting Mom. I think they're working things out—getting closer."

"What about Danny? When did he get clued in?"

"The fight, it woke him, and he came into my room to see if I knew what was up. I told him everything."

"A double shocker for him."

"Yeah, it dumbfounded Danny—ticked him off at everyone except me. We talked for an hour before he went back to bed. Neither of us got much sleep after that. Maybe we'll be closer now, even though we have different fathers. I still can't get used to it: he's not my father."

"Um, but what about your real father? Did you learn anything about him?"

"Yeah, from Anna. What she knew came from Mom at the time it all went down. After finding out about one of Dad's episodes, she went to a bar to spite him. She met a man named Ben something; I don't remember the last name—it doesn't matter. She had too much to drink and ended up going home with him. I guess it also happened another time."

"Then, it hit the fan. Your father, or should I call him that?"

"Whatever, it doesn't matter, Davey. He raised me, so I guess he's my father, at least the only one I'll ever know."

"Do you know what happened to Ben?"

"No, I don't think anyone does. Mom never told him she was pregnant. She heard that he left town; went out west somewhere. She never saw him again."

"It was a mess with your dad?"

"Anna didn't give me details, but of course it was. They argue a lot, and I'm not sure where their relationship is. Sometimes they're on the same page; at other times, they're in different worlds. I have to live with it now, Davey."

"Yeah, has your mother said anything about your grandma? Is she mad at her?"

"Probably, but she's keeping it to herself, not a peep to me. I'm not sure what to expect next. If Grandma and Anna both come for Christmas, it'll be worse than Thanksgiving, and I can't handle it."

"It could get ugly. With all that's happened, though, you seem solid, Cara. Mentally speaking, that is. Darn, that came out awkward. What I mean is this hasn't thrown you off, as everyone would expect. And learning that you haven't inherited mental illness has to lift your spirits."

"Yeah, you don't know how good it feels to be free of that. But I still have issues, Davey. Do you understand?"

"The mirror, is that it?"

"I go back and forth about the mirror because it's incredible. But then I know—as sure as I'm here in your arms, Davey—that I'm not hallucinating and Britta is as real as you are. It's some of the other things I see that I'm not so sure of."

"What you think you saw behind your drapes and in the closet?"

"Yeah, those and the incident with Luke in the basement and the other attacks. Is it possible they didn't happen, were only figments of my sick mind? That's what keeps bugging me, Davey. Maybe I've gotten it wrong, imagined it all. Then there's Snuggles; I don't know what to make of that either."

"It's a lot, Cara. I think it'll work out in time."

"I guess, but I don't know how or when. Ow, I'm starting to feel the biting wind on my face—time to walk home. I have to get a good night's sleep before going back to the school routine."

"We'll walk fast."

November 30, 1982, 5:11 p.m.

"Sit, please."

"On the couch, Doctor Reyna?"

"Yes. Just so you know, Cara, your mother and I talked on the phone earlier. I know it was a rough Thanksgiving for all of you. And we think it's beneficial for her to schedule a few sessions with me to sort out her feelings. She also told me about Sunday night. So, how are you doing, dear?"

"I'm still feeling crappy."

"Sounds like you might have a cold. Tell me about Sunday, Cara."

"Well, Davey and I went to the park in the afternoon. I guess I got chilled in the wind. After I'd been home for a while, I started feeling bad: coughing, a runny nose. I drank some cough syrup, maybe too much. Then I told Mom I wasn't hungry and laid down. Around seven, I woke when I heard Snuggles. He ran to the drapes barking his head off. Please don't say it, Doctor; I know he's gone. I thought I must be dreaming, maybe the cough syrup. When I got up and walked to the window, I saw the form of a man behind the drapes like before. I was shaking, but still I pulled back the drapes. Fear must have taken over to the point where everything went blurry and then dark."

"Is that when your mother and brother found you?"

"Yeah, they said I was screaming. I don't remember it, but I'd opened the window and knocked the screen out. I was on the sill. I guess I was going to jump and didn't know it. Anyway, they pulled me down, and Mom shook me until I snapped out of it."

"It must have been a frightening experience. How do you feel about what happened, Cara?"

"I still shake when I think of it. I didn't feel up to school yesterday or today. I haven't even talked to Davey. It scares me, Doctor Reyna; what would have happened if I hadn't screamed."

"And that's the problem, dear. Unfortunately, your stress has gone to a new level, one that requires us to rethink everything."

"Oh, well, what does that mean?"

"We'll all have to have a serious discussion about that, Cara, but not now. First, I'd like to know how you feel about learning that your father isn't your biological father. That would shake anyone to the core."

How do I explain my feelings to Doctor Reyna when I don't know myself? How am I supposed to feel? What does he expect me to say?

"It frazzled me. Like Mom, I was numb most of the weekend."

"Are you angry with your mom and dad—Brent?"

"I've been mad since May when I found out we'd be moving away from the eighty-sixers and what I knew and loved. So am I angry with Brent—that's what I'm going to call him now? I am, but probably no more than I was already. You know how I felt about him being cool toward me, never comforting me or saying he loves me. So, I guess, knowing *why* makes me feel better if that makes sense."

"I can understand that. What's his reaction to you knowing the truth?"

"We've barely talked since it came out. I guess he'd like to run away from it all, maybe he will. But I've talked to mom. She's dealing with her anger, and I think, in a way, she's relieved that it came out. I feel bad for her—he drove her to it."

"Your whole family has some heavy lifting to work through this. It'll take time, patience, forgiveness, and understanding. Go easy on your mother, Cara; she's not only dealing with your shock but her own. It'll take her quite a while to work through her own anger and all the other emotions that come with what she learned."

"I'll try, Doctor. It's strange that we'd learn these secrets at the same time. But it's drawing us closer. Mom's never been a touchy-feely person; I haven't been either. But now I want to hug and make her feel better—give her a peck on the cheek every time I see her."

"Umm, that'll help her immensely, dear."

"Doctor Reyna, why do I sometimes feel clear headed and happy, then at other times I completely lose it? Davey makes me feel comfortable and secure, but I don't want to hurt him. It scares me that I'll screw it up. I just want to know what's going on in my head. I know it sounds crazy about the mirror—and you'll never believe me—but I think Britta's real, not in my imagination. Ah, I'm confused; I guess I need a lot of help, Doctor."

"You do, Cara, I'm sorry to say. Your mother's now concerned about your safety, so we've talked about options."

Options! I kept saying they would send me away, but I didn't really think it was possible. "Options, what do you mean, Doctor Reyna?"

"Well, we've talked about Elmwood, an effective recovery center in Arvada. I practice there, also. It's a wonderful place that's helped many people sort out their issues. I think going there could protect you, dear. You'll receive treatment that I can't provide in our weekly visits."

"But when . . . when would I go?"

"We'd have to finalize the decision then make the arrangements. It would take at least a week or two."

"Um, how long would I be there?"

"Hopefully, not long, but truthfully, we'll have to wait and see, Cara. Your mother's going to be up in your grill—as you kids say—until this happens. Be patient with her. She only wants to protect you. Okay?"

"Hu, hu, hu, I understand."

"Here's the Kleenex. A good cry helps. I'm going to step out and talk to your mother. Join us when you're ready, dear."

December 1, 1982, 4:07 p.m.

"Oh, it's you, Cara! I've been worried; it's been two weeks since you called."

"Can you talk, Gee?"

"Yeah, Mom and Dad won't be home till five. What's going on, Cee? I lie awake at night thinking about you."

"Mom's in the kitchen, so I might have to hang up quickly. So much has happened, Gracie; it would take an hour to tell you. They might take me to a mental hospital at any time—"

"No! How can they do that? What happened?"

"Ah, a lot. They think I tried to kill myself. I was about to jump out of my window. But I didn't know it until Mom and Danny grabbed me. It was another bad dream. Now they're all freaked out and want to send me to Elmwood, a place for loonies."

"Darn! That's not good. It must scare the crap out of you, Cara."

"Scared, for sure, but that doesn't cover it. I'm confused about what's happening to me. My life's out of control with all the twists and turns since we last talked."

"What else happened?"

"Where do I begin, Gracie? Aunt Anna came for Thanksgiving and blew our family apart."

"Huh, what do—"

"No, Gee, let me get the whole thing out; I don't have much time. Mom cheated on Dad, and the man I thought was my father, all my life, isn't. At least now I know why he doesn't treat me like a father should. That's good, Gee, but it hurts like hell, knowing I'll never get what I need from him."

"Wow! That came from left field. I'm sorry, Cee."

"Well, then Aunt Anna shakes my mother out of her shoes—tells her that she's adopted. Mom's still trying to deal with that like I'm dealing with my news."

"Dear God, tell me how I can help."

"Be on my side, no matter what. I need help, Gracie, but I'm terrified! I want no part of Elmwood; it sounds terrible. If I go, I'm afraid I'll never come back. Maybe I'll run away instead."

"Where . . . where would you go, Cara?"

"Oh, I don't know. Maybe Davey would go with me. We've gotten closer with all that's going on. We could go to Texas and find a place near you, Gee."

"Really? Doesn't sound like you, Cee. You should think that one over."

"I guess. I'm grasping at straws. Anyway, Davey's been sick. He's missed school, and his mother won't let me talk to him. I don't know anymore; maybe I should give up and go away for good."

"No, that's not my Cara, either. You've never been a quitter, girl, and this isn't the time to start."

"But what do I do? I lose either way. What would you do, Gee?"

"I don't know, Cara. Talk to Davey; see what he thinks. If he cares for you—the way you say he does—he might have more wisdom than us."

"Yeah, if I could only see him I would. He has to be back in school tomorrow. Okay, I'll try it; Gracie—Davey will help me. But now I've got to go, Gee. Please keep me in your prayers."

"Of course. Bye, Cara."

12
WHERE'S DAVEY

December 3, 1982, 3:11 p.m.

Where are you, Davey? Why were you late to history class, slipping in so no one would notice? Darn, you said you'd walk me home when I told you that Mom couldn't pick me up, and Danny might not be able to walk with me. Where are you? Aww! Duck behind your locker door! Just pass by Andrea; don't look this way. Okay, she's gone. Finally!

"Where were you, Davey?"

"Getting my books for algebra and English. You're upset."

"I'm on edge—can't shake it. Why wouldn't your mom let me speak to you when I called Wednesday night? She only said you were sick. Is she peeved at me?"

"She was upset that I stayed out in the cold Sunday afternoon. Mom always thinks that sort of thing brings on a cold. I was down in bed by Monday night. That's why you didn't see me in school."

"Let's get out of here. I hate the dingy halls in this place; they need more lights. Crap! it's snowing; watch the steps, Davey; they're slippery."

"Yeah, I will. You got sick too; I'm sorry, Cara. Are you feeling better?"

"A little. How about you?"

"On the mend, I should be back to normal in a day or two. I'm not sure if I should ask, but did something happen this week that got you in trouble with your mother?

"How did you know, Davey? I went to the basement twice to see if Britta had left for good. I waited an hour each time, but she never showed. Mom caught me the second time. I told her nothing happened, that Britta was gone. I said that not seeing her might be a good sign, but it didn't impress her. It ticked Mom off; she's afraid for me, Davey. Then she said I'd have to stay at home—except for school—until I went to Elmwood."

"That's why she called my mother. I don't know what she told her, but Mom was upset. She said that she talked with your mother and was concerned about me having any further contact with you."

"Oh, crap! I'm sorry, Davey. So, what are you going to do?"

"Well, I'm with you, right?"

"All the way, thanks."

"Do you think the mirror thing is over with, Cara? I hope so."

"I don't know. But I can't lose Britta. I'll never be able to explain it, though. We have a special bond, and down deep, I think I can save her. Yeah, it's crazy, Davey, but since I finished Anne Frank's story, I believe I have the courage to do it. And I'm starting to see how—it's all in the mirror. Ahh, I don't know; maybe I'm fooling myself. Do I want to escape my miserable life for something worse?"

"Miserable life! I thought I made a difference, Cara, made your life better?"

"Damn, that didn't come out right, Davey, I'm sorry. You've saved my life—made it better. I'm confused about everything."

"Thanks, we're both on edge, being sick and all. The mirror aside, are things settling down at home?"

"How could they. I'm not sure time will fix what happened over Thanksgiving. But Anna called Mom yesterday after talking to Grandma. She's back from Germany and on the warpath after Anna told her what she did. Grandma wanted to break the news to Mom. Christmas is up in the air. Maybe it's best that I'll be away by then."

"You don't know that for sure!"

"Three weeks? It won't take that long for a room to open up at Elmwood. I'm torn, Davey! I need help—probably need to go. But I'm also scared and don't want to. Gracie and I talked about running away. She said I should ask you about it."

"Run away! What do you mean, Cara? Where would you go?"

"Back to Texas came to mind. Let's hurry; it's snowing hard, must be three inches now."

"How would you get to Texas, and why would you go there?"

"I don't know, only throwing ideas against the wall. I'm not thinking straight these days—forget it."

"Just get ahold of yourself, Cara!"

"Huhu, please don't be harsh with me."

"Oh, don't cry, I'm sorry. Being sick on top of all this has me in a bad mood. I don't mean to be hard on you, but something has to change; I'm having a hard time dealing with it."

"You're having a hard time?! What about me? If it's too hard for you, maybe it's all been a big mistake! Huhu, I'm poison to everyone around me."

"Don't go overboard; it's not like that. Please stop crying! You're not poison to me. We've committed to each other, and I'm not going away."

"Thanks, Davey. I'd hate to hurt you. Let's hurry; this snow is bad."

"Don't slip; we're only three blocks from your house. I can hardly see anything."

"What, watch out, Davey! Stop damnit! Let him go; what're you doing? Ouch!"

Get up, Cara, get up! No, they've got Davey—stuffing him in a car. "Davey, Davey, stop!" *Who are they? Get the license plate number. Wait . . . that woman in the front seat looked like Andrea. How could that be? Where are they going? Why would they take Davey? Was it a blue car? I think it was a dark blue Mustang, fairly new.* "Snuggles! Bad dog. How'd you get out? We gotta get home, hurry, Snuggles." *Careful, don't fall. Where's my left glove? Damn, I dropped it!*

4:14 p.m.

Stop it! Stop shaking, Cara. Where are they? You called twenty minutes ago. Even with the storm, it shouldn't take the police that long to get here. Why is nobody home when I need them? Why do you still have your wet socks on? Get 'em off, Cara, start thinking. Hurry up! When did Mom say she'd be home? Think, Cara, think. Was it half past four? "Thank God! They're here."

"Are you the young lady who reported the taking of a boy against his will?"

"Yeah, come in, please."

"Thanks. I'm Officer Lambert. Quite a storm—getting worse by the minute. Is anyone else home?"

"No, my mother should be home in a while."

"So, who was the boy?"

"The boy? Oh, it was Davey Windly. They came up fast—out of the blizzard. Two of 'em grabbed him before we knew what was happening. They held his arms; he didn't have a chance."

"They didn't try to take you?"

"No. They knocked me down and had him in their car before I could get up."

"The vehicle; did you see it, get the license plate?"

"Yeah, it was a newer blue Mustang. But I couldn't see the license plate in the snow."

"Please write down the boy's name, address, and phone number on this form. You do know them?"

"Yeah, here at the bottom?"

"Uh-huh, under your statement. Well, Miss Corrigan, we'll look into the matter and get back to you if we need more information. I have to tell you, though, I talked to Sergeant Sullivan before I came over. Your previous reports, you know. Hope this one pans out."

"Um, it has to." *He doesn't believe me. Will anyone ever believe me again? Oh, great! Now, Mom's pulling in the driveway. Wouldn't you know—perfect timing, of course. The officer's filling her in.*

"Cara, I'm home. Where are you?"

"Here, Mom."

"Oh, sweetie, the officer told me what happened. I'm sorry; let me hold you. You're shaking."

Dear God, this feels good. I feel her warmth—it hardly ever happens. Don't stop; let it flow.

"You're crying, dear. Here."

She's never given me one of her monogrammed handkerchiefs. Thanks, Mom. Give her a peck on the cheek.

"Oh, sweet of you, dear. Someone took Davey?"

"Yeah. He didn't believe me, did he? Is that what he told you?"

"No, Cara, he didn't mention that, only about Davey. You're sure this time?"

"I think, but everyone's making me doubt myself. I guess I'm not sure of anything, Mom."

"We'll get through this together, darling."

Sounds good, together. But where's it coming from? Must be everything going on; the fallout from Thanksgiving. Maybe it wasn't all bad. "Will Davey be okay?"

"I believe so, Cara. Do you want to help me with supper; it'll get our minds off this for a while."

"Yeah, what are we having?"

5:51 p.m.

I'm glad mom let me move my place setting between her and Danny. I need to be close to her.

"Pass the corn, Cara."

"It's left over, Danny; please clean it up."

"Dad's coming home tomorrow, Mom?"

"No, Danny, he called this afternoon; he's driving to South Dakota to look at sites there. Then he's going to Wyoming before he comes home. It'll be next weekend before he gets back."

"Not scheduled, huh?"

"No, it wasn't, Cara. He needs time; we need space now. It's complicated, maybe too much to put on you and Danny. But try to understand; you're old enough. At least that's what your aunt thinks."

"Will he leave us, Mom?"

"Leave, no, Cara, I don't think so. Well, I hope not. You want him to stay, don't you?"

How do I answer you, Mom? With what you want to hear or what I want. What do I want, though? Maybe I can answer when I know. "Yeah, I do. Do you know anything, Danny?"

"What, about Davey? No, how would I, Sis?"

"Just thought . . . about Luke."

"Haven't seen him for several days. He wouldn't tell me, anyway."

"Huh, that's unusual."

"Not so much, Cara. I doubt he had anything to do with this, but I'm not as sure about him anymore."

"Why, Danny?"

"Hmm, can't really say, Mom, only a feeling."

Oh, who's calling now? I hope it's not the police when I'm starting to enjoy Mom's fried chicken.

"Hello, yes, this is Sarah. Oh! Please don't be harsh; it's not fair! Okay."

"Who was it? What's going on?"

"It was Mrs. Windly, Danny."

Dear Lord, did they find Davey? He has to be alright. "About Davey, Mom?"

"Ah, how do I say this, dear? Davey's been home all day; he never left the house. He's in his room now, according to his mother."

"What?! That's not true, Mom! He was late to history class, but he was there. He walked me home, and they took him. Believe me, please, Mom!"

"I'm confused, Sis, don't know what's going down. Hell, maybe you're right, but how?"

"I'm afraid it won't be long before the police call or come back, Cara. What do we say?"

"Oh, I'm only glad Davey's okay, Mom. Nothing else matters. I guess my mind is gone. What am I going to do? It's time—time for Elmwood."

8:38 p.m.

Wow! That was a long entry—bad, bad day, diary. Glad you've been faithful to make entries every day since you started reading Anne Frank. Ahh, Britta, where are you? Dear God, did she leave? Is she gone for good? Three times now, I've tried, and I can't find her in the mirror. I miss you, Britta. But how much do you really love her, Cara? Yeah, the scripture in John. Could I lay down my life for my friend? Then there's the other question. Would I do it for her . . . or me? You can't answer that question, can you, Cara? You know you're on the edge—probably over it. So would you lay down your life to save Britta or to escape your miserable existence? And if you did, what would you be getting into? Crap, this going back and forth isn't getting me anywhere. What's next, what—

"Cara, get your robe on; the police are downstairs."

"Huh, oh boy!"

"Sergeant Sullivan and another officer want to talk with you. They didn't say why. Try to stay calm, dear; I imagine they've spoken to Mrs. Windly and are here to follow up. Be honest, sweetie; tell them what you know."

"Can I get you something warm to drink, tea, hot chocolate?"

"No thanks, ma'am, we're fine. The snow's stopped; must have gotten six or seven inches. Please sit over here, young lady."

Don't start shaking or crying, Cara—cool, cool, cool. "Yes, Sergeant Sullivan."

"Did Mrs. Windly call you, ma'am?"

"She did, Sergeant."

"Then, you know that Davey Windly was in his room all day and not abducted."

"No! He wasn't in his room all day. He was at school and then they took him. It's just like I told the officer this afternoon."

"Can I speak with you in private, Mrs. Corrigan?"

"Well, sure; in the kitchen."

What now? Why does the sergeant want to speak with Mom alone? This isn't good. Calm down, Cara; chill, and try to remember. Hurry up, how long can it take? Don't look at the officer. Is he staring at me? Oh, thankfully, they're coming back.

"We know you're not telling us the truth, Miss Corrigan. According to your mother, you think you are, but obviously, you're not. Some other—"

"But I am telling the truth. I don't—"

"No, hear me out before you say anything more. We have more information now. Do you know a boy in your school named Gary Groves?"

"Hmm, he's in my history class, but I don't know him, except for that. Why?"

"He said Davey Windly was absent today—never entered your history classroom as you said."

"But how was he involved, Sergeant? How do you know anything about him?"

"Well, that's the rest of the story, ma'am. Mrs. Windly thought Davey was in his room when she called you earlier, but he wasn't. She—"

"See, I told you. I was telling the truth!"

"Please don't interrupt, young lady, let me finish. Anyway, when Mrs. Windly went to Davey's room, he was gone. She called us right away and said he was now missing. We went out to get her statement and have a look around. When we went back to the patrol car, a young man was waiting for us—Gary Groves. A curious kid, like most, he wanted to know what was going on. Of course, we told him it was a private police matter. But after volunteering what he saw earlier, we took his statement. He said around three thirty, he saw Cara Corrigan leading Davey Windly down the street through the heavy snow. Groves said they were in a big hurry, and he wondered where they were going in such lousy weather."

"No, no, he's lying, Sergeant!"

"Why would he lie, Miss Corrigan? You don't know each other except for class."

"I don't know. I guess he's one of the toadies. If you check, you'll find he has something to do with Luke Glover and the others. They're all out to get me, and I don't know why. And that's the truth, Sergeant."

"Where is he, young lady? Stop with the games! Filing a false report is a crime."

"No, Sergeant! It's like we talked about."

"I'm sorry, Miss Corrigan, but we have to get to the bottom of this—find the boy now. We're wasting time, and it's cold out there. So one last time, do you know where Davey Windly is?"

What's he want. I've told him over and over again. Think, Cara, think. You saw Davey at school, right? He walked with you, and they took him, right? But what if you're wrong? Is it possible that it only happened in your mind? Oh! Snuggles was there. No, please, it can't be!

"Cara, Cara! Answer the Sergeant."

"Oh, sorry. What did you say?"

"This is going nowhere without your cooperation. Are you sticking to your original story that the Windly boy was snatched and taken away in a Ford Mustang? And you know nothing about what Gary Groves said?"

"Ah, I think so, sir."

"Okay, we're through here, Mrs. Corrigan. We'll be back. You might have the doctor you told me about take a look at her. I know it concerns you. We can show ourselves out."

"Good night, Sergeant, officer. Ah, what a night. Are you alright, Cara?"

"No, not at all, Mom. No one believes me. I'm not sure anymore, either. Please don't scold me."

"No, I won't. I love you, sweetie. Let me hold you."

"Um, feels great." *Is this my mother? I don't know what's happening, but, dear God, don't let it stop.*

"It's been a long day, Cara. Why don't you go to bed and try to sleep; that's where I'm heading."

"Can I sleep with you tonight, Mom?"

"Sure, sweetie, let's go upstairs."

December 4, 1982, 2:16 a.m.

"The window's too high, Davey. Can you move boxes over and stack them—maybe three."

"Good, the bottom one's the heaviest, so they won't slip. Be careful. That's it, that's it. What can you see?"

"A parking lot next to the building, Davey. Oh, now I see a Motel 6 sign and the highway behind it. I think it's I-70."

"Hm, sounds familiar; I think I know where we're at. I'd be sure if I could see it."

"No, no way you're coming up here with what they did to your legs. Damn them! I can't believe they threw you down and kept stomping you."

"Yeah, I can barely stand, Cara. How'd you find me, anyway? And, well, why don't you know where we are?"

"Hmm, I guess I don't recall. I was walking along and looked down. There was a key on the ground, and I picked it up. Then I kept walking until I got to this building. I heard you screaming for help and went to the basement door and unlocked it. That's all I remember. Where do you think we are, Davey?"

"I'm pretty sure we're south of I-70 on—"

Ahh, where am I? Dream, it was a dream. Mom? Oh, that's right, I'm in her bed.

"Are you awake, Cara? You were thrashing around. Did you have another bad dream?"

"Yeah, a dream, not a bad one, though. It seemed real, Mom. I found Davey locked in the basement of a building. Someone hurt him and tied him in a chair."

"Hmm, it's understandable that you'd dream about finding Davey."

"I want him back more than anything in the world. I woke up just as Davey was about to tell me where he is. But I looked out the window and saw a Motel 6 sign and I-70 in the distance. That should be enough to find him, shouldn't it?"

"But, sweetie, it was a dream—not real."

"I guess, but can't we find out for sure? We could go through the phone book and see where all the Motel 6's are; there couldn't be many along I-70."

"I don't know, Cara. What would you do then?"

"Look for buildings south of the Motel 6 sign with a parking lot on its north side. It wouldn't be that hard, Mom; we could do it."

"Oh, dear, I wish it were true, for your sake, but it can't be. Even if we found a likely building, what would you do, rush in and demand to see their basement? And stop to think, Cara, if by some wild chance you found Davey, what conclusion would the police draw? They'd suspect you knew where he was all along. And that you abducted him."

"Hmm, I didn't think of that. I guess we need to be careful. Ah, I'm not sure if I'll get back to sleep. But I'm sure I'll find that building if it's the last thing I do. We just won't tell the police."

"I'll help you, dear, to make sure you're safe. But now I'm going down to make hot chocolate. Maybe it'll help us sleep."

"I'm coming too. Thanks, Mom, for caring." *The way Mom's taking care of me, I must still be dreaming.*

2:51 a.m.

"Here, sweetie."

"Thanks, Mom." *She's so affectionate. I really like it; thanks, Lord.* "Always tastes good. If it doesn't help me sleep, nothing will."

"Danny! I'm sorry if we woke you."

"What's going on, Mom? You usually don't have hot chocolate at three in the morning."

"It's me again, Danny. I was dreaming and woke Mom up. We couldn't get back to sleep, so she suggested we come down for hot chocolate."

"Oh, another nightmare."

"Hmm, no, not this time. I dreamed about where Davey is. But I think it's more than a dream. I believe—at least hope—someone was trying to tell me something. It sounds crazy, but I guess that's where I'm at now."

"Wait a minute, Sis, I thought Davey was home in his room, according to his mother."

"We did too, dear, until the police came later."

"I didn't hear them. Did the story change?"

"Sit down, Danny; there's hot chocolate left in the pan. I'll get you a cup. After Mrs. Windly called us, she discovered that Davey wasn't in his room—he was gone."

"Wow! Do the police know what happened?"

"They said someone saw me walking up the street with Davey—Gary Groves from school. Do you know him, Danny?"

"Yeah, he's a toady, Sis. No surprise to you, I bet. In fact, he's Albert's cousin."

"Huh, it's all about them again, Mom. Their ganging up on me, I knew it. Crazy? No, I am not! Damn them to pieces!"

"Don't get riled up, dear; you'll never get back to sleep. Speaking of sleep, the hot chocolate did the trick. I'm going back to bed, kids; don't stay up long."

"So you think it was more than a dream, about where Davey is?"

"It has to be. Please pull your chair up close to me, Danny. Hold my hand."

"Sure. You're really hurting, Cara?"

"Uh-huh, can you help me? Please help me find Davey. Since you have your license now, do you think Mom will let you drive me around?"

"She's not cool with that yet. Maybe we could talk her into it, though. Do you think she'd go with us?"

"Probably not, I'd just rather go with you, Danny."

"We'll figure it out if you know where to look."

"I do. I'm glad Dad's not home; he'd never let us take the car."

"Yeah, he definitely wouldn't, Cara. But tell me something; how do you honestly feel about Dad now?"

"I would if I could. It's still too much of a shock."

"Sure, I understand. Brent Corrigan, is that who he is to you now? You know he's your father in every way that counts."

"Of course, I know he is. Maybe in time, we'll see. It's freaked him out, though—was a boogeyman hiding in the closet all those years. Is that why he doesn't touch me or tell me he loves me? Is it too much to ask for a hug or word of encouragement?"

"That might happen now, now it's out in the open. Now that the boogeyman's out of the closet."

"I hope you're right. I need a real father. I'll keep hoping but enough of that. I love you, Danny, and need your love now. I need as much love as I can get to help me to the other side of this. But now I need your help, need you to be honest with me."

"Yeah, it's time, Sis. It's about how I've treated you, not being truthful."

"It hurt like hell, Danny, going against me, not having you in my corner. Can you tell me why?"

"I'm sorry. I'll tell you what I know but you can't tell anyone. I'm scared and ashamed, so damned stupid! It started a week after I first met Luke and the others. Andrea came on to me, and I thought she was sizzling hot. We made out a few times and then she asked if we could do something crazy—kinky. I was stupid, Cara, foolish!"

"Uh-oh, what?"

"You'll get the drift, so I won't go into detail. It involved her family's new camcorder and her bedroom."

"Crap! She didn't?"

"Yeah, she did and had the movie to prove it. I'm the dumbest guy in the world. So, that's how it all started. Her hook sunk deep, Sis. Andrea was a drug I couldn't kick. They all threatened me, said everyone would see the movie if I didn't join their gang and do whatever they told me."

"I'm sorry, Danny. I'll help in any way I can. That's why you lied about Albert Hobbins shoving you around at school that day?"

"Yeah, I had to go along with their scheme to make you look bad. But I didn't know much about the other times they lied about you. I felt like a Judas—sorry, Sis."

"But, why'd they pick on me, Danny?"

"I don't know; they just target people they don't like."

"Bastards! They had you. But at least now I understand, and I forgive you. I need you, Danny. I suppose they pulled you into the drug scene."

"Ah, drugs and other stuff. That's why they blackmailed me with the movie in the first place. Now how do I get out? The film was bad enough, drugs, though; how stupid could I be! I'll end up in jail for sure. But know this, Cara: you haven't lost your mind concerning their lies."

"Thanks, Danny, it had to be awful for you—difficult to tell me. The other things, the mirror, and all the other stuff I still need to deal with, but at least I have peace about their lies."

"Yeah, we both have stuff, but we'll get through it together."

"Thanks, Danny. I think I'll try to sleep now."

10:04 a.m.

I'm so glad I have Danny back. I was sure Mom wouldn't let him take the car. I know she thinks it's fruitless, but I know there's something to the dream. At least now I know mother's pulling hard for me. When has that happened?

"Only two possibilities to checkout, Danny?"

"Yeah, Pecos and Kipling. Pretty sure it's Kipling. It won't be long; we're only eight blocks from I-70. What then, Sis—when we get there?"

"We'll scope it out; see if it's like I remember in my dream. If it isn't, we'll check out Pecos Street."

"God, I hope you're right, Cara. But how could you dream about something that's real? I can't get my head around it. You're stoked, starting to shake."

"Yeah, it has to be, Danny; has to be where Davey is. It's crazy, but I believe he's there."

"It's coming up. There's the Motel 6 on the right."

"Pull in here, Danny. Wow! What a turn; I hope no cop saw it. Okay, there's the Motel 6 sign to the north, and we're in the parking lot. And there, there's the building to the south. Now I'm psyched—it totally fits my dream."

"You've got me pumped too. It must be the building."

"Gotta be. Do you think it's open on Saturday?"

"Let's find out. Lock your door. Be cool, Sis; no crazy antics."

"Don't worry; they won't see me shaking. Great, the main entrance is open. I've never noticed this building; wonder what all's in it."

"Over there—a building directory that'll have the names of the businesses. Hanson & Hewlett, P.C., Farmers Insurance, Galvin & Associates—"

"There it is, Danny! Wicks and Groves Realty."

"Crap, Andrea Wicks and Gary Groves. Yeah, now I remember that Andrea's father's a real estate agent. Damn, Sis, I can't believe it!"

"Has to be the connection, Danny. So, Andrea and Gary have access to the building—the basement."

"Yeah. It looks like only a few people are around on a Saturday morning."

"The Wicks and Groves office is on the second floor. I guess it doesn't matter. We need to find the basement."

"Look, Cara; the door across the hall, over there."

"It's open. C'mon. Quietly shut the door, Danny. Okay, let's go down. Large basement—supplies and stuff."

"Is it like your dream, Sis?"

"No, it doesn't look like it. Something's wrong—missing. Hmm, let's see. Wait a minute; there's a door over there. Probably locked, don't you think, Danny?"

"Only one way to find out. Damn, it's open!"

"Look, Danny, the high windows on the north wall like in my dream."

"Really!"

"Really, and look, a chair; could be the one in my dream. Oh, is that rope?"

"Sure is."

"This is the place, Danny, the place where they held Davey. It has to be; it's all here like in my dream."

"Um, am I dreaming now? I don't understand how it could possibly be?"

"I don't know, either, but it is! Where is he, though; where'd they take Davey?"

"Crap, what's that! Someone's down here, Sis, walking around in the main storeroom. No place for us to hide in this room."

"Just hope they don't come in here."

"Damn—"

"What the hell are you kids doing down here? This is private property for employees only."

"I'm, I'm sorry, sir, we got lost. Someone told us Wicks Realty was in the basement."

"No, no, sounds like a story to me, young lady. You'll have to do better than that."

"No, really, it's true; someone told my sister that. We didn't mean any harm by it. Where is that office?"

"Upstairs, on the second floor. Read the board by the elevator; it'll give you the location. I should call the cops, but I'll cut you some slack this time—don't want to see your faces again, though."

"Thanks, come on, Sis."

"Whew! now what, Danny?"

"Go home and figure it out. What else can we do? Wait! Is that Andrea over there?"

"Where, Danny?"

"By the basement door—she's opening it."

"It's her, alright. And now she's gone through the door to the basement. But why, Davey's not there? Should we follow her?"

"No, I don't think so. Let's go home; this is getting way scary."

"Yeah, I'm starting to shake again. I'd like to know what she's doing down there, but I guess you're right; we should play it safe—figure out where to go with it all."

"Let's get out of here."

11:22 a.m.

"Before we go in, what do we tell Mom?"

"Ah, I think mum's the word, for now. I'll handle what happened."

"Glad you're home safely."

"Danny did fine, Mom. He's a good driver."

"Just kidding, I know he is because he had a good teacher. Did you learn anything; find the place in your dream, Cara?"

"Yeah, a place south of the Motel 6 on Kipling was kinda like my dream. I couldn't tell anything else. That's about it."

"Well, it was a dream; couldn't expect much more. Oh, I got two calls while you were gone. Your grandma called just before you got back. Gracie called earlier. I said you'd call her this afternoon, Cara.

"Really, Mom. I thought Dad laid down the law about calling Gracie."

"I think you need to call her, so I'll permit it this time. And your grandmother's coming on the twentieth. Anna decided not to come this Christmas as her children are coming home for the holidays."

"I didn't think grandma would come after what happened at Thanksgiving."

"To be truthful, Danny, I didn't either. But it'll make it easier with Anna not being here."

"Is grandma still ticked at Anna? How about you, Mom? Are you still mad at her?"

"It's fading. But after talking with her, I'm starting to see your grandma's side. It'll take time, Danny, for all of us to deal with what happened."

"Are you going anywhere this afternoon, Mom?"

"Ah, no, I'm not planning to. Why?"

"They're having a thing for Albert's birthday at noon. Luke said I needed to be there."

"Luke said you needed to be there. Who's he to tell you where you should and shouldn't be, Danny?"

"It came out wrong, Mom; he doesn't tell me what to do."

"You can have the car but be home by two. I'm not liking this much—Luke and the rest of them. Something's wrong; I wish I could put my finger on it."

"It sure is, Mom. Can I talk with you outside, Danny?"

"Yeah, see you in a couple hours, Mom. What is it, Cara?"

"Be careful, Danny. I didn't know anything about the party. Can you snoop around and see what you can find out about Andrea and her father's office? Anything you learn might help us find Davey."

"I'll keep my eyes and ears open, but I don't want to push it or tip my hand, Sis."

"Of course not—see you later."

4:19 p.m.

"My God, Cara, I can't believe what's happened since we talked on Wednesday. I've felt a heaviness about you but couldn't imagine this."

"Yeah, me neither, Gee."

"I can't get my head around you dreaming about something that actually happened. It's sci-fi stuff. I don't know, Cee. Do you really think they held Davey in the building near the Motel 6?"

"Well, why is Andrea's father's office in the building? Why did we find a room with the same chair and rope like the one in my dream? And why did we see Andrea there this morning? You tell me, Gracie."

"Good points, I'm fried."

"I hoped Danny would find out something this afternoon at Albert Hobbins's birthday party."

"Yeah, did he?"

"He should have stayed home, Gee. Andrea took him into a bedroom and reamed him out. She saw us in the office building this morning—don't know how. She asked what we were doing there. Then she said, 'you'll be damned sorry if you stick your nose in this.' After that, she threatened to circulate their movie and frame him for selling drugs."

"Oh, hate that for him. But at least he's on your side now, Cee, the Danny I remember, the good guy."

"Yeah, I'm glad to have him back; I really need his help now."

"I don't think you should mess with that gang of thugs. Can't you tell the police and let them handle it from here?"

"We should, Gee, but there's a problem with that. The police will never believe I dreamed about the place where they held Davey. They'll think I knew because I took him there."

"I suppose you're right. Do you or Danny have any idea about where they took Davey?"

"We've racked our brains, Gracie, nothing."

"Hmm, something just popped into my mind. Probably nothing but maybe an idea. I think it was on *Bonanza* or some other western. The bad guys held a woman at an abandoned farmhouse. Her husband learned that she might be there, so he went to the farm and searched it without finding her. After the crooks knew he had already searched the farmhouse, they took her back there, knowing he wouldn't recheck it."

"I follow you, Gee, but do you think they'd do that?"

"It's a thought. Maybe have Danny disguise his voice and call in an anonymous tip to the cops about where Davey is."

"Huh, that might work. That's why I love you—always there with the right words to help. As long as I'm not involved, we have nothing to lose. And hopefully, they'll find Davey and return him to me. God, I want that!"

"Yeah, I hope it works out for you. Not to put a damper on things, but anything more about Elmwood?"

"We'll know more at Tuesday's appointment with Doctor Reyna. We heard there might be a room opening up but now Mom wants to wait until after Christmas, unless something else happens."

"That's good news, isn't it, Cee? I mean, you seem stronger now, like you've got a handle on things. I know you and your father are going through stuff, but I don't sense much anger about the move anymore."

"Hmm, it still hurts, but everything else makes it trivial, even selfish. Mainly now, my heart's breaking for Britta."

"I thought it was over, the mirror and Britta."

"No, I snuck down to the basement Thursday. She wasn't there, but I've had this gnawing feeling ever since I finished the Anne Frank book that I'm not through with Britta—I'm going to save her if I have the courage."

"Oh, what the hell's in store for you, Cara? How can you do it?"

"It's still the scripture we talk about. The greatest love is laying your life down for a friend. That always scared the crap out of me because I knew I could never do it. I was never big on courage or love. But now I have to do it because I love her and helping her is greater than my fear, Gee. Please understand."

"I'm trying, and you know I'll always support you, Cara. But what can you do for someone in World War Two Germany?"

"Ah, I don't know how, but I know I have to try. Somehow, the mirror's the answer. Mom's setting the table for an early dinner, so I better go. Thanks for calling earlier. I love you, Gracie; take care of yourself."

"Love you too, Cee. Be careful, please!"

"If I'm here, I'll call you before Christmas—bye."

December 7, 1982, 4:49 p.m.

"Hmm, Cara, dear, you must have known how that would turn out?"

"I guess, Doctor Reyna, but I was desperate to get Davey back. It seemed reasonable at the time."

"So, the police showed up last night?"

"Yeah, Sergeant Sullivan. They traced Danny's call. We weren't as smart as we thought. And, yes, Sullivan put it all together and suspected I took Davey. He went on to say the storeroom had a high window but no Davey and no chair or rope."

"How do you feel about it now, Cara?"

"Ah, so scared for Davey, and so damned mad at Andrea and the rest of them! Excuse my French, Doctor."

"So, are you going to let the police handle it and leave it alone? That's my advice, dear."

"Yeah, I should, but if there's anything I can do . . . . Would you give up, Doctor, if it was someone in your family?"

"Well, maybe not. But let's move on and discuss Britta. Help me understand, Cara. I thought you agreed that Britta and the occurrences in the mirror were only in your mind—not real. But now you're telling me that you love her and want to help her. I have to say that now I'm quite concerned about you."

"I know you don't believe me, Doctor, but I also know what is and isn't real. And I know what I have to do. I guess that means I'll be going to Elmwood at any time."

"Right now, it's the best thing for you, Cara. And a room becomes available Thursday, but your mother wants to wait till January. Frankly, I don't think it's good to do so."

"I guess, but I don't want to go now. I'm fried! Is that it for the day, Doctor?"

"One other thing, first. How do you feel about your grandmother coming for Christmas?"

"I guess mom keeps you up to date on everything. I'm cool with it. Grandma's always been good to me. But I know they've got issues to work out. I don't understand why people keep secrets that are important to know. Do you, Doctor Reyna?"

"It's complicated, dear, and mostly they do it because they think they're doing the right thing—protecting those they love. In reality, though, it often makes things worse when the truth comes out. You're dealing with that firsthand, Cara, and I want to ensure you successfully handle it."

"Thanks, Doctor. It's helped me understand my father, the way he treats me. I don't like it, but at least I can deal with it. He might need to talk to you now. Dad never wanted it to come out, and now that it has, it's all in his face again. I think he'll need help dealing with it—deciding if he wants to stay with us or leave."

"You're quite perceptive, Cara; your father might need professional help for a while. You're certainly an enigma, dear."

"I hope that's good; I won't even ask what it means. So, is that it for today?"

"It is, Cara. Be careful and try to enjoy the holidays. Our next appointment won't be until January 11. Then we'll see about Elmwood."

13
GRANDMA

December 18, 1982, 2:44 p.m.

They're finally here; what took so long? Stay back in the dining room, Cara, where you can hear but not interfere. Grandma looks upset, no surprise, I guess. Of course, Dad's going upstairs right away—surprised he went with mom to the airport. It couldn't have gone well. Mom's crying. I feel for her; I know what she's feeling. Oh, good! Grandma's taking mom in her arms— both sobbing. Healing, I pray you're healing their hearts, Lord. Hmm, I want to hug each of them; help my mom the way she's helping me. No, wait a few minutes, Cara, let them have their time and then go in.

"Hi, Grandma! I need a hug too." *She always gives the best hugs—so good.*

"My dear, Cara, you look sweet. I love the dress, a special occasion?"

"You're the special occasion, Grandma. I'm sorry about all that's happened, but I'm glad you're here to help us."

"Yes, sweetheart, and I'm happy to be here to help mend mistakes of the past—bring understanding, healing. It's time for hugs and tears,

Cara; then we'll all walk to the other side of it. But your mother and I need time to work it out. I know you and your mother are doing the same—such a shock for you, dear."

"We're healing, Grandma, getting closer."

"Hmm, I'm thankful for that, Cara; I hope for the same grace. You look so . . .

"So normal?"

"Well, I wouldn't have said it exactly that way, but yes, you look normal. With all I've heard, I didn't know what to expect; if you'd be here or in the place your mother mentioned."

"I'm sorry, Cara. I didn't want any more surprises when your grandmother got here."

"It's cool, Mom, I understand."

"Any news about your friend Davey? It was a shock to hear of such a horrible thing."

"Umm, no, Grandma, nothing."

"Unfortunately, the police are still looking more at Cara than the thugs who she said took Davey. But Danny and Cara are devoting their time away from school to find him. They've talked to people in the area and hung posters. And I'm with Cara on this a hundred percent."

"Mom's right; we won't give up till we bring Davey home. And now I'm furious. I think the anger's cleared my mind, given me a focused purpose. That's what you're seeing, Grandma. But it's probably covering the other stuff."

"It must be hard on you, Cara."

"Well, I sleep only a few hours a night, cry a lot, and get cranky at times—ask Danny and Mom."

"Umm, you've grown this year, sweetie, in many ways. And we're all here to help you."

"I know, Grandma, thanks."

"Of course, dear. Oh my, the trip's worn me out; think I need a chair."

"Sorry, Mom, let's sit in the dining room, and I'll brew a pot of your favorite tea."

"While your mom's in the kitchen, Cara, I need to ask if you and your mother have really gotten past her not telling you that Brent isn't your biological father. You can be honest with me, and I hope you will, dear."

"Yes, I think we have, Grandma. Being shocked like that—at the same time—has bonded us in a way I would have never thought possible. We're getting a grip on things, the not understanding, the hurting—all of it. And we're doing it together. I can't tell you how much that helps."

"So, what do you think, is she furious with me? She's doing a good job of covering it up, but she has every right to be."

"Hmm, at first, probably. I think as we're working through our stuff, she's also sorting things out with you. The similarities are right in her face. She does need answers from you, Grandma, but, no, I don't think she's furious anymore."

"Oh, that's quite a relief, Cara. Thanks for your insight."

"Here we go, Mom."

"Peppermint tea at Christmas, my favorite as you always remember, Sarah."

Soothing hot tea for a cold day. Good, Mom's putting her hand on grandma's. Thank you, Lord. It looks like there won't be any blowups after all.

"We're glad you came early, Mom, but you never explained why it was necessary."

"I'm sorry that I didn't come right out with it, but I wanted to tell you in person."

"Ahh, sounds kinda scary, Grandma."

"Not scary, Cara, but important. It's something that both your mother and you need to think about."

"Okay, we're ready to hear what it is, Mom."

"It's your mother, Sarah. You know I recently went to Germany to see an old friend that your father and I knew when we were there in the forties."

"Yeah, when you adopted me."

"Yes. I hadn't heard from the woman for years. Then, in October, I received a letter from her. She said your birth mother wanted her to make arrangements for her to meet you. Of course, I was against it at first. But as I thought about it, I concluded it was finally time to tell you the truth about your mother. I didn't know that Anna would do it for me. What Anna did angered me, but then I realized it was for the best. Anyway, after the war, my friend helped arrange adoptions for American servicemen through an orphanage. Your mother was almost a child herself and had no way to provide for her baby. Your father and I never met your mother, but my friend felt sorry for her—poor thing was in desperate straits."

"Makes me feel sad for her. But you raised me, so you're my mother. What am I supposed to think about her? How did she ever find your friend, and why after all these years?"

"She said your mother's had a tough life. But, after going through difficult trials, she's ready to meet you. She needs to know if you're alright, if you had a better life. I think she's feeling guilty too. That's all to be expected, but the thing is, she came to America last week—"

"What?! Why? What happened when you went to Germany, Mother?"

"Well, I never spoke directly with your mother, but my friend told me of her plans to come to America. She felt bad for the woman and told her that she would do what she could to arrange a meeting with you. The bottom line is—after changing my mind—I told her I would only help arrange a meeting if you wanted it, Sarah."

"Wow! Really, Mom. Talk about being hit with a ton of bricks. Hmm, I don't know; what should I do? It'll take a while for it to sink in."

"Of course, darling, but that's why I needed to get here as soon as possible. Your birth mother will be here in three days if you agree to it. She's in Chicago now, visiting a friend, and will only fly to Denver if you agree."

"Oh, crap, what do I do? How much time do I have?"

"You need to decide by tomorrow, Sarah; she'll need time to make reservations."

"Yeah, would you want to meet your birth father, Cara?"

"No, never! But it's not close to the same. He's a scumbag, but who knows what hell forced your mother to give you away. She might have a broken heart, Mom."

"Could be. I need to do a lot of thinking tonight."

December 20, 1982, 9:12 a.m.

"Pass the butter and jelly. Do you want a piece, Sis?"

"No toast for me; a waffle and banana's all I can get down."

"Didn't sleep much again?"

"No. At least we didn't have to get up for school. Thank God for Christmas vacation; couldn't have come sooner. We need to boogie, Danny; got a hundred flyers to put up, and I've mapped out four blocks to search."

"Whoa, Cara, we can do it all in three or four hours. At least let me wolf down my toast. You know, I'm still thinking about Mom's decision. Were you surprised?"

"No, not at all. I would have been shocked if she didn't let our mystery grandmother come. Mom's struggling with it, though. I guess it's to be expected. Can you imagine what's going through her mind?"

"Um, not even. I feel for her, but what can we do? What should we do?"

"Not get in the way, Danny; that keeps running through my mind. At the right time, Mom will introduce us—let us be a part of it."

"Yeah, that makes sense. At least Mom and Dad aren't yelling at each other all the time; that's progress."

"Mom talked to me about that last night. They're doing some heavy lifting. All the hurting and hell they went through, Danny. It all got stirred up again and came to a head. And now, each of them is doing their best to deal with the stink."

"Think they'll stay together?"

"Well, they love each other, I'm sure of it. They'd've separated years ago if they didn't. I've been furious with Dad for a long time. But the anger is going away; I feel sorry for him if you can believe that."

"I hear you, Sis. Poor guy's still paying for what he did—Mom too. I'm glad you're handling this so well, Cara. I mean it."

"Means a lot to have you back, Danny. I was confused about you and everything else. But no more; my mind is clear, and we're going to find Davey."

"Amen, Sis. So what do we—"

Who's calling this early?

"I'll get it, Cara. Hello. Who? Okay. Myrtlewood Lane, the vacant house just east of Youngfield. Sure, I've got it. Uh huh, Cara too. Yes, this morning."

"What was that all about, Danny?"

"Bastards! They have Davey, Cara"

"What! Who has him?"

"Andrea, it was Andrea on the phone. They have Davey in a vacant house off Youngfield."

"Myrtlewood is what you said, right? I know it—it's only fifteen minutes on foot. What do they want from us, Danny?"

"She said we should both come to the house this morning, no one else. And we better not call the police or anyone else."

"They're letting us have Davey, just like that. I don't think so."

"We'll be walking into a trap, Sis. What do we do?"

"We're going, Danny; we're damned well going! But we need to think it through. What's their game; why call now and tell us where Davey is? I guess the first question is, is Davey really there? And then why do they want us too?"

"I think they want us. I don't know if Davey's there, but we need to get over there right away—surprise them. We'll have to be careful, though, and come up with a plan on the way."

"Okay, let's do this! At least it's a decent day. Get your coat and gloves, Danny. It'll take less than ten minutes if we jog."

"We're out of here, Sis!"

9:33 a.m.

"Whew, not far now, Sis. We're on Myrtlewood. Only a block away."

"Oh, gotta rest, Danny; can't believe how fast we got here. Now what?"

"Let's walk up slowly—hide in the bushes closer to the house and scout it out. We'll see—"

"Wait! It's the blue mustang, in front of the house. Quick, Danny, the bushes—hide! Down! Down! They're taking off. Wow! Close call."

"Pretty sure Albert was driving; Andrea was in the front seat with him."

"Was that it, Danny; no one in the back seat?"

"Yeah, either they took Davey earlier, or he's still in the house. Nobody around, Sis; let's run and hide behind the bush beside the house."

"Okay, the coast is clear; let's look in the windows. We'll work around the house; you check the upstairs, and I'll look in the basement—be careful."

"Be quick and keep down, Sis. What happened to my frightened, timid sister, anyway—where'd she go?"

"Don't make me laugh; it's not funny. I never said or felt it before, but now I'm angry, Danny! I'll lay my life down if I have to, but we're bringing Davey home."

"Well, the house looks vacant; I'm not seeing anything."

"Maybe in the back? Wait, Danny, there he is!"

"My God, they have Davey tied up in the basement. Tap on the window, Sis."

"Oh, thank the Lord, he sees me! How do we get him out, Danny? The backdoor's locked, and we don't want to go around front."

"The window . . . we have to break it and climb in. It's a tight squeeze for me, but you can get through, Cara."

"Ah, hope no one heard that. Knock out the little pieces of glass along the bottom—crap, glass all over the place."

"Put your coat on the window frame and slide through, Sis. Feet first, careful. Perfect!"

"Davey, Davey! Are you okay?"

"I'm weak, Cara. How'd you find me?"

"Tell you later; we gotta get out of here now! Throw me your pocketknife, Danny. You do have it?"

"Yeah, here, Sis."

Be cool and calm, Cara. "Okay, Davey, I'm cutting the ropes. Pray for a steady hand."

"I'm definitely praying—don't rush it."

"Good, that's the hands. Can you untie your feet, or should I use the knife?"

"No, they're not that tight; I'll do it, Cara. There. Out the window or the front door?"

"What do you think, Danny?"

"Davey may have trouble getting through the window; better go out the front. I'll meet you there."

"Open the door, Davey; let's get you home."

"Run, Cara, hurry! I'm going for the cops."

"Okay, Danny. No, Davey, the Mustang's back—they're coming up the walk! Can you make a run for it?"

"No choice, run as fast as you can, Cara; I'll try to keep up."

"What the hell! Get him, Albert; I'll take care of the bitch."

Keep running, Davey. Run. Cara, make your legs go faster. No use, I'll never outrun the two of them. Well, it's time to fight for Davey. Turn around and face them.

"Crap, she's gotta a knife, Andrea!"

"Take the damned thing away from her, Albert! She's a girl!"

"Be cool, Cara; now give me the knife, and I won't hurt you."

"Here, take that, bastard!"

"Damn, she sliced my wrist, Andrea; I'm bleeding—bleeding all over the place!"

"I'll kill you, skank; choke the breath out of that scrawny body!"

"Just try it, Andrea. Take that, you bitch, and that too!"

"Ow, ow, oh."

Get out of here, Cara, run like you've never run before. Keep going. Oh, Danny waited for us. He's with Davey.

"My God, how'd you get away, Sis?"

"Tell you later, let's go. They'll be on our tail. Let's split up. Our house is closer; I'm going there to call the police, take Davey home—hurry!"

"Crap! Luke and Gary Groves; run like hell, Cara!"

10:04 a.m.

"Yes, Sergeant, they're after us now! Probably somewhere between Youngfield and Davey's or my house! Please hurry!" *Oh, Lord, the police have to get to Davey and Danny first. I wish mom and dad were back. What? Crap, I forgot to lock the door, stupid—has to be Mom and Dad, with Grandma. Hide, Cara, just in case.*

"I know you're here, Cara. Time to pay up like I always said you would. Even left the front door open for me; how easy."

Luke, damn! Stay down behind the couch. Okay, now he's looked in the kitchen and dining room and is going upstairs. Hurry, slip down the basement and lock yourself in the storeroom until the police get here. If Mom and Dad walk into the middle of this, protect them, Lord. I wish the door had a lock; at least there's one for the storeroom. Okay, the door's locked. Now all you have to do is hide and pray. Snuggles! No, you can't be here! But wait, Cara, think. You need to do something. Crap, he's on the stairs—Luke's coming! He'll kill me this time unless I kill him first with this knife. Help me, Lord. What should I do? Get under the blanket, hurry, get it off the mirror!

"I've checked out the whole house, bitch; I know you're in there. Tick tock, time's up."

Get under the blanket. What? Really, now! I thought Britta left a long time ago. But the mirror's sparking again. "Are you there, Britta?"

"Oh, you're there, Cara! Help me, please; they're downstairs. The Gestapo's in the house, and they'll be here in seconds!"

You have to do this, Cara. I'm not sure how, but you need to help Britta while there's still time. It's the mirror—destined from our first meeting. It won't take long for Luke to bash in the door, and it'll be too late. But will Britta be better off with the danger here? I know I won't be if the impossible happens. Muster the courage, Cara—do it! "Put both hands on the mirror, Britta; right where my hands are. Don't take them off, no matter what!"

"It's getting warm like before, Cara."

"Starting to get hot, please keep your hands on the mirror, Britta!"

"Oh, dear, God, it's burning now; I have to take them off!"

"No, no, you can't, even though it hurts like hell. Keep your hands on the mirror!"

"Ah, why? I'm burning!"

"Because we can't let go now." *Crap, the door's open. Luke's here!*
Crackle, BANG!

14
ESCAPE

October 31, 1943, 6:18 p.m.

"Britta, Britta! I heard a loud bang coming up the stairs. What happened? Ah, the acrid smell and smoke. Oh, the lamp cord's melted. Ouch, the base is red hot, and the table's singed!

"Oh, what?"

"Get up, Britta, hurry! What're you doing on the floor?"

"I . . . I don't know. Did I faint?"

"The yelling, they're here, Britta. Get your suitcase—hurry, we have to go now!"

Umm, what's going on? I'm dizzy—weak. "Help me up. Hold me and make it go away."

"No, not now, sweetheart. Get your things; let's get out of here before it's too late!"

Oh, the pain; I can hardly hang on to my suitcase. What's happened to my hands? They're on fire! "Okay, father."

"They're already on the stairs. The Kellers weren't able to stop them. Down the backstairs, follow me, Britta."

Dear God, please, please don't let them catch us—please!

"The alley's clear. Close the door gently and follow me. We'll go south."

"Whew, I can hardly run; please slow down."

"What is it, Britta? I've never seen you like this. Come on; we'll go west and try to get to the safe house."

"I'm not sure if I can go that far—so weak."

"Give me your suitcase. I'll hide it behind the bushes and come back for it later. I can carry you; it's not far. Hmm, heavier than I thought, hold me tight."

Strong arms holding and protecting me. It's strange, but I feel safe—loved. "Watch out!"

"I see them on the corner ahead, Britta. I'm sure they're on our tail from behind too. We need to hide. The alley ahead; hang on."

Dear God, this won't work; they'll find us. I need to get down as close to the building as I can, but my palms burn. Not enough light to see why— the pain! "Be careful, father, get down! I hear the Gestapo in the alley."

"Shush, sweetie."

"They're here, someplace; I saw them turn into the alley. Get them now!"

Stop panting; they'll hear us. Oh, God, save us! Aw, gunfire; they see us; they're going to kill us. I don't want to die—please!

"Stay down, Britta. Pray hard."

"Gerhard, are you back there?"

"My God, is that you, Aaron?"

"Yes, we have to get out of here—quick! Oh, your daughter?"

"Yes, Britta, she's not doing well. I'll have to carry her."

"I can carry her, Gerhard. Follow Hans to the safe house."

"But how did you—"

"No time now; I'll tell you later. Steady, I'll pick you up slowly, Britta. There, put your arms around my neck; I'll be running fast."

Oh, bodies. How many did they kill? Three men with Aaron; how did they do it? Thank you, Lord, help us get to the safe house. He's strong, like father told me, a good man. Umm, I feel secure in his arms. "You're Aaron; I've heard a lot about you."

"Oh, only the good stuff, I hope. Were you injured?"

"Ah, no, I don't think so. I don't know what happened; it's blurry. I have no strength, and my hands burn."

"Did you scrape them on the cobblestone?"

"No, no, when I came out of the fog—they burned like fire. I feel like I could faint."

"Hold on, Britta. Five minutes, and we'll be safe."

I'll try, but I'm weary—need to sleep. What's going on? Wait! I remember being in front of the mirror but don't know why. Think, Britta, think. Was my face in the mirror, and did I hear, "Britta, Britta, Britta?" Let it fade away for now. Oh . . .

8:23 p.m.

"Ah, where am I?"

"You're awake, sweetheart. How are you feeling?"

"Not well, Father, queasy and confused. And my hands hurt."

"Let me see them, darling. Ouch! Oh, this is Mary Schmitt, my daughter, Britta. Mary and her husband, Otto, coordinate trips to Switzerland from this safe house—their home. She's a nurse; let her look at your hands."

"My goodness! What happened, child? Blisters on the palms of both hands. Was there a fire, Gerhard?"

"Apparently. Britta, do you know what happened?"

"It's a blur; I can't remember, maybe something with the mirror, I'm not sure."

"Well, let's see if we can make them feel better. I'll clean your palms and cool them with cold compresses. Then I'll wrap them. They'll be alright, dear, but it'll take time for them to heal. Strange, though; I've never seen burns like these."

"Thanks, Frau Schmitt, for helping, they hurt terribly. But who'd think I'd find a nurse to take care of me. Oh, I remember Aaron carrying me. How did he know we were in trouble, Father?"

"Herr Keller called the Schmitts before letting the Gestapo in. He knew we'd head for the safe house and hoped someone was there to help. Fortunately for us, there was."

"It was awful! I've never seen dead bodies and blood all over. I'm having a hard time getting it out of my mind. It scares me, Father— hold me." *It always makes everything better and breaks the fear, restores my confidence that everything will be okay.* "Where's Aaron? I'd like to thank him for saving us and carrying me."

"I think he's in the kitchen, Britta, helping to clean up. It looks like you missed dinner at the Kellers and here. But we saved you a plate. You must be starving."

"Yes, Frau Schmitt, I think my stomach's settled enough to have a bite."

"Then let's go to the kitchen and put compresses on your hands while I warm your dinner. Then you can thank Aaron; he's a special young man."

8:48 p.m.

"Okay, Britta, that's taken care of, and your dinner's warm."

"Thanks for tending to my hands, Frau Schmitt."

"You're most welcome, dear, and you can call me Mary; we're informal here. Oh, here's Aaron. Britta's been looking for you."

"Hmm, what can I do for you, Britta?"

"I wanted to thank you for saving us, the others too. And, well, for carrying me all that way."

"I'd do anything to protect Gerhard. He's saved my life more than once. We look after each other here."

"Ahh, that makes me feel safe." *Are you tongue-tied, Britta? Is that all you can get out?*

"Yeah, safe is good. You better eat before it gets cold."

"It's been a long hard day for you, dear. After you're through, I'll show you where you and your father are bedding down for the night."

"Thanks, Frau, Ah, Mary. I'm frazzled."

"Umm, frazzled, I've never heard that. You know your father and Aaron are taking you and two Jews to Switzerland tomorrow. I'm just getting to know and like you, and soon you'll be leaving."

"Father's always wanted to get me safely to Switzerland. I guess we don't have a choice."

"It's best, but we'll meet again someday."

November 1, 1943, 3:11 a.m.

"Britta, Britta, Britta!"

What, who's calling me?

"Britta, Britta!"

Oh, it's the mirror—so distorted, hidden in the fog. Wait, a face in the mirror. Is it me? Who else would it be?

"Britta, Britta, Britta!"

I'm calling out my name, but why? It's strange; my face, my voice—everything. Ah, I'm falling into the mirror. It has me! No, no, what can I do? I'm falling faster and faster.

"Britta, Britta! You're having a bad dream. Wake up, sweetheart; you're wet with sweat."

"Oh, thank you, Father, I'm burning up—the mirror."

"The mirror from our hiding place?"

"Um, yes. It kept calling my name. Or maybe it was me calling. I can't describe it, but the mirror was different. It had me; took me into the darkness."

"It was only a dream; I'm here now, sweetie."

"Please hold me tight, Father, until I get back to sleep."

"Close your eyes, Britta, and let peace come."
So good, so good. His arms around me—so good!

10:05 a.m.

We're leaving this haven of safety soon. A mid-day meal and we're out the door, on a treacherous journey to Switzerland. Make a diary entry while you have time—at the desk in the corner.

Morning, November 1, 1943

No entries yesterday. The happenings of the day are shrouded in fog, all but our escape in the evening. Our departure was sudden, narrowly avoiding capture by the Gestapo. With others, Aaron Gabel saved and led us to this sanctuary, the home of Otto and Mary Schmitt. Aaron is strong, reliable, and handsome. Though older, he'd fulfill all my dreams. I bonded immediately with Mary. I hope my mother had all her qualities. This morning I asked Mary why. My father told me before, but his answers faded. Hate and evil, she said, turn hearts black, driving them to commit insane acts of barbarism. But our hearts of love and compassion are compelled to stand up for the afflict- ed. That's why Father leads Jews to safety. I'll miss Mary's warmth and hope our paths cross again. I'll be with Aaron on the journey and hope I do nothing to make him think less of me. I don't know why, but I continue to feel odd, like something is missing and not right. Hopefully, we'll survive the journey so I can make another diary entry.

—Britta S.

1:07 p.m.

"Is your suitcase ready, Britta? We're leaving in fifteen minutes."

"Yes. Who went to get it?"

"Aaron. I told him where we hid it. Oh, a last-minute surprise; Mary's going with us to Switzerland. This morning she heard from her sister in Winterthur that their father's ill. It'll work out well for her, as our destination is a farm south of there."

"What a blessing. I like her a lot, Father."

"It's a dangerous trip, sweetheart, so pray hard for everyone's safety."

"I haven't stopped praying since we left our hiding place. I guess we're only trading our old hiding place for a new one. How long will it be, Father—how long will the war go on?"

"Not long, Britta, the Allies will invade Europe in the coming months. We have to hold on till then."

"So, how do we travel, and who's going with us?"

"Six is the limit for this trip. We'll be taking a young Jewish couple, Anna and Rolf Eisenberg. That only leaves room for Mary and Aaron. We usually have two or three autos so that we can take seven to ten Jews. This afternoon, we'll drive forty kilometers south to Balingen in Mary's auto. A friend will drive the automobile back to Stuttgart tomorrow. Tonight, I'll tell you about the continuing journey."

4:28 p.m.

"You have a special name, Anna. Where are you from?"

"A farm near Herrenberg—my parents' land. We passed until someone snitched to the Gestapo. We thought they were friends, Britta. They were on us before we knew it."

"Ahh, how did you escape?"

"Weeks before, father gave me the name and address of a friend who would help us if we ever needed a hiding place. Father told us to run and not look back. We heard gunfire as we ran into the forest."

"Dear God—your parents?"

"We don't . . . we don't know. I pray every night they're alive. But I fear they're in a prison camp. Someday I have to see them again, Britta."

"So, you found the person who would hide you?"

"Thankfully, we found Joseph Becker, an underground operative who knows your father. It was eight days ago, and finally he arranged our escape to Switzerland. Thank God, here we are."

"We're glad you're escaping to freedom."

"Thanks to you and the others, Frau Schmitt. We'll be in your debt for life."

"Are you alright, Rolf? You haven't said a word."

"I'm okay, Frau. The fall colors have turned to winter's gray, and I fear all our lives are heading into an endless winter we have no control over.

"It's been that way for four years, Rolf. But I look at it differently, like we're coming out of a dark tunnel with the light ahead getting brighter each day."

"I like that, Herr Schumann—hopeful. Isn't that a better way to look at it, Rolf?

"I suppose, Anna, but it's hard to keep my head up and see much that lifts my spirits."

"I understand, Rolf. I don't mean to pry, Britta, but I've noticed the bandages on your hands."

"I burned them, but I . . . I don't remember how. I have an idea—that's all."

"I'm sorry; they must hurt. Tell me, Herr Schumann, what's the terrain like where we're going?"

"Well, Anna, it's not much different from what you see out the window—probably more open meadows and farmland. Balingen is only a few kilometers away; the house we'll be staying overnight at is on the south side. The SD and Gestapo are everywhere, so we have to be cautious. Everyone double check your new papers. And keep repeating your new name until it's part of you."

My new name, new identity. How do I leave Britta Schumann and assume the identity of Lydia Wolf? Who is Lydia Wolf? I'm not sure who Britta Schumann is. Lydia, Lydia—

"Damnit, not now, a blowout!"

"Oh crap, I'm sorry, Gerhard. I told Otto to check out the Mercedes to ensure it was in tip-top condition."

"It's not your fault, Mary, tires go. There's a place here where I can get off the road. Aaron, we need to get the spare on quickly. We can't be a spectacle."

"I'll get the jack from the trunk, Gerhard."

"Hold up; someone's pulling off the road behind us. They're getting out. I don't like it, Aaron, black auto and suits—Gestapo!"

"It's okay; we're only changing a tire."

"No, it's who we have in the auto that has me on edge—the fancy Mercedes too. Let me do the talking, Aaron. Here they come."

"Well, a little problem, huh? Very nice automobile, expensive. Pesky tires, always blowing out—too bad."

"Yes, it happens too often. We can manage to change the tire."

"Oh, I'm sure you can. Out for a pleasant drive in the country? Hmm, probably not with the loaded Mercedes. Where are you headed?"

"To visit family in Rottenburg."

"The suitcases, must be a long visit. How many people?"

"Six. We'll be staying for several weeks, hence the suitcases. Thanks again for your concern."

"Ask the others to step out of the automobile. We need to check papers."

"Tell them, Helmut. I'm Ricard Wolf, a banker from Nuremberg. I'm traveling with my daughter, Lydia, my younger brother, Helmut, my cousin, Hilda Lange, and her niece and nephew."

"We'll see. Open the suitcases, Hofmann. Check everything. Hmm, your papers look in order, Herr Wolf."

"Well, well, what do we have here? Three Lugers in this suitcase, Herr Kraus."

"What do you have to say for yourself, Wolf? Why are you hiding pistols?"

"The roads are dangerous, and I carry sensitive bank documents and large sums of money. So you can see the need for protection."

"No, no, I don't. This is looking suspicious."

"Look at this, Herr Kraus; maps with coding on them."

"Hmm, well, Hofmann, do their papers checkout?"

"They appear to, but something's amiss; I can't put my finger on it."

"I'm afraid we'll have to detain you until we sort this out. Wolf, get in our auto with your daughter. Hofmann, drive their automobile to Gestapo headquarters."

My God, doomed before we've started. Dear Lord, help us, please! Ahh, gunshots, no, no! "What happened? Father, Father!"

"Everyone get down, quick! Aaron will have the tire on in seconds; then, we'll get out of here."

"Okay, Gerhard; go, go!"

"What happened, Aaron?"

"We did what we had to, Anna. This business is never easy. They were careless, or we would have all ended up in prison, or worse."

"What do you mean, careless?"

"Well, Rolf, they thought all our Lugers were in the suitcase, so they mistakenly assumed we were unarmed. When all three of them turned toward Gerhard, I pulled out my pistol and shot each one in the back."

"Oh, Father! I'm scared; how will we get away?"

"Believe me, we will, sweetie. Pray hard. We rolled the bodies into the ditch. It's deep enough so passers-by can't see them from the road. A few autos went by, but none when the shooting started. I doubt if anyone's suspicious. But it's only a matter of time until the Gestapo comes looking for them and sees their auto."

"For all our sakes, hopefully that won't happen until we're safely in Balingen."

"Amen to that, Mary."

"It must be hard for you to do what you did, Aaron. I don't know how you and Gerhard continue to do it year after year. You're too young for such things, dear."

"Maybe, Mary, but no one stays young for long; they grow up quickly or die."

"How much further, Father?"

"Fifteen minutes to the safe house. I need to keep my speed down and not draw attention. We all need to be calm; we'll make it."

November 2, 1943, 2:03 a.m.

"Hi, I see you found your way to the kitchen too, Britta. Or should I call you Lydia?"

"I don't know . . . don't know who I am anymore. This kitchen's huge. The Weber's home surprises me, so big and luxurious."

"I expected a modest home too. Wouldn't a rich person's house arouse more suspicion than an average one?"

"I guess, Anna, but I'll enjoy what it offers."

"You can't sleep either?"

"No, not with my dreams. I keep having them over and over and don't know what they mean."

"Nightmares?"

"No, they're not always frightening. They involve the mirror from our hiding place with the Kellers. I see my face in it, and then it distorts and looks like another girl."

"Hmm, never heard of dreams like that."

"They're eerily real. Some dreams are snippets that come and go. I see things I don't understand that I've never seen before."

"Strange, and you have no idea what they mean?"

"That's why I'm awake. I keep going over them and can't get back to sleep. I want to forget about them now—get them out of my head."

"Okay. I hope they'll go away in time. I've been curious, Britta, about the way you look at Aaron. It might be bold of me, but do you have feelings for him?"

"What? Ahh, no, I mean, I don't think so, maybe."

"I'm sorry if I caught you off guard, but it seems the answer's clear. He's a desirable young man. I catch myself looking at Aaron—thinking about him."

"But, Rolf, you love him?"

"Of course. Rolf's tender and caring. He loves me, is my protector."

"I see it in his eyes, Anna. But you still give Aaron a second look."

"Looking at someone else—dwelling on them for a while—happens, Britta. You'll understand someday."

"I guess. How old are you, Anna?"

"I'll be nineteen in two months. Aaron mentioned that he'd be nineteen next month. You look seventeen, the right age for him."

"I wish I were, but I won't be sixteen for a while."

"Oh, you look older, and you're beautiful, Britta."

"You're kind; maybe if I didn't have this little turned-up nose."

"It's cute, be thankful for it. I was wondering, did you hear Mary talking about Aaron's friend?"

"Friend, no, what friend?"

"I didn't catch the name, but Aaron has a girlfriend in Winterthur."

"Hmm, I guess it's not surprising. What young lady wouldn't want Aaron?"

"Maybe it's not serious enough for a young girl to swoop in and steal him away."

"Thanks, Anna; I doubt I'd do that. Can we drop it? Why couldn't you sleep?"

"Well, don't tell anyone, but I'm with child—over two months along. We don't want to say anything until we arrive in Switzerland."

"Oh, dear, a baby's usually a blessing."

"Not in the middle of danger. It's the worst time to bring a new life into the world. I can't see how it'll work, Britta. That's what keeps me awake, thrashing around, trying to make sense of it."

"Sure, I see how it would. I'll pray for you, Anna."

"Thanks, I'll pray for you too. I don't relate well to people, but I sense you'll be a close friend."

"I hope so. I need a close girlfriend now. I can't explain it, but there's an empty spot in my heart, a place filled by a friend who's no longer there. And your name, Anna, brings peace and assurance; I'm not sure why. I'm going back to bed now. Hopefully, sleep will come."

9:09 a.m.

"Where have you been, Father?"

"Making plans for our trip to the lake. Nothing to concern you, sweetheart; we've arranged everything. How long have you been sitting here alone?"

"I finished breakfast an hour ago. Everyone scattered, so I've been thinking, trying to make sense of what happened and what's in store for us. But I'm not getting anywhere."

"Maybe you're trying too hard, Britta. Let it go; it'll fall into place. How're your hands?"

"Mary put ointment on them and re-wrapped them. She thinks they look better, and they don't hurt as much. Tell me about the Webers. They have such a beautiful mansion and grounds."

"Kurt Weber's a successful businessman respected throughout southwestern Germany. That's why they have the finest things in life."

"Doesn't being in the limelight make it difficult to do what he does?"

"You might think so, but in this case, it makes it easier. The Gauleiter of this region grew up with Kurt, and they're still close. The Webers know the right people, which gives them information valuable to the underground."

"It sounds dangerous to me, Father; they must walk a thin line."

"Yes, but with great skill. They're invaluable to Jews escaping Germany."

"Hmm, the courage of the people I'm meeting humbles me. I couldn't do what they do. It scares me to death. Can I ask you something, Father?"

"Always, sweetheart."

"Something Anna said. Does Aaron have a girlfriend?"

"Well, he's spending time with Ortrud Graf when we're in Winterthur. She lives on the farm where you'll be staying. I suppose she's his girl. Why do you ask?"

"Ahh, only curious about what Anna said. How old is she? Is she pretty?"

"Huhu, I see."

"Don't laugh, Father. And you don't see anything!"

"Sorry, sweetie. Yes, she's pretty. I think she's a few years older than Aaron."

"Hmm, thanks."

"I'll be gone for a few hours; get plenty of rest. It'll be a long night."

2:29 p.m.

Afternoon, November 2, 1943

Mostly bad news today, and it could get worse tonight when we continue our journey to Winterthur. I only know that we'll ride in the back of a delivery truck to Lake Constance and then cross in a small boat. We'll meet an underground operative on the other side who'll take us to the safe farm. The trip will be under cover of darkness. We'll leave around nine and have to be at the farm before daylight. Father spared further detail, trying to ease my fear. To be honest,

I'm scared—scared to death! I've sat around today, trying not to dwell on my strange dreams. Something about the mirror continues to irritate me, but I don't know what. Did the mirror burn me? Father thinks an electrical short in the lamp caused the fire. Thankfully, my hands are getting better. But for reasons I can't explain, I don't feel like myself. I'm also frustrated about my feelings for Aaron. The way father built him up before I met him affected me. When I first saw him, and for what he did, how could I not have these feelings? Is it love? I don't know; I have no experience with it. But still, it hurt me to learn that he has a girl. I think I hate Ortrud, and I've never met her, know nothing about her except that she stands between Aaron and me. I've never had such thoughts. It's not like me. I'm going to nap for a few hours and pray that I'll have no dreams. Hopefully, this won't be my last entry, and tomorrow I'll be able to detail our trip to Winterthur—Britta S.

9:12 p.m.

"Quick, we're running behind! I'm riding up front with Gunter and Mary; Aaron will show you where to hide—hurry!"

"I'll jump up and open the flap, then help each of you up. You're first, Britta, that's it. Okay, Anna, yes. Your turn, Rolf."

"Thanks, Aaron, but I can get up on my own."

"Sure. Go to the back behind the large boxes."

"Uh, dear God, the smell is awful. I don't know what it is, but they need to clean this truck. And all this stuff, Aaron. What is it?"

"Sorry about the smell and dirt—definitely needs cleaning. Each week they carry different products: iceboxes here, a sofa over there. Like you said, Anna, just stuff."

"Where's it going?"

"Konstanz, Rolf. Every Tuesday, it's the last delivery from Stuttgart. Gerhard told Gunter to put in four large empty crates for the journey. We shouldn't need them, but we have a hiding place if the authorities stop us. Otherwise, we can sit on the blankets in the back until we reach the lake."

"Gunter's with the underground?"

"Uh, he or Martin always make the trip. We'll be an hour and a half in the truck. Try to get some sleep."

Sure, just relax and take a nap while we slip through the night to who knows where. No, I'll be wide awake and hopefully not alone with my thoughts.

"Will you sleep, Britta? I don't think I can."

"No, Anna, I'm not sure I want to. But we can talk—get to know each other."

"Sounds like a good way to keep our minds occupied—off of what-ifs. What about you, Aaron? Will you sleep?"

"I'll rest but won't sleep till we're at the farm."

"Was it hard for you, Britta, being in a tiny hiding place all the time? How small was it?"

"Three by four meters, Anna. Only room for a small bed for me and a stuffed chair for father to sleep in. We also had a desk, a wooden chair, and a small chest of drawers. Oh, and, of course, the mirror."

"Windows?"

"Only a small one to let a little light in but no view."

"Dismal, what did you do to keep your sanity? How long were you cooped up there?"

"Over a year. Sometimes I thought I'd go crazy, especially when father was gone for days at a time. But he brought me several diaries and three packets of paper. To break the boredom, I made daily diary entries and wrote poetry and short stories."

"What about the family downstairs?"

"The Kellers are good people, though I rarely saw them. But their son, Ernst, was a different story. He was entangled with the Hitler Youth, and got worse and worse. He's the one who told the Gestapo about us."

"What a bastard! It's a miracle you got away, Britta."

"He did something even worse, Anna. He kept coming in when father wasn't there, making passes, and finally tried to rape me."

"He did what!?"

"Oh, I didn't know you were listening, Aaron. Huhu, he tried to rape me and would have if his mother hadn't come in. I'm sorry, I don't mean to cry."

"Dammit! It's okay, sweetie; he'll never hurt you again."

Ah, this is heaven; Aaron's arms around me—strong yet tender. I could only hope to be in your arms, darling Aaron.

"Sorry for asking, Britta; I didn't know."

"You had no way of knowing, Anna. I have to live with it and shouldn't keep it hidden. Thanks for comforting me, Aaron."

"You're precious, and no one should ever do that."

"I can't find my handkerchief. Do you have one, Anna?"

"Here, dear. I can see, Aaron, that you care for Britta."

"Of course, I do; she's my best friend's daughter. Anyway, I'm sorry, Britta."

"It looks like the only contact you had with the world was horrible."

"Well, the mirror also happened, Anna. I'm not sure if it was good or bad. It could have burned my hands. I can't figure it out, but there's something about it. I'm also missing someone and don't know who."

"Uh-oh, we're slowing down, stopping."

"Could be bad, Anna. Two honks, the trouble signal! Something's gone wrong; get in the crates now!"

Oh no, trouble again—will we ever make it to safety? Dear God, please, please protect us.

"After you're in the crate, I'll secure the lid with nails. It'll be cramped and hot, but you can't say a word; a cough or heavy breathing could cost all our lives. Be calm, and we'll be okay. I'll put the lantern out and keep it in my crate."

"Who's going to nail your lid, Aaron?"

"I'll balance a box on top of it as I get in, Rolf. Hopefully, they won't try opening the crate."

Oh, it sure is hot, and it stinks in here. I'm starting to hurt already, and my palms are burning from sweat. The hammer and nails—is this my coffin? Aah, Lord, Lord.

"We've stopped and pulled off the road, and I hear faint voices. It isn't good, so be as quiet as you can. I'm getting in my crate now."

It's so hot, and my left leg is cramping. Dear God, it hurts! How long will this torture go on? It seems like I've been in here an hour, but I know it's only been a few minutes. Wait! Someone's coming through the flaps; they're in the truck.

"Seidel, search in back with your flashlight. Brandt, check the crates and boxes—be thorough."

Footsteps are getting close. Stop panting, Britta, get ahold of yourself. Calm, calm, calm! Oh, what's that?

"Nothing but boxes back here, sir."

What's crawling on me? It's big. No, it can't be. Ow, a rat bit me! No screams, Britta; think about the mirror, anything to take my mind somewhere else. It hurts; where is it now? Don't move! Stay away, stay away!

"Open one of these crates, Brandt; let's see what they're hauling."

No, Lord, please! It's over—the creaking of a lid, not mine, but whose?

"Iceboxes, that's what they're carrying, sir."

"Nothing here. I can't stand the stench any longer. Get out, Seidel, hurry!"

Ahh, thank you, Lord. Oh, the rat again, please! I have to get out of here! It won't be long, Britta—hang on. At least five minutes have passed; what's going on? It hurts! Ah, the horn honked. I hope that's the all-clear signal. Thank God Aaron's prying the lid off. Aww, finally, air to breathe, even if it's foul.

"Britta, are you okay?"

"Oh, I'm stiff and hurt all over. There's a rat in there that bit me."

"What?! There's the varmint in the corner. Well, he'll never bother anyone else. Where'd he bite you?"

"On the arm, here. Thanks, Aaron."

"Hmm, doesn't look that bad, sweetie. When we stop, we have something up front to put on it."

"Thanks." *Oh, I'm exhausted. Thankfully, Anna and Rolf fared better than me. Dear God, how long do we have to breathe this putrid air? I'm afraid to sleep; too many bad things can happen, and I don't need more strange dreams.*

"Are you alright, dear?"

"I'm thankful that we're alive, Anna. But no, I haven't been alright this whole trip, and now I've been bitten by a rat."

"You what!? A rat?"

"See my arm. Aaron smashed the varmint. Just something else to hurt. My hands are on fire."

"Come here, Britta, let me hold you. This is no damned place for anyone, let alone a fifteen-year-old. There, there, let all the tension come out. A good cry is what you need, dear. I'm afraid my handkerchief is still damp."

"That's okay. Thanks for holding me, Anna; I guess I need a mother now."

"We all need each other more than ever. And I'm thankful to have a friend like you, Britta—someone who cares for a Jewish woman trying to survive in a world that doesn't want her."

"Can I rest in your arms, maybe sleep?"

"Of course, I'll lean back against the crate, and we'll both take a nap. It looks like Rolf is well on his way to getting back to sleep, and Aaron has his eyes closed."

"They're closed, but I won't sleep. I'll wake everyone when we arrive; get all the rest you can."

11:52 p.m.

Ahh, what!? where am I?

"Wake up, Britta; time to get out. Everyone get your suitcases and take these blankets."

"But, where are we?"

"Near Lake Constance, Rolf. We need to get going; it's two kilometers to the boat."

"We walk?"

"No other way to get there, Anna. The wind's up; it'll be damned cold crossing the lake—blankets will make the difference."

"Why do we cross the lake when the truck is going to Konstanz?"

"The border crossing into Kreuzlingen is more dangerous than going across the lake. It's crawling with Gestapo, Britta. We've had close calls trying it."

"Okay, get down, hurry!"

"What happened back there, Father, when they searched the truck?"

"It looked like the Gestapo shot up a truck that caused a traffic jam. They thought we looked suspicious—a close call. Thank God you were all able to hide quickly. Let me help you down, sweetie."

"Oh, it's a lot colder, Father."

"Everyone wrap up in blankets, and let's get going. It's a twenty-minute walk to the boat. Thanks, Gunter; we'll let you know if we're traveling next Tuesday night. We can't use our flashlights, and there's little moonlight, so watch your step and keep close to the person in front of you. It's slippery this time of night."

"You finally got some sleep, Britta."

"Uh-huh, but I couldn't avoid dreaming, Anna. I'm to the point where I fear sleeping—what comes with it."

"The same dreams?"

"They vary some. I was looking in the mirror from our hiding place. I always see my face before it distorts, looking like someone else. It vexes me that I can't figure out what it means."

"Strange, alright. Have you seen faces in the mirror when awake?"

"Not that I remember."

"I'm walking behind you, Britta."

"Thanks, Aaron, I need to keep my mind off things."

"The dreams you were talking about to Anna?"

"Uh-huh, I'd rather not talk about them." *I love that Aaron wants to walk by me. Why? What do I say? Could he like me in that way? Dear God, what am I to think?*

"Britta! Are you with me or someplace far away?"

"Oh, I guess I'm having trouble taking all this in. I'm tired and cold and want to get to the warmth and safety of the farm."

"It's not far to the lake. But no more talking until we get there; boats often patrol near the shore."

That's okay with me, Aaron. I don't know what to say—don't want to look foolish in your eyes. I only want to know what your feelings for me are. And to understand what my feelings for you are.

"There's Helmut with the boat. How long have you been waiting, my friend?"

"Ah, twenty minutes, Gerhard. I brought heavy coats for your passengers."

"Thanks, it's cold as hell with this wind."

"Indeed, Aaron, and the waves are high. I'm not looking forward to the trip."

"Ah, this coat feels good, Father. Where did Helmut come from?"

"From his home west of here."

"How far is it to the other side?"

"Normally six kilos. But tonight's wind might force us to take an indirect route to lessen the waves' drag. It could take an hour and a half to cross."

"This must be the daughter you've talked about."

"Yes, Helmut, this is my precious Britta. This is Helmut Bohm, who's been ferrying us across the lake for over a year. Helmut, this is Rolf and Anna Eisenberg, and you know Mary."

"Glad to meet each of you. Put your suitcases in the back; it's a small boat requiring we use the space precisely for balance. Rolf and Anna sit in the rear seat. Aaron, Mary, and Britta take the middle while I have Gerhard ride with me upfront so we can hear each other over the waves and wind."

"Wrap another blanket around you, sweetie. Okay, we're off."

"Put the blanket over your face; it'll help."

"Thanks, Aaron, it does. Dear God, the waves! I'm feeling queasy."

"Hold on; try to get your mind on something else."

What, when I'm scared to death? His arm around me is comforting—keep your mind on that, Britta. He's strong and will protect you if something goes wrong. Like anything could go wrong in the middle of a lake in a ferocious storm. Bite your cheeks; clench your fists, and hold on—going to be the longest hour of my life.

"Britta!"

"I'm trying to do what you said, get my mind off of this, Aaron."

"Good. Are we swinging east, before going south, Helmut, to cut through the wind?"

"Exactly, Aaron; you know the drill, though this wind is the worst I've seen this year."

"If you can hear me, why the small motor and slow speed? I'm freezing my butt off back here."

"I can barely hear you, Rolf. German boats patrol these waters, and a roaring motor and large wake would draw their attention. We have to creep along, so we're not detected."

"Oh, hell, Helmut, okay."

"Hang on, everyone; we'll be to the other side in forty minutes."

Ahh, let it all fade away, Britta. The mirror is better than this. Yes, the mirror. What am I missing—it's driving me crazy. Is it my face in the mirror or someone else's? Will I ever know? The mirror, the mirror. Hmm, getting drowsy, that's good."

"Wake up, everyone, lights to the south; most likely a German patrol boat."

"Aww, I fell asleep; what did Father say, Aaron?"

"German patrol boat, over there, going east. We're going west; we'll cut the motor if they get closer."

"Dear Lord, keep them away from us!"

"Uh-oh, they're turning, Gerhard, coming our direction!"

"Kill the motor, Helmut. Everyone get down and cover yourself with a blanket. Be calm; they should pass without seeing us."

"Crap, no, what do we do now, Rolf? We'll never make it to safety!"

"We will, Anna, but keep quiet."

"Sorry, Gerhard, I'm so damned scared—my teeth are chattering, and I can't stop shaking.

"Everyone quiet! Keep down and pray."

"I think they see us, Gerhard."

"Yeah, they're coming directly toward us—ten times our size. Start the motor and go right, Helmut—hurry!"

"It's too late, everyone jump!"

"But I can't swim, Aaron. Ow! Oh, the waters freezing—can't get my breath. Huh, huh, I'm swallowing water, Aaron; save me!"

"I've got you, Britta. I grabbed a life vest. Keep your head up and hold on to my coat while I put it around you and inflate it. Good, you won't drown now."

"Thanks, Aaron, but freezing to death might be worse."

"Hang on, sweetie. Gerhard, is that you? It's hard to see in the dark with the high waves."

"Yeah, Aaron. I have Anna and Mary; they have life vests. Where's Britta?"

"I have her; we need to get to shore; do you know how far out we are?"

"Maybe a kilometer, but the springs warm the water closer to shore. Do you see Helmut or Rolf?"

"No. I'm starting for shore; Britta's numbing up."

"We're both over here, Aaron. Rolf hit his head; it looks bad. I have a life vest on him, and we're heading for shore—damn, it's cold!"

"We're right behind you, Helmut. Wait! I hear the patrol boat."

"They're coming back; it's getting closer! Everyone get as far south of our boat's debris as you can. You'll have to go under if their search-light gets close."

"Okay, Gerhard. Kick and paddle as hard as you can, Britta, that way!"

"With the heavy coat and life vest, I can hardly move, Aaron. I barely feel my hands or feet." *Dear God, help us, please! I'm going to die in the middle of a lake at fifteen. They'll never find our bodies. I was trying to save her. What, what's that, you're confused, Britta, delusional.*

"Here they come with spotlights. God, they're firing. Go under! Go under!"

"Hold your breath, Britta; here goes!"

Ahh, bullets went right by my head; thank you, Lord. Help me to hold my breath. How long? How long? Oh, Aaron's finally pulled me up. "Thanks, Aaron, thanks for saving me again."

"That was too close, Britta; bullets were zinging everywhere. Gerhard, Helmut, are you alright?"

"Anna, Mary, and I are on our way to shore; we're okay."

"I got hit in the wrist, but I can manage to get Rolf to shore."

"Okay, we all need to get to warmer water before we freeze."

Oh, this will never work, Father. I'm freezing—can't feel anything. Huh, huh, keep coughing up water. Hang on to me, Aaron. Please don't let me drown. Um, fading fast.

15
THE FARM

8:12 a.m. November 3, 1943

"Britta, sweetheart, are you back with us?"

Ahh, what? Where am I? Wait, the water, the waves—numbness. I'm dry and warm, not dead! Thank you, Lord, thanks, Aaron. "Oh, Father, we made it. Everyone did make it?"

"They did. What a tough bunch, huh?"

"Not sure about that; Aaron saved me. I was dead without him. Are we at the farm?"

"We got here after two."

"But how, Father? I was almost gone—couldn't feel or think. What happened?"

"Well, we got to warmer water where the springs mix with the lake water. And, by God's grace, the wind died down. We still had a distance to shore, and everyone was exhausted, but we made it. Then Aaron carried you a kilometer to our rendezvous point with Robert. Our skirmish with the Nazis threw us that far off course. Robert was concerned that we perished. Most of us slept on the ninety-minute trip on backroads to the farm. We dropped Mary off at her father's home on the way. And now, with a few days to recuperate, we all should be fine."

"I'll miss Mary. Robert's part of the escape network?"

"He runs the safe farm with his wife, Katrin. They have two children, Lina and Horst."

"What about rescued Jews, Father? Do any of them stay here?"

"Right now, Hans, Emilie Horn, and Ida Stein live in the house. The Eisenberg's will also live here. Usually, five to eight Jews stay here."

"So, they're the only ones living here?"

"No, Thomas Haas and Ortrud Graf live here permanently. Thomas lost his parents and Ortrud her father. They were part of the escape network."

"Oh, I'll also be staying here, so does that make twelve who'll live here permanently?"

"Uh, thirteen is the maximum who can stay here comfortably. You must be starving, Britta. Do you feel up to coming down for breakfast? Katrin and Ida are preparing a big feed, and it should be ready in a few minutes."

"I'm wiped out, but I could eat anything in sight. Oh, where did these pajamas come from?"

"They're Ortrud's."

Not hers; couldn't you find someone else's pajamas?

"We had to get you out of your wet clothes and wrapped in blankets immediately after leaving the water. Your suitcase, with all your clothes, was lost. Fortunately, you put your diary in the waterproof pouch with all our papers, which I held on to until we reached the shore."

"But, wait, who took my clothes off and wrapped me in blankets?"

"Anna and Aaron. They had no time to think, sweetie, only to get you out of your clothes as soon as possible—sorry."

"Ah, how can I face Aaron again?"

"It's not like that, Britta, don't feel bad. He was helping to save you. I'm sure he paid no attention to what you're thinking."

"I hope not. I'm horrified! Why did everything go wrong, Father? They normally don't, do they?"

"I have no answer, sweetie. We've made the trip fifty times with few incidents."

"It's me, Father; I'm cursed. Something's wrong, and I don't know what."

"No, it has nothing to do with you, Britta—you're not cursed! Enough of that; let's get down to breakfast—I'm starved."

4:02 p.m.

"Oh, sorry, did I wake you, Britta? I need to get my clothes from the closet."

"No, I've been awake for a while, Ortrud. I've had enough sleep. Was this, did I take your room?"

"It's okay; with people moving in and out, we get used to changing bedrooms. You're feeling better?"

"My throat's sore from taking in water, and my legs and arms are stiff from thrashing around in the waves."

"I'm sorry to hear about your hands. Katrin's good at patching us up."

"Um, I'm thankful for that; my hands took a beating last night. They feel better now. The ointment she put on before wrapping them was soothing."

"How were they burned, Britta?"

"That's the problem; I'm not sure. Father thinks it was an electrical short in the lamp; I believe it was the mirror in our hiding place. I can't explain how and don't want to try."

"Oh, okay. You were quiet at breakfast; anything I can help you with—questions?"

"How long have you been here, Ortrud?"

"Fourteen months. I don't know if you've heard, but the Nazis killed my father. He worked with Gerhard in the transport network."

"I'm sorry. My mother's gone, and I worry about my father all the time."

"Um, it's hard. We worry a lot here; every time there's a transport, we hold our breath."

"What do you do here, to pass the time?"

"That's not a problem, Britta; we keep busy. It's a working farm, so we all have chores. We take care of the livestock and vegetable gardens along with the upkeep of the house."

"I guess I didn't think that far ahead. What do you do?"

"Feed the livestock, gather eggs, clean out the barn, help in the butchering—whatever they need. I also help Katrin and Ida with cooking and housework. There's always work to do. And that's good; it keeps us from being bored or depressed from having too much time to dwell on what's happened and what will become of us."

"I can imagine. They told me, but it's hazy; who lives here now?"

"You'll be most interested in your roommates. Lina is adorable; she's just blossoming at twelve. She'll ask a million thought-provoking questions, but she's precious—you'll love her the way I do. Then there's Horst; he's eight and will be a pain in the butt at times. He's alright, though. Watch out for the pranks; he loves them. All in all, Katrin keeps them in line, and they're good kids."

"What about Katrin and her husband, Robert?"

"Katrin keeps this place running. I've never seen anyone work so hard and long. She has to be tough at times, but she has a heart of gold. Robert's quiet but kind. He's brave like the other men, though; Katrin wishes he would cut down on his direct involvement with the missions."

"Is Ida harsh?"

"Ah, well, she's gruff at times. Ida's health is bad; she's always in pain, but when you get to know her, you'll like her. You'll love the Horns. Emilie's funny and easy going, though she works almost as hard as Katrin. Hans takes care of the livestock; he's always up at the crack of dawn. Thomas is a good man. He keeps to himself. But I like him; he pulls his weight. So, that's who lives here, and now your father it looks like."

"Aaron too."

"Yes, he's here half the time."

"I'm surprised at how big the house is. How many bedrooms are there?"

"Um, seven, I think. Let me see—your bedroom here with the children. The Koch's have a bedroom. The Horns and Ida share a large bedroom, though it's awkward. Thomas and I each have a small bedroom. Aaron and your father share a small bedroom when they're here, and there's another bedroom for two or three more Jews. Four bedrooms upstairs and three down, and thank God there's a bathroom on each floor. Even with that, the bathroom schedule is hectic."

"Large kitchen and living room, what about a basement?"

"A small one with some room for storage. There's also an office where the men plan missions. Any other questions?"

"Well, I guess you've covered everything, Ortrud."

"Um, you're sweet, Britta; let me know if I can help you in any way."

"I will. Ah, there's one thing I've heard, maybe I shouldn't ask."

"Oh, what's that?"

"About you and Aaron. Someone said you're his girlfriend. I was wondering, not that it's any of my business."

"It's okay, Britta. I think, I hope I'm Aaron's girl. We don't talk about it, but I assume. There's no time or place for a normal relationship, like before the war. But we're still close—he's tender and loving."

"Oh, well, okay."

"Sure, Britta. Your father never told us how pretty you are."

"I'm not with this turned-up nose, mousy hair, and no decent clothes to wear. I can't compare—"

"Compare? Don't be hard on yourself; you're a lovely girl. If there's nothing else, I need to get my clothes and then help the women with dinner."

"Sure, I'll be down in a while."

Afternoon, November 3, 1943

I've survived to make another entry. But our trip to the Winterthur farm was perilous. The truck we rode in was stopped and searched, and the Nazis destroyed our boat on Lake Constance in a terrible windstorm. I thought I'd drown or freeze to death—both possibilities were bone chilling. I blacked out before we were out of the water, not waking until the following morning. Breakfast was a blur, though I met those who live at the farm. This afternoon, Ortrud came to my room. I tried to dislike her for being Aaron's girl, but I couldn't. She told me about the farm and those who are here. It took me by surprise that she's sweet and kind; I thought she wouldn't be. She's beautiful, with sparkling blue eyes and flowing blond hair. Her nose is straight, not turned up like mine, and her mouth is perfect. Her slender figure would attract any man; I'm doomed. How can I compete with Ortrud for Aaron's heart—do I want to? I have to set the idea aside. My hands took a beating on the trip, but with Katrin's help, they're getting better. I still struggle, spending half my time dwelling on the mirror and what it's done to me.

—Britta S.

November 15, 1943, 7:07 a.m.

"Oh, three in the last nest, Britta."

"Gives us twenty-four; must be a record, Anna."

"I've heard thirty-one is the record egg day, with fourteen the least. I think we're good luck; we haven't gotten less than twenty in the five days we've been collecting eggs. Shoo chicken—go away! They're so protective of their nests."

"I'm glad we're sharing chores, Anna. Gathering eggs is easy, but I wouldn't say I like getting in with the pigs to feed them; they scare me. I prefer taking hay to the cattle. And I loved learning how to drive the tractor; it's fun."

"Haha, you're becoming a regular farmhand. I do enjoy outside chores more than helping with meals and cleaning the house. I like being with you, Britta; you've had a hard go of it but still keep your sweet spirit."

"I don't know; I feel beaten down with little fight left in me. I don't understand half my feelings, Anna, but at least I can talk to you about them. Getting outside helps. I'm still getting used to how large the farm is: barn, henhouse, and the other outbuildings."

"You mentioned earlier about another mirror dream but seemed hesitant to go on."

"I think my dreams bore you; please tell me if they do. I can't figure them out, so I don't know how anyone else can."

"Anything new last night?"

"Um, yes. Remember that I said my face was distorted and strange looking in the mirror? Well, now the face is clear. But it's not my face, Anna."

"Oh, who is it?"

"I don't know, and it's annoying me. But her face is familiar."

"A woman—your mother?"

"No, no, it's the face of a girl. She's about my age with dark hair. Who could it be, Anna? She seems real, but I can't remember anything else about her."

"Hmm, do you think the mirror put a spell on you? If it did, you're away from it now, so it can't hurt you anymore."

"Well, I don't think so. I've never thought of the mirror fearfully. Though it draws me in, it's always given me a sense of peace. I've got to let it go, Anna, or it'll drive me crazy."

"That's probably best. I've been thinking about something else, Britta, but I'm hesitant to say anything."

"What? Why would you hesitate?"

"I don't want to get in the middle of something that's none of my business."

"Please tell me, Anna."

"Do you remember when Aaron returned from the mission last week? He was playful; I thought he was relieved to make it back safely. The radio had a love song playing, and he kiddingly took you in his arms and started dancing."

"Sure, I remember it was fun."

"But then he said you were the sweetest girl in all Switzerland and such a good dancer."

"Hmm, I felt joy. My feelings were all over the place, Anna. I wanted to stay in Aaron's arms."

"But Ortrud was watching it all from the kitchen door."

"Oh, I didn't see her."

"I wondered what she thought about your dance in the living room but didn't have to wait long to find out. That's what I wasn't sure about telling you, Britta."

"Go ahead, please."

"The following afternoon, I was starting down the stairs when I overheard Aaron and Ortrud talking. I ducked back so they wouldn't see me. Ortrud was upset. She rehearsed the previous afternoon and asked Aaron if he thought you were sweeter than her. Then she asked him if he liked you more, even though you're a girl and she's a woman. She caught poor Aaron off guard; he couldn't get any words out for a minute. When he finally did, it only made things worse. Then, Ortrud ran back to the kitchen, sobbing. It was a mess."

"Dear God, I never thought. Ortrud's been good to me. What does she think now?"

"It's not your fault, Britta. It's probably a misunderstanding. But you might want to find out."

"Find out? What do you mean, Anna? It would mortify me to talk to Aaron about his feelings. And now I'm afraid to see Ortrud if she's angry with me. What should I do?"

"Try not to worry about it. On second thought, I'd wait for one of them to bring it up."

"I guess." *Oh, I don't need this; how can I sort out my feelings? Settle down; you have to face them both at breakfast.*

Morning, January 2, 1944

My yearly summary follows. 1943 was a long and eventful year, spent mainly in the Keller's upper room hideout. I think a portion of the year is missing, something important. I still reflect on the mirror and what part it played in my life before we left for the farm. I've seen a face in the mirror that I can't identify. I'm sure the mirror was responsible for my burnt palms, though no one else does. My hands have healed, thanks to Mary's and Katrin's care, though scarring remains. Otto and Mary Schmitt came for Christmas. Both ladies treat me like a daughter; I love them dearly. Anna Eisenberg became my closest friend. We share everything, trusting each other completely. I'm thankful that she and her husband, Rolf, were allowed to stay with us on the farm; most Jews rescued by the transport team move on to other locations.

This year I fell in love for the first time, if I know what love is. My feelings for Aaron are deep, though I have no idea what to do with them. One day my emotions are in one place, and the next day they're in another. Confusion over Aaron, the mirror, and Ortrud have my head spinning. Ortrud Graf is Aaron's girlfriend, who's lived on the farm for over a year. She's the most beautiful woman I've ever seen. Though I feel like I'm competing with her for Aaron's heart, I still like her. It's all too confusing. I thought Ortrud would despise me after seeing Aaron dance with me and express endearing sentiments, especially after arguing over his intentions. But she didn't. Instead, she continues to be kind, helping me in any way she can. Twice she's taken Anna and me on the weekly shopping trip to Winterthur. Anna and I assumed responsibility for daily chores at the farm, both inside and out.

I share a bedroom with Katrin's and Robert's children, Lina and Horst. They're good companions after being alone for most of the year. Emilie Horn is also a close friend. Her husband, Hans, Ida Stein, and Thomas Haas keep to themselves, so it's hard to get close to them. I'm hoping that we'll all be safe in 1944, and the war will end; most are encouraged that it will. I worry about father and Aaron each time they're away on a mission. I pray all on the transport team will be safe along with my new friends. I hope I'll finally identify the girl in the mirror, and feelings for Aaron will be clearer

—Britta S.

January 20, 1944, 3:12 a.m.

"Britta, Britta, wake up, sweetheart!"

"Ah, oh, you're finally home, Father! I worried the whole time—thought I'd never see you or Aaron again. What happened?"

"The delivery truck from Stuttgart broke down, pushing our schedule back three days. We couldn't take the chance to call the farm and tell you about the delay. You should be in bed, Britta, not down here worrying about us."

"I couldn't help it, and Katrin said I could wait with her."

"She was upset, Gerhard; I felt it best to let her stay down here with me—after Robert received word that it was on for last night. Thankfully, she finally went to sleep."

"Thanks, Katrin, for watching over my little girl."

"Hold me, Father, make my fear go away. I'm sick from worry."

"Don't cry, sweetheart. I'm surprised, though; you were brave in our hiding place, even when a mission took me away for a week. You're much safer here; what's changed—what is it?"

"Something's happened; I don't know what. But fear of losing you and Aaron won't go away. When I'm in your arms, though, it leaves me."

"Sweetie, sweetie, it'll be okay; you'll see."

"Thanks, Father. Would you help me up, Aaron?"

"Sure, dear. Ah, what was that for, Britta?"

Oh God, where did that come from; why did you do such a stupid thing, Britta? What do I do now? What can I say? "I'm sorry, Aaron; don't know what came over me—not thinking straight, I guess."

"Britta, usually you kiss someone on the cheek when greeting them, not the mouth."

"I know, Katrin, and now I'm embarrassed. I'm losing my mind."

"Don't, don't say that again, Britta!"

"Please, don't be hard on her, Gerhard. We roused her from a deep sleep. I'm sure it took time for the cobwebs to clear—know what she was doing."

"Maybe, Katrin, but I, I didn't mind it. You're sweet, Britta, and you know I think the world of you."

Oh, my face must be turning red. Could Aaron have felt what I did when our lips met? Lord, I pray he did. What can I say? I need to get out of here before I make things worse. "I'm sorry; I need to go up to bed now."

"Glad to see you, that you're home safely."

"Oh, sorry we woke you, Ortrud. The disadvantage of having a downstairs bedroom."

"It's alright, Katrin. Aaron and the others were on my mind, making it hard to sleep. Where are the people you transported, Gerhard?"

"Ida's feeding them in the kitchen. We brought three couples on this trip. One might stay for a while; we'll see."

"Did you stay down here all night, Britta? Poor dear, I know you were worried. But now that your father's home, you can breathe easy and get some sleep."

I need to tell her what happened. She needs to know how I feel about Aaron. I need to fight for him. "I can't sleep, Ortrud, and I have to tell you what happened."

"No, not a good idea, Britta—not now!"

"Not a good idea; why, Aaron?"

"Nothing to be concerned with, Ortrud. Only an innocent kiss of gratitude that they made it home safely."

"What did you say, Katrin? Who kissed who?"

"Britta was thankful that we finally made it back. She got carried away and kissed me. Like Katrin said, nothing for you to worry about."

"Well, how I feel about it is up to me, not you, Aaron."

Now what? Aaron only responded to my affection. "Blame me, Ortrud; I kissed Aaron on the lips and held it. But you need to know that he also felt what I did." *Oh Lord, I've doomed myself now!*

"Don't say that, Britta! You don't know what I felt. And you shouldn't upset Ortrud."

"Too late; she already has. And you've also upset me, Aaron. First, you dance with and flatter Britta, and now you kiss her in front of everyone. She's only a girl! I feel like leaving the farm—goodnight!"

"Oh, I'm sorry, Aaron, I don't know what's wrong with me—what I'm saying."

"This isn't like you, Britta, hurting Aaron and Ortrud the way you did. You should go to bed now and apologize to them later."

"Yes, Father, I feel awful, sick. I doubt if I'll be down for breakfast."

10:22 a.m.

At least you slept. Now you have to humiliate yourself for being stupid and selfish. Who'll be waiting for my apology in the dining room? Listen outside the door, Britta; see who's there before going in.

"She's a precious girl, Gerhard, but I sense that you're puzzled."

"Yes, confused about what's happening to my girl, Katrin. She's changed since the night we escaped the hideout. Britta's emotional and wants me to hold her when the slightest thing happens."

"Hmm, I understand how she'd be upset with the sudden changes. But, like you, I'm perplexed as to how she burned her hands. Thank God they're getting better."

"I haven't shared this with anyone and probably shouldn't now. But I trust your keen judgment, Katrin, so here goes. In the summer of 1936, we lost Britta's mother to cancer. She suffered terribly, and it was devastating for Britta."

"Poor darling, it had to be awful."

"It was more than that—something happened. Britta drifted away for several months."

"Drifted away; what do you mean, Gerhard?"

"Understand first how close they were. Britta depended on her mother for her emotional needs. We were close, too, but her mother was near all the time. When she passed on, Britta couldn't cope with the loss. It affected her in peculiar ways, requiring psychological help."

"Oh my, I'm sorry to hear that, Gerhard. I would have never—"

"I know you are, but let me get it out, Katrin. Ah, the thing is, Britta started seeing things that weren't there. For a time, she couldn't tell what was real or imaginary. Thankfully, with therapy, she came out of it."

"What about the mirror? She attributes her burns to it."

"The whole business of the mirror is troubling, Katrin. I can't explain the burns, except I know the mirror had nothing to do with it. There might be something more to the mirror, though. But she's covering it up after seeing a face in it."

"Oh, I see; you think Britta imagines things again—digressing due to stress."

"I suspect it. What do you think, Katrin?"

"Well, it's possible. The poor girl's gone through a lot that would throw anyone. But I don't sense Britta thinks she imagines her experiences with the mirror."

"I'm sure you're right. Another concern is Britta's blanking out the three months of therapy from her past. When I've asked her about it, she says it's only a blur."

"Hmm, I see your concern. And what happened this morning with Aaron and Ortrud is unlike Britta. She's kind, not wanting to hurt anyone."

No, father, I do remember losing mother. But no matter how hard I try, I can't remember her face. Oh, why not? I focus all my concentration on her, but she doesn't come into view. It's a blur, father, though I don't recall imagining anything. And I don't imagine what the mirror did. It's real, and it hurt me.

"Are you eavesdropping, Britta, or building up the courage to go in?"

"Ah, Ortrud, where did you come from?"

"My room. I startled you?"

"You did. And yes, I was building my courage to apologize for what I did. Since you're here, I guess I get to apologize to you first. So, I'm sorry, Ortrud. It was wrong to kiss Aaron the way I did and terrible how I threw it in your face. I wouldn't blame you if you never forgave me."

"I was furious with both of you! To be truthful, Britta, it'll take time to get by this. You're a young girl going through a lot, but still, I don't know if I'll be able to forgive you. I love Aaron, and you purposely tried to come between us, which hurt deeply."

"I can't deny it. I've been foolish in dealing with my mixed-up feelings for Aaron. I can't make them go away, but I hope you can understand and forgive me someday."

"I know it troubles you, and I think you're sincerely sorry, so I'll try . . . try to look beyond it and forgive you. But it won't happen overnight. I thought you were my friend, and then this—no, it'll take time."

"I understand. I best go in and apologize to father and Katrin—get it over with."

"Yes, I'm going for a walk; I need some fresh air."

"Britta, you're up, sweetheart."

"I slept some, not much. I'm sorry for what I did. I hope you and Katrin will forgive me, not only for kissing Aaron and hurting Ortrud but for listening outside the door."

"Listening, you heard what I said?"

"I did, Father. I was coming in to apologize when I heard you talking."

"Oh, dear Britta, what am I to think? You know how much I love you, sweetheart."

"Am I losing my mind, Father? Why did I erase the pain of losing Mother? As you said, only bits and pieces come to mind. Why?"

"It was too painful for you, Britta; that's all the doctors said. But you're not losing your mind, sweetie, only dealing with what's happening in the best way you can."

"What about the mirror? The face I see but can't make out. It's familiar; now I wonder if it's Mother. It's too confusing, Father. And I know the mirror burned me, even though you don't think it did."

"Don't cry, Britta. Here, let me hold you. There, there, that's it. As you settle in here, it'll get better. You'll see. As for what happened earlier, you need to make it right with Ortrud and Aaron not me."

"I've already apologized to Ortrud. But I doubt she'll ever forgive me."

"Time has a way of smoothing things out, dear."

"I hope so, Katrin. I'm embarrassed and have no idea why I did it. Doing anything on the spur of the moment, without thinking, isn't like me. And I can't sort out my feelings for Aaron; I've never had to deal with such thoughts."

"You're better at understanding this than I am, Katrin. You're so young, sweetie; I never dreamed that you would feel this way about Aaron. You know he and Ortrud love each other, and there's no place for you."

"I don't want to hear it, Father! I love him too."

"I understand, Britta, but now you need to have an honest discussion with Aaron."

"Discussion, did you mention my name, Katrin?"

"Ah, Aaron, I didn't hear you come in. Yes, you heard your name. I have chores waiting, don't you, Gerhard?"

"I do. Britta wants to talk with you; we'll see you at lunch."

"Talk with me?"

"To apologize, Aaron. Can you forgive me for kissing you the way I did and then hurting Ortrud?"

"I want to, Britta, but I don't understand why. What's going on?"

"I have feelings for you that I've never had before. I guess I don't know what to do with them. And it hurts me the way I treated Ortrud. Do you love her?"

"Um, to be honest, I'm not sure. I mean, I like everything about her, and we enjoy being together. And she's beautiful and smart; what's not to love."

"Oh, really, thanks a lot! Do you have feelings for me, Aaron?"

"Please don't ask me that, Britta. You'll be sixteen next month, and I'm nineteen. Maybe if you were older."

"If I were older, you'd feel differently, have feelings for me, maybe love?"

"I feel uncomfortable talking about this. I think of Gerhard; how would he feel if I got involved with his daughter, who's too young? It wouldn't be right."

"Right or wrong, you're not telling me how you feel. Be honest and tell me!"

"You know I like you. You're special in many ways, and I feel bad for what's happened to you. How could I not love you, but not in the way you want. Maybe I could someday when you're a woman, but there's Ortrud, who'll always be in my life."

"Thanks, thanks, Aaron, for being honest with me. I won't bother you anymore, but I'll hold on to the hope you've given me. I'll shut up now—go for a walk and clear my head. Please forgive me."

"I have, Britta; enjoy your walk."

16
A SILENT DECISION

February 2, 1944, 10:12 a.m.

"Thanks, Ortrud, for reconsidering and letting us go with you to Winterthur. We needed to get away from the drudgery of the farm."

"Sure, Anna. But I wouldn't change my mind for you, Britta."

"I understand."

"I love walking in the snow, Britta. Oh, the chill in the air is refreshing, makes me feel like singing again."

"Well, but I . . . I wish Ortrud wouldn't look at me with anger. I'm doing what I can, Anna, to repair the damage I caused. I'm surprised she let me come."

"Get the groceries to the truck before they get wet! You're not that far away, Britta. I heard what you said. Let's go. Thankfully, there's little traffic on the slick roads."

"The square, with the market and shops, and the snow, it's such a beautiful scene."

"You're enjoying this outing, Anna; too bad we all can't."

"It's your choice, Ortrud. You might ease up on Britta; you'd be happier for it. Remember how young she is."

"Hmm, you've become close, and now you're taking her part. You've gained a friend, and I've lost one."

"I'm sorry, please don't bicker over me. I'm feeling bad enough."

"A young man's looking this way from across the street. I saw him staring at us earlier."

"Hmm, wonder who he is?"

"Oh, my Lord! Duck, he can't see me!"

"What are you talking about, Britta?"

"It's him, Ernst Keller! What's he doing in Winterthur?"

"You're getting wet on your knees, Britta. Who's Ernst Keller?"

"The boy who hurt me in the hideout, Anna. He's in the Hitler Youth and God knows what else. Did he see me?"

"He saw you, alright. He's seen us all."

"We have to get out of here, Ortrud!"

"Get the groceries in back, Anna, let's get on the road—hurry!"

Late night, February 8, 1944

It's nearly eleven, and Lina and Horst are sleeping soundly. Their beautiful faces are precious as they stroll through magical dream worlds. I read an adventure story to them every night. I've neglected my diary for days, not having the will to set my feelings to paper.

My conversation with Ortrud this morning was encouraging. I apologized again, telling her that I miss her friendship. Aaron—my deep feelings for him—and all that's ensued have me doubting if I want to make the transition to womanhood. It's harder than a girl knows. I love Aaron on some level but must accept that he'll never love me as I wish. He belongs to Ortrud, and as much as I hate it, he always will. Does the pain ever go away? Hopefully, my heart will mend someday. But now, I have to bind the wounds and bridge the chasm I've created. If Aaron and Ortrud allow it, we can live in harmony in this uncertain world.

Seeing Ernst Keller brought back the memories of his attack. Father had no idea why he was in Winterthur, and Ortrud is sure he saw me. What Ernst will do next runs through my mind continually, stoking the embers of fear into a raging inferno. How long has he been in Winterthur? How long has Ernst been watching us? Ortrud saw him before, and he was staring directly at us. I pray that God will show us what to do. Father insists that I not return to Winterthur until we know that Ernst is no longer there.

I'm thankful for Anna Eisenberg, a loyal friend who provides sound counsel.

My hands are healing, but I'll always have scars to remind me of what happened. Mary visited and treated them again. Thoughts of the mirror are decreasing as fear of Ernst increases, but they're still lurking in my mind. My dreams continue to baffle me. Somehow, I need to put it all together—remember what happened that evening. Two nights ago, I dreamed about a girl trying to get my attention. She was yelling, but I couldn't hear her. Finally, I heard her say two things that mean nothing to me. She repeated a girl's name, "Gracie." Then she repeated, "The eighty-sixers." I can't make sense of it. I don't know what to do, though I'm sure sleep won't come.

—Britta S.

February 9, 1944, 7:19 a.m.

Two more bites; force the oatmeal down. You need some strength. Everyone around the table is quiet—fourteen silent chairs. Lina and Horst need to hurry if they want to get to school. I hate that Father and Aaron are leaving on a four-day mission today. I need them to come back. I need to pray a lot; it's all I can do. The Issenbergs and others aren't orthodox, so why don't they eat ham?

"Britta!"

"Yes, Father."

"Mind's off somewhere else, huh?"

"I guess. I hate it when you and Aaron leave. When, when does it end; this life of waiting and cringing in fear?"

"This is the year, Britta, focus on that—it'll end soon. Only oatmeal today?"

"No appetite. I got to bed late and couldn't sleep."

"You know, sweetheart, it's okay to stay in bed if you don't feel well. Others can help Anna with the henhouse and barn."

"No, I'll do my part, Father. I need to keep busy. I'm sad not sick. I enjoy working with Anna."

"You're not going with Ortrud and Anna to Winterthur, are you?"

"I'd like to, but not if you don't want me to, Father. I'm scared to death yet need to know why Ernst is in Winterthur."

"Hmm, we all want to know, but I've told Ortrud and Anna to keep away from Ernst if they see him—run the other way. Give me a kiss goodbye, sweetheart—don't worry. Aaron, I'll double-check supplies with Robert. We'll leave in fifteen minutes."

"I'm almost finished, then I'll join you, Gerhard."

"It's time, children; get your books and be out the door in five minutes."

"Yes, mother; come on, Horst."

"Are you finished, Anna? Can you help us clean up in the kitchen?"

"Sure, Katrin, I'll start clearing the dishes. We'll talk later, Britta, before I leave for Winterthur."

"Okay, looks like everyone's deserting us, Aaron."

"And I'll be leaving soon. Can I ask you something, Britta? How are you honestly doing? No sugar coating."

"I don't understand; are you asking if I'm physically ill or have recovered from the kiss and what followed?"

"Ah, no, I wasn't thinking about that but since you asked. I mean, are you okay? I never wanted to be harsh or hurt you."

"The kiss, Aaron; I know what you said, but I also know you felt what I did. Now you need to be honest with me."

"Be honest, Britta? You don't know how I've struggled with being honest with myself, let alone with you. Of course, I felt it—felt what you did. But it complicates everything, and I don't need that now."

"Thanks, Aaron; I knew it deep down. Where do we go from here?"

"I can't say, but I still have strong feelings for Ortrud. I think about you too much, though. I try not to but can't stop. When I return, we need to settle this."

"I need to go back to bed; I'm feeling dizzy. Please give me a hand up, Aaron."

"Sure, no, don't faint on me, Britta!"

"Sorry, hold me up, hold me in your arms for a second."

"I've got you. Please don't do that. Oh, hell."

"What! What are you doing with her, Aaron?"

"Dammit, Ortrud! I mean, ah, hell; I'm sorry."

"You kissed her with more passion than you've ever shown me. Why, Aaron? And you, Britta, after trying to make it right, you stab me in the back! I can't stand it—I'm done!"

"Please, Ortrud, let me—"

"Let it go, Britta! I'll make it right when I get back. I'm sorry for this, but I have to go."

Dear God, what have I done? And I might never see Aaron again. Now I am sick. Sit down until you're stable, Britta. It's over, all over. Ortrud will never forgive me; she'll hate me forever. Oh, it has to all go away—please, Lord!

11:22 a.m.

Ahh, going back to bed didn't help; maybe moving around will get me going. Where is everyone? No one in the kitchen. Oh, the front door. "Anna, where is everybody?"

"We just got back from Winterthur. Ortrud asked Katrin and Ida to go with her to the barn—I'm puzzled as to why. She's acting strangely. Katrin said the Horns and Thomas are cleaning the henhouse; that you're the only one in the house."

"They have to come back soon to prepare lunch."

"I'm sure they will, but first, I need to tell you something, Britta. It's about Ortrud and our trip to Winterthur."

"I hoped Father would let me go, even though I felt bad. What is it?"

"I wish you were with us, so I could get your take on what Ortrud did. She asked me to return to the market and see if she left her glove on the counter. It seemed peculiar that she didn't do it herself. When I returned, the clerk was waiting at the door with Ortrud's glove. I started walking back to the truck when I saw Ortrud down the street, talking to the young man who upset you."

"Ernst Keller?"

"Yes, Britta. I hung back behind a sign so Ortrud couldn't see me. She must have thought I wouldn't return as soon as I did. I didn't hear their conversation, but it was intense and then she started crying. Then Ortrud shook his hand before crossing the street to the truck. I waited a few seconds before returning. I wanted to ask her about the conversation but thought better of it."

"She said nothing about it?"

"No, nothing at all, and that's what I want your take on. Frankly, it's worrying the hell out of me, Britta."

"Hmm, what is it, what's she doing? Look! The hairs on my arms are standing up. I have a tingly sensation all over, not from something good. Ortrud's furious with me over what happened earlier, and now she's consorting with someone who hates me even more."

"What happened earlier?"

"Another kiss that set Ortrud off. Shaking hands with Ernst can only mean one thing, Anna, and it's bad. I'm not sure what, but we need to do something before it's too late."

"Now you're scaring me. You don't think—

"Yes, I do. We know there's Gestapo all over Winterthur, and Ernst is surely involved with them."

"And Ortrud got everyone out of the house except you, and now me."

"We need to leave now, Anna!"

"Oh, pounding at the door—too late!"

"Hurry, let's run upstairs to my bedroom and hide!"

"Okay, I can hardly breathe. No, not under the bed, Britta; too obvious."

"We have no time. They're coming up the stairs. The closet? No, no, what about the floor-length drapes, one on each side?"

"Our best chance, Britta, hurry!"

Dear Lord, help us! Settle down, Britta; you have to do this—have to be quiet. No, no, I hear Anna—her breath.

"In here, quick! Search the bedroom; they're here someplace."

No, stay away, please God! Anna, not a cough. That's it.

"The drapes; get her Schulze! And who's behind the other drape? Let's take a look. Hmm, just as I suspected. Get both of them down to the auto."

"Ow, you're hurting me. Stop! Stop!"

"Shut up and get down the stairs!"

Where is everyone? Why doesn't someone help us? "Help! Help! Ah, my nose." *It's bleeding badly. Where are Katrin and the others; where are they?* "Don't hurt me, please!" *Where are they taking us. Where's Anna? Oh, between two men in the front seat; I think she's unconscious. Dear God, where are we going? Is this the end?*

17
A NEW REALITY

2:18 p.m.

"Get out!"

"Where are we? Why are—"

"Shut your mouth; never speak unless spoken to!"

I'm so stiff all over. What a horrible, cramped ride. Oh, don't stumble; you can't fall, Britta. Oh, no, Anna's swollen eye. There's blood on her dress. They struck her hard before shoving her into the auto. Don't say anything to her; keep your head up. The surroundings are unfamiliar. Where are we? Back in Germany, we went north and east. Are we entering a Gestapo office?

"Britta, are you alright?"

"Quiet!"

Oh, this hallway is so dark. Are those cells on either side? I guess this one's ours; they're unlocking the door. What's on the other side? How long will we be here? What will become of us?

"Get in there now!"

Stop shoving. Oh, that clank of the heavy door is our death knell. Such a dark, dank narrow cell. Oh, two woman are in here.

"Welcome to Ulm, girls. Unfortunate for you, but now I'll have someone to talk to."

"Ulm, isn't it south of Stuttgart?"

"About seventy kilometers southeast. A pleasant place; at least it was. Our family visited my aunt here several times when I was a child. I'm Vera Vogel. This is Friedl, the only word she's spoken in the three days she's been here."

"I'm Anna Wolff, and this is my friend, Britta Schumann. We're from Stuttgart."

"So am I. You're so young, dear."

"I'll be sixteen in three days if I survive. What will happen to us, Vera? I'm scared to death and worried about my father and Aaron."

"Well, I've been here five days. They haven't bothered me, haven't even questioned me. They bring in crappy food in the morning and evening, and that's it. I assume they're holding us until they figure out where to send us."

"Well, maybe they won't shoot us."

"No, Anna, I don't think that'll happen. Why did they bring you here?"

"Some fool Hitler Youth brat had it in for Britta, so he turned us in for helping Jews escape from Germany. The Gestapo caught us before we knew what happened. Several hours later, they dumped us here. Why are you here, Vera?"

"SS soldiers showed up at my home six days ago to inform me that my husband was dead. He was a Wehrmacht captain in Russia. They executed him for crimes against the Reich. I knew nothing about it, but they said I conspired with him; that's why I'm here."

"I'm sorry about your husband, Vera."

"Umm, that's sweet of you, Britta. But to tell the truth, girls, our nine-year marriage was shaky from the start. Love was never a part of our relationship. I don't know why I married Rudy. He was a devoted

Nazi while I never bought into any of it. It split us from the beginning. So it wasn't the traumatic loss one would expect. But thanks for your sentiments."

"Where do we sleep?"

"The floor, girls; don't see beds, do you? The blankets in the corner are it. Be warned; the floor isn't kind to anyone wanting sleep. Now we need to figure out how all four of us can lie down at the same time."

Oh, Lord, what are we doing here? I could hardly sleep at the farm, and now this, I won't sleep a wink. No bathroom—like the hideout. Will they let us out?

"I can see the wheels turning, Britta. See the can in the corner; that's where we go. It's empty now, but with four of us, it won't take long for it to fill up, especially with the slop they feed us. The other can is water; they fill it daily, so we'll have to ration it."

"Dear God, hopefully, we'll leave soon."

"Be careful what you wish for, Britta; this might be the best place we see."

"I guess. I need to sit and rest. Right now, I don't know if I can face what's coming next, if I even want to go on."

February 11, 1944, 6:19 p.m.

"Wake up, Britta!"

"Oh, what?"

"You had another bad dream. Are you alright, dear?"

"Thanks for waking me, Anna. Flames lapped out of the mirror, drawing me in. I tried but couldn't resist its lure; it consumed me."

"Not unlike previous dreams."

"Yes, it's always in my mind. Will this trip ever end? Does anyone know where we are?"

"Somewhere in the north. While you slept, we stopped in Leipzig and picked up four women. An hour ago, there was more traffic and frequent stops. We probably passed near Berlin."

"But we can't see out, Vera; how did you know we were in Leipzig?"

"The women now sleeping said so. We've stopped three times, and they've crammed nine more women into the truck."

"Is it dark again?"

"Looks like it, Britta; we left in darkness, and we'll arrive in darkness."

"But where are we going, Vera; do you know?"

"I shouldn't tell you until I'm sure. It might be good news or bad, depending on how you look at it. Oh, I might as well tell you what I think. I've read stories about a large prison camp for women north of Berlin. I think that's our destination; we'll know soon."

What next, dear God. I can't face whatever it is. Please hold me, Father, take me from this nightmare, let me wake up and find it was only a bad dream. I'm sick; my stomach aches from hunger. It's been hours since we've eaten. What do they expect from us? I'm only a girl; it's not fair! Crying won't help, Britta; you have to face it all—it's not going away.

"There, there, Britta, we're here; we'll take care of you."

"I'm sorry for breaking down, Anna. I know you and Vera will do your best for me. I can't help it; fear has a grip on me that I can't shake."

"What, we're stopping . . . voices. I can't make them out."

"We've arrived, Anna. Brace yourself and pray if you believe in God. Come to my arms, Britta. Let me wipe your tears away. We'll make it; keep that in mind, no matter what."

"I can't, Vera; I don't have it in me."

"You will, sweetie. Vera and I will take care of you and Friedl. A girl shouldn't face this. Steel yourself against the bastards, Britta; that's the way we'll make it."

"I'll try, Anna, for her sake."

"Her sake? Who are you talking about, Britta?"

"Um, I don't know, don't know why I said it."

"Everyone out—now!"

Take a deep breath. The only choice you have is in what you do in the face of it. Stand up, stand up for her and muster all your strength. For her, I'm confused. Be strong on the inside—fight!

"It looks like they're herding us into a large group of women, another transport that recently arrived. We need to stay together. Anna, keep your arm around Britta, and I'll keep mine around Friedl."

"Believe me; I won't let you go, Anna. My Lord, there're women everywhere. Are we going in the building over there?"

"Looks like it, Britta. They'll process us; not sure what that involves—be prepared."

"How Vera? Look at Friedl; she's confused. I wish she'd say something; let us know what she's feeling."

"Maybe she's better off."

"Quiet, quiet! No talking while we process you into the camp. Violators will meet with severe punishment. Have your identification papers and possessions ready for inspection. Those hiding items will regret it. Move through the process quickly, and then you'll be fed and get a warm bed."

Ah, the thought of food and a warm bed is comforting, but the dreams will return. It is freezing out here. I guess I was too afraid to notice. Thankfully, we're near the front of the line; we'll soon be in the processing building. Is that good or bad?

"Single file, go directly to the table in front of you with papers out."

Thank you, Lord, that we're still together. What do I do? I have falsified papers, and I'm sure Ernst Keller told the Gestapo who I am.

"Next, these are false papers, correct? Your name is Britta Schumann."

"Yes."

"Take these patches and move to the next station by the window."

Anna's ahead of me, and Vera and Friedl are behind. Please keep us together, God. Oh, no, they're shaving heads. Not my hair!

"Let me see your patches. Hurry up! That chair—now!"

Scissors, she has scissors, not a razor. She's only taking some off the sides and back.

"Move to that table with the clothes."

Still together, good.

"Patches. Hmm, you'll keep your clothes. We'll issue a heavy coat and cap. Select one of each from the piles over there. Then go through the door. Take these with you and hurry!"

I need to find a heavy coat that fits quickly. Nothing suitable on top. There, that one looks warm and almost new. So many caps. Who's were they? That one's in good condition and will cover my ears. What next? Oh, go through the door; I think that's what she said. Ah, dear God, some are naked; some are dressing, and others are undressing! I can't . . . I won't—that soldier's gawking at everyone? No, no, Vera and Friedl have taken off their clothes. I'll die having to do it—wake up, Britta, wake up, please!

"Give me your papers, patches, and the hat and coat. I'll have the patches sewn on while you're waiting for inspection. Give me your blouse."

"But, I—"

"No talking—blouse now!"

You have to do it. Here, damn you! I need to stop crying. It won't help—stop it! Friedl is so frail, poor girl. She might be my age, but I doubt it. There, my skirt, shoes, and socks are off. I can wait till—

"Everything, get the pants and brassiere off immediately! I'll examine you shortly."

Okay, there off. Use your hands and arms, like the others, hide as best you can. Keep your eyes closed, so you don't see his leering stare. Put it out of your mind; go someplace far away.

"You're next. Lean and healthy—to be young again. Stand straight; this hurts but won't take long."

"Ow, ow! Oh, why'd you do that?"

"Hidden treasure; the pain will go away. Wait over there till your clothes are ready."

Stop the tears. Don't show your pain; bite your tongue, do something. Oh, it hurts. I'm bleeding. Why'd they have to do that—damn them! How can they do this to a girl? Hurry, please get my clothes ready, please! I'm freezing. Vera and Friedl are getting dressed, and Anna is undressing. Keep us together, Lord. What an awful, decrepit, drafty place. It smells so fowl, and the screaming is nerve-wracking. Hopelessness is our reality. What do I do now? Wake up or die—please!

"Your clothes; get dressed and go through the rear door."

Hurry! Vera and Friedl are gone; you can't lose them. Anna has to keep up. Okay, dressed—the coat feels good. What's on the other side of the door?

"Let's see your number, the one sewn on your coat. Line up over there with those women."

"Twenty-seven is your barracks. Report to the guard outside the door."

Be there, Vera, please! Ah, the wind is biting. Is that the barracks?

"Barracks number?"

"Twenty-seven."

"Follow those women to the mess—hurry!"

Run, Britta; there's Vera, catch up to her! "Vera, Vera, wait for me! Ow, what?"

"No talking, bitch! Get in line and be quiet."

Oh, that hurt the back of my head. What did she use to hit me? Stand up and walk behind Vera and Friedl. Don't stumble and fall; shake off the dizziness. Thank God, here comes Anna. Don't say anything. When can I go to sleep and make this go away?

"Attention! Go inside the mess and take a bowl. You have ten minutes to eat."

Take another one, Britta, that one's filthy. Whatever it is, it smells sour. Watery broth, I guess. A warm piece of bread, a minor miracle in hell. Benches; Vera's waving me over. Finally, I can sit down. I'm dizzy, and my head's hurting. Eat, don't talk. Aw, what is this stuff? It tastes horrible. But the bread's tasty and will fill my stomach; make the aching go away.

"Attention! Barracks twenty-six line up in front of me. Barracks twenty-five line up to their left. Barracks twenty-seven line up to their right—now!"

Keep quiet, Britta, no more whacks on the head. I'm feeling steadier on my feet, and my stomach's better. Sweet sleep, that's what I need now. I guess this long two-story building is it, barracks twenty-seven, our home for who knows how long. They all look the same—dreary.

"Over here, Britta, Anna. By luck, the bottom and middle bunks are vacant. Let me boost both of you up. We'll be below you. I'm concerned about Friedl; she's not doing well. I've tucked her in with the two blankets they issued."

"Thanks, Vera; I was afraid we'd be separated and alone."

"I saw them hit you, Britta. Are you alright?"

"Um, will we ever be alright?"

"Attention! Thirty-one women have joined us, nine in this bay. They replace those expelled—more will follow. For those of you who are new, I'm Dagmar Roth, matron functionary of the barracks. When here, you'll follow all rules and instructions. Those who choose otherwise are subject to severe punishment. We fall out for morning roll call at four thirty. You'll receive your work detail assignment at that time. Others will advise you of what to expect. Lights out in five minutes."

"I'm Lina Krause, and this is Marie Berger. We've been here five months, I think. Dagmar means business, so heed what she says. We'll answer questions and help you with this life from hell. We took the high bunk for protection, to keep an eye on everything. You can't trust what anyone will do; some are out of their minds; watch your back every minute."

"Thanks for your hospitality, Lina. I'm Vera Vogel. This is Britta Schumann, Anna Wolff, and Friedl. She doesn't talk."

"You best get what sleep you can; the days are long, and the work is hard."

"It looks like Britta, Anna, and Friedl are well on their way; goodnight, Lina."

Evening, March 11, 1944

Thanks to Marie Berger, I can resume my entries. She came across this diary at her work location and smuggled it into the barracks. Knowing my desire, and having no intention to use it herself, she slipped it under my blanket last night, a surprise that lifted my spirits. We've been at the Ravensbruck labor camp for women for a month. Vera and Lina are searching for a place to hide my diary. Keeping it is dangerous.

Life here is unbearable at times. I can't put words on paper that describe the daily horrors. Typhus and Pneumonia have taken many from our barracks along with starvation. Others had no will to go on, so they didn't. New women come and go while, almost miraculously, our close-knit group stays intact. Lina Krause and Marie Berger mentor us in carrying out our daily activities, which are fraught with danger. Avoiding the wrath of Dagmar Roth, our barracks functionary, is critical. She's vicious and void of compassion. I've had one run-in with her when she hit me with her club for no reason.

We work in the camp industry that makes Wehrmacht uniforms. Some purposely did shoddy work but were caught and seen no more. The days are endless. They roust us at four thirty. We stand for an hour at roll call before waiting in line that long for breakfast, if anyone can call it that. A large piece of bread sustains us. Most save half for later in the day. The bowl of broth is watery with little taste or value. I don't drink the coffee that others say is putrid. We get partially rotten apples or questionable dried fruit for a meager lunch. After returning from work around six thirty in the evening, we wait another hour for a meal not worthy of a one-minute wait. It's usually a thin soup with no meat and few vegetables. But, again, we receive a generous slice of bread, which temporarily relieves the gnawing in our stomachs.

We've all lost weight and are losing strength by the day. Friedl's health concerns us the most. We still haven't heard her say a word. Anna's been sick for the last week; she gets better as the day wears on. I've avoided illness, though perplexing dreams still vex me. I see another girl in the hiding place mirror. I talked with her but can't recall the conversations. I can almost call her name—maybe in time.

Thank God for Sundays—no work. Roll call and breakfast are an hour later, leaving us free for the remainder of the day. With the coming of spring, we enjoy patches of green grass and flower boxes blooming with vibrant colors against a dreary backdrop with little color. We talk to women from other blocks and get helpful information about what's occurring in the camp. Hearing the news is a useful distraction that momentarily takes me away from the world I want to escape. The saddest story is the medical experiments on Polish women. They call them "rabbits" or "guinea pigs." The doctors butcher them to infect tissue or bones to see if varied medications will heal them. Some die, most are left maimed and crippled, none recover.

Many women show ingenuity. They've made cards to enjoy games. Some developed new games for Sunday, while those who were teachers developed study plans for school-age girls. I've participated in geometry and history classes. We welcome anything to keep occupied.

Rumors are rampant in the camp. We continually ponder the status of the war, discuss our fate, and scrutinize the validity of wild stories. Avoiding illness and prodding our minds and bodies to go on when they don't want to are essential to our survival. Such is our existence. Dear God, help us all. I'll only make diary entries periodically when it's safe.

—Britta S.

March 16, 1944, 11:24 p.m.

"Wake up, Britta, you had another nightmare."

"Uh, Vera?"

"Yes. Whisper so we don't wake the others. Are you alright, dear?"

"I guess."

"The same dream, Britta?"

"Oh, I woke you, Anna. I'll be okay, but I'm sorry to disturb both of you. For the first time, the girl in the mirror came into focus. Then she told me her name; it's Cara."

"Well, did that jiggle your memory? Do you know anyone named Cara?"

"No, Vera, I've never heard the name. She's friendly. I don't know why, but I feel we have a special bond."

"It's beyond me, Britta, but it must mean something."

"It does, though I have no idea what. Are you alright, Anna? Your health concerns me. I hate ruining your sleep."

"Since you brought it up, Britta, it's time to tell the others why—I'm pregnant."

"Dear God, of all things, not that!"

"I should have told you sooner, Vera."

"How in the hell did you hide it?"

"It wasn't easy, Vera, but I always made sure I covered it."

"How far are you along?"

"Five or six months, I'm not sure."

"It must be on your mind all the time?"

"It is, Vera. What can I do? Remember the woman in the barracks who was pregnant—here one day and gone the next, never heard from again. My God, will that happen to me?"

"They must have a place—a barracks—for expectant mothers."

"I don't mean to interrupt, Britta, but they don't."

"Is that you, Lina?"

"It is, Vera. Two women who know told me what happens. A doctor confirms the pregnancy. Then they'll give you double rations, which is good but not enough. You'll stay in our barracks and continue to work until you go into labor. Few make it to full term before losing their baby."

"Then what can I do, Lina?"

"It's up to you, dear, but I'd tell Dagmar Roth tomorrow. She'll eventually find out."

"You've hidden it well, but soon you won't be able to. Lina's advice is sound; I'd follow it."

"Thanks, Vera. What do you think, Britta?"

"I don't know, I guess. I'm afraid for you, Anna, and can't stand the thought of losing you."

"We're all concerned, sweetie, but it's time to let the mother get back to sleep."

"Of course, Vera; goodnight."

June 23, 1944, 2:54 a.m.

"Oh no, it hurts—burns! Father, where are you? Why won't you ever hold and comfort me? I need you now more than ever. Please, help me, Father. No, Cara, don't go through the flames that burn. Go back; you can't do it. You can't help. Ow, oh, it burns! Help! Help!"

"Wake up! Wake up! You're dreaming again."

"Mother, thank you, Mother! Can we go to church now; it's been a long time, and I miss it. Gracie will be there, won't she?"

"Is she out of her head, Vera?"

"It sounds like it, Anna. Is she warm?"

"Burning up! What do we do? Oh God, do you think it's typhus?"

"Check her chest and arms for a red rash, if you can see in the dim light."

"It's hard to see, Vera. I don't think there's a rash, though. What now?"

"Mother, why can't we go to church? Why can't I see Gracie?"

"She's delirious, Anna; it's the high fever. It doesn't sound like typhus, though. Strip off her blanket and clothes. I'm going to the latrine to dampen my blouse and skirt with cold water. We have to get her fever down."

"Where's Father? He's never home when I need him, Mom. Why doesn't he love me? Oh, no, run, run away—hurry!"

"Dear me, Britta, what are you saying? It doesn't sound like you. That was fast, Vera."

"Damn, she is burning up!"

"Thank you, Mom; the warm bath feels good. It soothes my mind. I'm not losing it, am I? The doctor thinks I am. Oh, it feels wonderful. I think I'll lay back and close my eyes."

"She's breathing hard, Vera, but I think she's gone back to sleep. Dear Lord, I hope so. I can't sleep, so I'll watch her."

I can hear you, Anna. It's foggy, though, as I go in and out of the darkness to an unfamiliar place.

"Thanks, Anna; I won't sleep either. It won't be long until they roust us anyway."

"What will they do with Britta?"

"Hmm, rarely do they take them to that damned excuse for a hospital. Usually, they leave the poor souls in their beds to die or make it on their own—ruthless bastards!"

"What was she mumbling, Vera? I know she's out of her head, but nothing fits what I know about her life."

"Hard to tell—she's one sick girl. We need to pray she makes it. She might leave us now. The hell will only get worse, Anna; escaping might be best."

"No, I won't accept it, Vera! Britta's a fighter; I can't lose her."

You won't, Anna; I can't let you down. But now the darkness, the darkness—

4:28 a.m.

"No, no, you're from the coven. You can't take me to that place. It's only a bad dream. Wake up! No!"

"Wake up, sweetheart, you've had another dream. We'll stay with you until sleep comes."

"Horrible, horrible dream, Mom; it's like I was there. They were dragging me to the dark place again."

Aw, I'm falling, Mother; help me, the darkness is closing in.

"Why's this one not up?"

"She's ill, Dagmar; let her be!"

"Ah, Vera, always a pain in the ass, asking for things you know you can't have."

"Look, she's wet with sweat; her fever's broken."

"My God, Anna, you're right. Can you hear us, Britta? Wake up!"

"I am awake and heard what you said. I was in a dark fog and thought I died, but Mother brought me back."

"It's a miracle she recovered that quickly; hours ago, she was deathly ill."

"It has to be, Anna. Do you understand, Dagmar? You can't take her away."

"If she can get up and stand in formation, she can stay. What about the mute? Why isn't she up?"

"Get up, Friedl, now!"

"What's wrong with her, Vera? Friedl's not waking; she's burning up like Britta."

"She must have what Britta had; a bug that passes quickly. Please let her stay in bed, Dagmar. She'll recover in a few hours."

"Not this time, Vera! We're taking her to the infirmary. She's worthless anyway, has never carried her weight in the factory. Don't you have enough burdens without taking care of her?"

"No, you can't take Friedl!"

"Such a pesky one for just getting off your deathbed. You'll all do well to shut your mouths and survive another day. Now get outside and fall into formation! They'll take this lifeless one soon."

"Can you walk, sweetie? We'll help you."

"I'm weak, and my stomach's gnawing, but I can walk if you and Anna steady me. What happened? Was I sick? I remember dreams and conversations."

"I thought we were losing you, Britta, and I don't want to go on without you."

"Please don't say that, Anna. In this place, we have no guarantee. But one of us has to go on to tell our story. God must have healed me, don't you think? And if He did, will I be sacrificed later?"

"I doubt it, Britta."

"What about Friedl? What will become of her, Vera?"

"God only knows, dear, but now we have to survive to face this day."

Evening, August 5, 1944

I almost lost my diary last week. I pulled it from behind a loose board, and as I began to write, Dagmar and five guards burst in for the second surprise inspection of the month. Vera hid the diary in her blouse as we stood at attention while they searched the barracks. She put her life on the line for me again. For some reason, they skipped her as they patted the rest of us down—another miracle. The surprise inspections have increased, requiring extreme caution. I have to tell the story, but now entries will be briefer and infrequent.

I've finally recovered from whatever I had; no one knows what it was, but it wasn't typhus. I'm still weak and expect my strength will only wane. Conditions at the camp worsen by the day as transports increase from the east, mainly Poland. The souls in our barracks far outnumber available beds. Some use the benches between rows of bunks as their bed while others sleep on the floor. The weakest—those without friends to help them—are expelled from their beds by the stronger new arrivals. Ugly violence is a part of daily life. We're turning on each other as our captors increase their brutality. But Vera's and Anna's protection often saved me, though we don't know how much longer we can go on.

Sunday, we'll go to the infirmary to see if Friedl's there—if she's alive. We've heard nothing since they carried her off, and we have to know. If she's there, we somehow have to free her.

—Britta S

August 6, 1944, 10:04 a.m.

"This should work, girls; we have to try for Friedl. You each have your pack of cigarettes?"

"Yes, Vera, but you and Anna paid a high price for them."

"It's not too high, Britta, if it means freeing Friedl. Okay, you know what to do."

"We're here, Ma'am, to see our friend, the mute girl. We have cigarettes for you."

"Do you know bribing a functionary could cost your lives?"

"We're past caring; we need to know if she's alive."

"Brave, huh? What's your name, dear?"

"Vera, why?"

"I'm looking for someone like you. I'm bored with the other ones."

"Ah, let us in, and we'll see."

"Hell, I don't give a damn if you go in or not. But stop and see me on your way out."

What a wretched place. The building's rundown, almost falling apart. Paints peeling off, cracks in the boards. What are those screams? Do you want to go in, Britta? You have to for Friedl.

"Hurry in, girls, the functionary's walking away down the hall. Try that door, Anna; it's probably one of the wards."

"Two nurses and a doctor, Vera."

"Follow my lead. Hello, we're representatives from the general population council."

"What, what council are you talking about?"

"Oh, the screw-ups did it again. They didn't tell you—damn it!"

"No one told us anything. Why are you here?"

"To cheer up the sick. The council approved it, and the patients need our support."

"Crap, this place gets crazier every day—what the hell am I doing here as a renowned doctor? Go ahead but keep out of our way!"

"Thanks, doctor, we'll keep out of sight. Come with me, girls."

"She's not here, Vera!"

"Don't panic, Britta. Let's slip out and check the other wards."

"Shall we try this door, Vera?"

"Enter quietly, Anna. Damn, it's dark in here! You'll have to get close to recognize Friedl."

"Wait! Here she is!"

"Thank God, Britta. Is she alive?"

"I don't know, Anna. I'm afraid to touch her, afraid she won't move. What do we do, Vera?"

"I can feel her breath on my hand, girls—she's alive! We have to stiffen our necks and carry out our plan. No one's in the ward. Check the door, Anna, and see if anyone's in the hall. I'll carry Friedl. Put a blanket over her, Britta."

"Oh no, a nurse is coming this way!"

"God, please don't let her come in. What should we do, Vera?"

"I'll handle it, Britta. Anna, stay back in the shadows, out of sight. Pray hard."

"What, what are you doing here? Who are you carrying?"

"The mute girl."

"But why? She's weak and can't last much longer."

"That's why. If she's going, please let her die in the barracks with those who love her. Is it that important to you, Frau? Have mercy!"

"Well said, Britta. So, will you let us take her?"

"Oh, why not. The poor girl should have the chance to die somewhere other than in this crap hole. I never wanted to be here; I hate every minute of it! I'll have to fix things, though. But being Sunday, with few workers around, I can fill out a death report, which will keep them from looking for her."

"Thank you, nurse. Can you show us the safest way out?"

"Follow me to the back door. The fence gate opens from the inside and has no guard on Sunday. Be careful. I hope she makes it."

"Now that we're through the gate, girls, it'll raise suspicion if we carry Friedl. Drop the blanket, and we'll drag her as if we're helping her walk. Help me, Anna; get on the other side of her."

"Thankfully, the barracks is empty. Is the plan still to have Friedl sleep in your bunk, Vera?"

"Yes, Britta; it's the reason why I fought off women who wanted to share my bed."

"There, there, cover her with the blanket, Anna."

"Her breath is shallow, but she looks at peace."

"So fragile, Anna. Have you girls ever seen a bird with a broken wing? That's what I think of when I look at Friedl."

"I did once; it hurt me to see it."

"Then you know how helpless she is, Britta, how scared she must be. You have to wait a long time for the wing to heal. I'm afraid it won't happen for Friedl, but we must help her to the end."

"How do we hide her from Dagmar?"

"We can't, Anna. It depends on any mercy that Dagmar has in her heart for Friedl. We can only make her comfortable and see what happens."

Evening, September 5, 1944

Dagmar surprised us with an inspection last night. They removed three women with contraband. When this happens, we never see them again. Though usually heartless, Dagmar confounded us twice. As Lina said, she allowed Anna to stay in the barracks without medical care. The workdays were hard for all of us but impossible for Anna in her condition. Tragically, complications took her baby at birth. No one could help her. We grieved for weeks, but Anna believes it was for the best, knowing her baby had little chance to survive. She's broken, but we seldom talk about it. It took time before I could think of putting it on paper.

Dagmar also surprised us by allowing Freidl to stay in the barracks. Does she have a chink in her armor that reveals a heart? We never thought Freidl would wake, but on August 14, she did. We pilfered extra bread to feed her. She's gaining strength and returned to work in the uniform factory last week. Thank God the broken wing is healing.

My nightly dreams continue. They're a puzzle I'm trying to put together. Some pieces fit, but most don't, or they're missing. I've learned more about Cara, the girl *in the mirror. She's my age and quite bright and lovely. I think she's from America, which makes no sense. She speaks English, and her phrases are sometimes puzzling. I know things about her but don't know how I do; they're pieces of the puzzle I haven't put in place. My hands have healed, leaving behind unusual scarring.*

Rumors are spreading that the Allies invaded France and are beating back the Wehrmacht. We pray it will be over soon, and the Allies will free us from this hell. I hope we have the strength to last until they do.

—Britta S

September 24, 1944, 9:42a.m.

"Where do you want to sit, girls?"

"Oh, today I'd like to sit on the benches in the northern yard. It's been weeks since we sat there. Is that okay with you, Anna?"

"Sure, Britta, is it alright with you, Vera? And how about you, Friedl? Someday she'll answer me."

"It might be too late to get a bench, girls."

"It doesn't matter, Vera, we have blankets, and there's some grass. Ahh, I love the coolness of a cloudy day after a gentle rain cleanses the air. No smells of the putrid camp. Isn't it glorious, Anna?"

"It is, sweetie, a few moments to steal away—let our minds go to another place."

"Oh, I just got a whiff of the fall flowers. Do you smell them, girls?"

"Um, Vera. How can it be? A respite in the middle of hell. We've never had a day like this, Anna. Women are lounging on benches and lying in the grass, talking with smiles on their faces. I must be dreaming, but I hope not."

"You're right, Vera, no empty benches, but there's a nice patch of grass over there."

"Perfect, Anna. Stretch out your blankets, girls, then lay back and take yourself far away."

"Wait! Is that . . . it couldn't be!"

"Who, who do you see, Anna?"

"I'm not positive, but I think it's Katrin, Katrin Koch from the safe farm. Stay here, Britta; I'll go find out."

"I don't see her, Vera. Oh, now I think I might, but she looks different, gaunt. Look, Anna's talking to her. It must be Katrin."

"They're having quite a conversation; it looks like your friend's trying to walk away from Anna. Ah, now Anna's pulling her this way."

"Is it you, Katrin!?"

"She's distraught, Britta, and doesn't want to talk. She might be, you know."

"No, Anna, I'm not out of my mind. I'm hurting and don't want to face what I must."

"None of us do, but we don't have a choice, Katrin?"

"You don't understand, Anna. I accept this place; it's better than where I was. No, it's not that; it's cutting someone to the bone that I care for."

"I guess I don't understand, Katrin; what do you mean?"

"Ah, Britta, Britta, I hate it! The Gestapo killed your father in May. I'm sorry, sweetheart."

Oh, what, what did she say? Everything spinning, going dark.

"Wake up, Britta!"

"What happened, Anna?"

"You fainted, dear."

"Why? Katrin, oh no! No, no, no, dear God, no! How? What happened?"

"I don't have details, Britta. Someone tipped off the Gestapo that your father and Aaron planned to transport Jews from Stuttgart to Switzerland. They waited for them near the safe house in Balingen. The Gestapo opened fire and hit your father. It was quick; he didn't suffer, dear. That's right, cry it out, sweetie, let it all go."

Oh, Father, why? Why God? I can't go on without you; I'll die or go back.

"We'll help you, Britta. It killed me to tell you."

"Aaron, is he gone? Please, Lord, no!"

"He's alive, Britta. By some miracle, Aaron escaped with only a flesh wound in the arm. But he only remembers running until he was safe. Only two of the Jews escaped with him."

"Is he safe? Where is he?"

"When the Nazis captured me in June, they lived in a safe house near Konstanz."

"They? Who's with Aaron?"

"Ah, Ortrud, sweetie. They married in April."

"Oh, I see." *It can't be! No, I need you, Aaron, more than ever before. I can't lose both you and father. Ah, our lovely day's gone forever. I take it all back. It's too much; I have to go back! What? Why do I have these thoughts? What do they mean?*

Evening, November 21, 1944

I fear this might be my last entry. Conditions in the camp have worsened. Out of fear, my previous descriptions didn't portray our horrible circumstances and the chilling horror of being brutalized. My insides quiver with the thought of being caught with this diary. Yesterday, the guards found a woman with a Bible. They instantly took her away. She returned in agony several hours later. Two women in the barracks with medical training ministered to the open wounds on her backside from the beating. We've heard this is a typical punishment for possessing banned items. Other changes jeopardize our survival.

New women arrive weekly as others die to make way for them. Vera thinks the population of our bar–

racks is now over a thousand. We're mandated to sleep four to a bunk, which is near impossible. Vera and Friedl moved to the bed Anna and I share. The only way it works is to lay head to foot facing the same way. Anna and Vera insisted on being on the outside, but each has fallen to the floor twice. Fortunately, they weren't hurt badly. The corpses of women are stacked in the latrine until someone takes them away. It's ghastly, and I wonder when they'll stack mine there. Disease takes some, but many die of starvation or the lack of will to go on. We've made a pact to go on no matter what and bring Friedl with us. I don't know if I can.

Reducing food rations while increasing work will kill us all if it continues. The black bread and watery soup can't sustain women working eleven-hour days. I've lost so much weight that my ribs and hipbones are showing. They wake us earlier, and the time we stand in formation doubled. Many times, Vera and Anna held Freidl and me to prevent us from falling. For several weeks we've worked in a freezing building repairing and laundering German army uniforms. The bloodstained fabric brings visions of horror.

I try to steal my mind against it, but the bitter loss of Father haunts me day and night. I have to come to terms with it but still can't. I think of Aaron every day. I long for him to hold and comfort me. My love for him is greater than ever. I wish Aaron hadn't married Ortrud. Anna and I know she's responsible for our imprisonment. I won't let her stand between the love I have for Aaron and the love I know he has for me. I sleep little, so dreams are infrequent. Cara and the mirror fade as our circumstances worsen and my health *declines. I don't think I'll ever understand the meaning of the girl in the mirror.*

I need to conclude now and take my place in line for the latrine. It's a necessary endless wait. Hopefully, the line will be shorter by now, and the toilets won't be clogged and overflowing. Ice cold water to wash our face and hands sends us shivering to the body heat of those in our bed, yet another few hours of misery trying to escape in elusive sleep. Maybe tomorrow will come, perhaps not.

—Britta S

February 7, 1945, 12:24 p.m.

Ah, sick again. Do I want this? Do I want to go on? I can't keep eating black bread and soup. But that's all we have until tomorrow. How do they expect us to work, even survive on this? I feel like retching again but there's nothing to vomit.

"Where have you been, Vera? We were worried."

"I was talking to a woman who arrived yesterday from Hamburg, Anna, then with Annika from block twelve."

"Britta and Friedl are deathly ill—they can't get a bite down."

"Lay your heads back for a minute. Let your bodies settle. Do you understand, Friedl?"

"Nothing will help, Vera. Is there news?"

"Good news and bad, Britta. The Allies are advancing from the west and east. The war will be over in weeks. But we need to pray the Americans or Brits get here before the Russians—they're butchers, no better than the Nazis. I also have bad news. Katrin died last week. Annika thinks she starved."

"Katrin!? I loved her, Vera. She was so precious."

"You can't afford the tears or expend the energy, Britta. It's gotta end; it has to. Stay with us, sweetie, hang on. But you have to eat!"

"It'll come back up, Anna. Let me lie here until they come for us. Maybe I won't wake up. It's okay, isn't it?"

"No, Britta, it isn't. We're not letting you die in this cesspool. Do you hear me?"

"Damn, damn, my blanket's wet! I can't even lie down and rest on this muddy ground. I'm freezing, Anna, can't you let me go? The drizzle is chilling, and the gray skies are lowering to take me."

"Get your asses up now! Russian uniforms are waiting for you. Why are these two lying in the mud?"

"No other place to lie—let 'em alone!"

"Wait a minute, you're the bitch I allowed in the hospital. I never forget a face, and I liked yours. But you cheated me—never came back as you promised."

"Crap! Did you think I would, lady?"

"We'll see about that. Have the SS take these two away—the ovens need fuel."

"No, you can't! Let them lie; I'll keep my promise."

"Why do you want to bargain now? They're worthless as the crap piling up around the barracks."

"Leave them alone! I promise you'll be glad you did."

"No, you can't, Vera! Don't degrade yourself. I want to keep them with all my being, but Britta and Friedl want to leave us now—it's time."

"I won't let any of my girls go, Anna. What's your name?"

"Sigrid."

"Well, come for me tonight, Sigrid, and let these two lie."

"Eight-thirty every night this week, and you can keep these bags of bones."

"Let Anna help them back to our barracks and excuse them from work today as part of the bargain?"

"Why not? You've cheered me up, Vera."

Evening, April 25, 1945

Thank God I got my diary back after a woman took it. She was out of her mind, so I don't blame her. When Anna learned who took the diary, she persuaded her to return it. The barracks is rampant with rumors that the camp will close soon. No one knows what will become of us. We've heard they'll move us to another place further away from the advancing Russians.

The explosions tell us the war is nearer every day. Now the Red Cross is allowed to come in and distribute rations. Though, not enough, the food has nourished our racked bodies these past days. Fear of the unknown haunts us. I can't explain it, but knowing what to expect each day, even if it's hellish, brings a sense of stability. We pray where we go is far from the Russians. I fear that my body is too weak for the journey; looking at it brings tears.

I owe my life to Vera, as does Friedl. The brutal functionary, Sigrid, humiliated her for a week. I can't imagine the horror she endured for us. She hasn't been the same since and probably will never be. We're indebted to Vera for life and love her deeply. We pray that God will wipe away the memories and heal her body.

Once more, we thought Friedl was leaving us. But, though extremely weak, she's still with us, never uttering a word but speaking with pleading eyes. I can't express how I've come to love Friedl. Her heart is gold, and light shines through her. I want to hold her, but she's too fragile. Anna plods along, watching over me. She's my closest friend. My love for her, Vera, and Friedl sustain me. I know it will carry me to days of bliss.

Though the Red Cross is a Godsend, many died these last months, and many more will before leaving. Every time we think conditions couldn't get worse, they do. We recently had another infestation of typhus, and some said cholera was in the camp. Camp medical staff abandoned us weeks ago, but Red Cross doctors and nurses have blessed the women of Ravensbruck.

Flowers are again in bloom, but the stench of feces and vomit everywhere prevents us from enjoying their fragrance. The irony speaks to the state of life here, leaving little else to say. Wherever we go, I'll keep my diary. I have to guard it with my life, so you'll know the horror of this place. Is this my last entry; only God knows.

—Britta S

May 1, 1945, 3:21 p.m.

Ah! What? Shooting. Wake up, Britta. Come to your senses—quick! Oh God, we're still walking. When will it end? Who's carrying me? It must be Anna; Vera has Friedl over her shoulder. Dear Lord, how do they have the energy to do it?

"You're awake, Britta?"

"Shots woke me, Vera. Not more, please, God!"

"Don't look, sweetie; it's brutal. Thankfully, the SS are leaving in droves to escape into the woods. They know their end is near, but the brutes can't resist more senseless killings as they leave."

"When will it be over, Anna? When, oh, when? Please put me down; I'm stiffening up."

"Are you strong enough to walk?"

"No, but I can't burden you anymore. How do you and Vera manage to carry us? You must be as weak as we are."

"We have no choice, Britta; we won't leave you, and that's that. Besides, you're both light as feathers."

"How do I repay the love you have for us? Thanks, Anna, from my heart." *Ah, I'm lightheaded. But I have some strength in my legs.*

"The bread and chocolate rations from the Red Cross are lifesavers. Without them, we wouldn't have made it this far."

"But now they're gone, Vera. What do we live on until someone rescues us?"

"Pray, Anna, that the Allies find us soon. We've been going northwest for two days, and the sound of small weapons gets closer by the hour. And now we're mixing with hundreds of civilians."

"The gunfire is east of us, Vera. Does that mean what I think?"

"Yes, sweetie. The Russians will overtake us soon. The stories scare me to death; we can't let them take us. We'll flee to the woods and look for a hiding place."

"Won't they shoot us?"

"We'll be careful, Anna; wait until the woods are closer, and we see no SS soldiers."

5:17 p.m.

"Get ready, girls! I see a village ahead. There must be places to hide, and I see only two SS guards. With all the people, they won't see us run to the woods."

"But Friedl and I can't run, Vera. How can you and Anna run and carry us? You should leave me and save yourselves."

"No, we won't do that, Britta!"

"I love you, Anna, but the time's come to save yourself. I'll be alright; they'll rescue us soon."

"Pick up Friedl, Anna. Relax, Britta, I'm picking you up. You can't let the Russians take you. Okay, Anna, run to the woods as fast as you can."

Aw, the bouncing up and down hurts! At least we're in the woods now. Is anyone following us? Somehow, lead us to safety, Lord.

"Look, Anna, a house."

"I see it, Vera, but I don't know if I have enough strength to get there. Can we stop and rest?"

"Put Freidl down. Are you okay, Britta? I'm going to put you down gently. There we go. Whew, that wore me out."

"There's a small building next to the house. Do you think anyone's there, Vera?"

"No lights, Britta, and it's getting darker. We'll sneak up and see after we rest for a while. How does Friedl look, Anna?"

"She's not awake. I hope she's alright. I worry about her all the time—that she'll silently leave us for good."

"We won't lose her, girls; remember our pact to escape hell together."

"I'm ready if you are, Vera."

"Okay, this is it. Can you carry Friedl to the house, Anna? And can you walk that far, Britta?"

"I can."

"Me, too."

"Go slow and follow me, girls. Good, good. No one's around, and I can't see anyone through the windows. It's abandoned."

"Looks like someone shot it up."

"It's a mess, Britta, but it might be the perfect place to hide for the night. Good, the door's unlocked. Carry Friedl in, Anna, be careful. Look in those cupboards, Britta; maybe there's food or something we can use."

"Hmm, nothing but this rouge case and a few dishes. There's rouge left with a tiny brush. I guess we can fix ourselves up and have a party."

"Sure. I'm glad we can still laugh, though I'm not sure how that's possible."

"I don't know, Anna, but it's better than tears. This place is a mess—looks like it might fall on us."

"There's a bed big enough for the three of you in the other room, girls, and a stuffed chair for me. If we get some sleep, we can go north in the dark. I've saved a chocolate bar to divide before we leave."

May 2, 1945, 12:07 a.m.

"What! Where am I?"

"You were restless, Britta, about to fall out of bed, so I woke you."

"Oh, I'm groggy. Is that you, Vera? It's dark. What time is it?"

"I have no idea, except it's time to leave. Did you have another dream?"

"A strange one. I was talking with people. They seemed familiar, though I couldn't see their faces. But I recognized the room, which made me feel safe. It was unlike any dream I've had—so real."

"These dreams, Britta, I don't know about you. But now, we need to rouse Anna and Friedl and get going."

"Are you going to put rouge dots on Friedl before we leave, as you did for us earlier?"

"It's too dark now, sweetie; we'll do it when I can see."

"Do you think they look enough like smallpox to fool the Russians and make them leave us alone if they catch us?"

"It wasn't the best job, having to spit in the rouge case and use a tiny brush. But it should scare the bastards enough if it comes to that. Wake up, Anna; wake up, Friedl!"

"Oh God, I was sleeping so well. It's time already?"

"Past time, Anna—get up now, Friedl."

"What's that, Vera? I hear voices outside—not German, either!"

"Crap! It's the Russians, Britta. Get under the bed—hurry!"

"Oh, the door's open; flashlights are shining everywhere. What do we do, Vera?"

"Nothing we can do now, Anna; it's too late. Pray and act like you're sick as hell."

Oh Lord, they have us; we need your protection. Ah, one of them is speaking German.

"Who are you, and what are you doing here?"

"We're refugees from the Ravensbruck prison camp. We were looking for shelter and found this house. We're going to the home of a relative northwest of here. Please stay away; we're all sick—smallpox."

"Smallpox? Let me see. Damn, you've got something disgusting!"

"This one does too, and that one. But this one's clean, young, and ripe for the picking. It's your turn, Yuri; enjoy some German love. We'll take turns after you. You three get the hell out of here; you're dead if we see you again!"

"No, you can't! Run Friedl! Oh, no God, no!" *My Lord, they didn't have to hit her with the gun. So hard. So much blood. She didn't understand what was happening.*

"She's dead. Put her body on the bed. Then the three of you get out before we kill you."

"There, sweetie, rest in peace. God bless your soul. Let's go, girls—hurry!"

Precious Friedl, she can't be gone. I love you, dear one. Why am I here? Please, I want to go back.

"Britta! We have to go now!"

May 6, 1945, 2:19 p.m.

"Let's go off the road and rest. I'll put you down in the grass, Britta."

"The cool grass feels good. It's hot for early May, Vera."

"It's not hot, sweetie; you're running a fever. There must be something we can do for her, Vera."

"Let's face it, Anna, we all need food and water soon, or we'll lie down and fade away. It's been three days since we've had anything to eat, and the water along the way is bad."

"Where's the Red Cross? We need help now; they could sustain us. Look at all these hopeless souls going west. Where are they all going, Vera? Is there any reason for this madness?"

"Russians, they're all fleeing from the Russians, Anna. Thank God we escaped them once. Now we have to pray that we keep ahead of them."

"Ahh, poor Friedl, she had no chance, and now she's gone. Why, Vera? Why did they have to hit her? I'll never get that sight out of my mind—never! And then to burn her, I can't believe such cruelty. They didn't have to burn the farmhouse. Why, Anna? Why?"

"It's beyond us, sweetheart. Nothing explains it. And their excuse for revenge for what the Wehrmacht did to their people can never justify it."

"Is that it, Anna? Are the rumors true? Did Germans really do the things we've heard? It's fuzzy in my mind; they never told us the truth, did they?"

"No, girls, their propaganda had us in the dark. We suspected but never knew. I'm sure we'll be shocked as we learn more about it. I have to be honest; I'm spent and can't go any further. I know I can't pick you up again, Britta, let alone carry you."

"Maybe it'll end here; we'll lay our heads down and join Friedl. I'd welcome it; I know I can't go back."

"It still puzzles me, Britta, three or four times you've said I can't go back. What do you mean?"

"Um, I don't know, Anna, but it keeps popping out. Where would I go back to?"

"I thought it might have something to do with your dreams and the mirror."

"Maybe? Whatever it is, I guess it doesn't matter now. We'll never reach the American lines, Vera, before the Russians catch us?"

"We will, Britta. We've come far enough west that the Allies have to find us. We passed a sign that said Crivitz is a few kilometers away. I visited there once, a lovely town. They'll have food and water to save us. But we have to get there first, and that sounds impossible. But now we need to rest. Do you still have your diary, Britta?"

"It's in my jacket. I'll never lose it—I can't. I'm fading; wake me when it's time to go."

18
MOVING ON

My precious diary, I've finally pulled you from the drawer. I had no will to do so until now. The damage upset me: wrinkled pages from water; most of the back cover missing; several pages smudged, making them hard to read.

We're back in Stuttgart. I remember little of the journey. Again, I owe my life to Vera and Anna, who cared for me every step of the way. I can write only what they told me. Americans found our procession on May 6—the three of us were near the end. They gave us food, water, and shelter. It took about a week to revive enough to travel. Then they sent us to a refugee camp for five weeks. The conditions there were far from ideal, but the care we received, and the absence of bru-tality, made it seem like being on holiday. According to

Vera, the lack of food and water racked my body and affected my mind. By mid-June, we began our journey home, arriving in Stuttgart in early July. By then, I regained my wits.

Allied bombing destroyed the apartment building where Vera previously lived. Anna and I had no home to return to, so Vera took us to the St. Paul orphanage, where she worked before her capture. They're still operating and welcomed Vera's return. With the shortage of staff and children, they allowed the three of us to live and work there. Anna and I do laundry, clean, and help in the kitchen while Vera resumed her duties administering the adoption of orphans. I'm still recovering, so I only work five hours a day. The food supply in Stuttgart is sparse, and conditions in the city are horrendous, including the lack of safety. We're blessed to be where we are.

I had a season of sleeping deeply without dreams, but now they've returned. I dream more of Aaron than Cara. He's attentive to me, and we appear to be a couple deeply in love. If only it weren't a dream. I have no idea where Aaron is or if he's alive. The thought of him being dead makes me shudder. Our limited efforts to find him were fruitless. I try to snap back to reality, knowing Ortrud is his wife and the love of his heart. But I can't bring myself to dream; I love him too much.

Though doing all she can, Anna has no idea where her husband, Rolf, is or if he's alive. Now that I'm recovering, I try to support Anna and Vera. I owe my life to them and can never make up for what they've done for me.

Cara is still a mystery. I wonder if I'm mentally ill concerning her and the mirror. I recall little about

my mental problems when I was young, as described by my father. I continually wonder if they are still with me. And why do I repeatedly say I want to go back? It makes no sense, yet somewhere in the recesses of my mind, I sense a place that's both familiar and foreign.
—Britta S

February 26, 1946, 10:42 a.m.

Oh, so weak, are you calling me? Who's calling me? Hmm, sick!

"Are you awake, Britta? Britta, Britta, can you hear me?"

"Yes, familiar, familiar voice."

"Can you open your eyes, sweetie? We've been waiting for you to come out of it."

"Oh, dear Lord, it's you, Aaron! Where . . . how? How did you find me? Ah, how long have I been out?"

"Anna said you've been in and out since Saturday. I got here yesterday. For months I've looked high and low for you, beautiful girl. Or should I say, beautiful woman?"

"I guess. I think tomorrow's my eighteenth birthday. But beautiful, I don't know. Where have you been, Aaron? We tried to find you."

"Are you up to talking now, Britta, or should you rest, and we can catch up later."

"No, I need to know now—know about you and Father. What happened to him, Aaron? Tell me the truth."

"Someone tipped off the Gestapo; we don't know who. They ambushed us. I'll spare you the details, but you need to know it was quick. Your father didn't suffer."

"I wish that helped; I guess it does. Oh, damn, damn, Aaron, I miss him! I need him, need someone to lead me out of the darkness."

"You have Anna and Vera, sweetie; And I didn't search for a year to let you be without whatever you need from me. But first, we have to get you better. The doctor said it was meningitis. They did a spinal procedure yesterday and say you're through the worst of it. Your fever broke several hours ago; you're a lucky young lady."

"Could you hold me, Aaron? I know I'll sleep if you do."

"Well, sure, whatever you need."

Ah, in his arms. I must be dreaming; I love you, Aaron. I feel peace; I can sleep now—heal my mind and body.

March 1, 1946, 9:07 a.m.

"Good morning, Britta. My, your color's better today; you're bouncing back."

"I feel stronger, Anna, but won't be running races for a while. Did Aaron leave?"

"He's checking out the whereabouts of a transport team member. He'll be back later. I saved a bowl of oatmeal for you. Eat it all, Britta; you need to get your strength back."

"I'll try. Are the workmen coming today? It's been a year since the bombing damage; I hope they finish soon."

"They should finish next week. Ah, I'm curious, Britta. Did Aaron tell you how he located us?"

"Yes, it's amazing. Remember when Emilie Horn came to the orphanage looking for her niece?"

"Yes, Emilie from the safe farm."

"I believe by God's providence, Aaron happened to see Emilie last Sunday. It surprised her to learn he was looking for me but thrilled her to tell him that we were all at the St. Paul orphanage."

"Um, something's going on. I hope it's for the best."

"What do you mean, Anna, for the best? Of course, it is."

"Well, to be honest, I mean Ortrud. You've been floating on air since Aaron found us, not hiding your feelings for him. Don't hurt yourself, Britta; he loves Ortrud not you. And she had his baby in December."

226

"Oh, I know, but he has feelings for me that match those I have for him."

"Ah, Britta, what are we going to do with you? I swear, you're one tough girl, and stubborn, oh my, are you stubborn. You've got this fantasy which is only that; it'll only lead to more pain, and I don't want that for you, dear."

"I know you have my best interest at heart, but I love Aaron, and it's not going away. I need him now and want to be with him for the rest of my life."

"I might as well be talking to the laundry, which has no ears. And speaking of laundry, we better get after it. It won't get done on its own."

"Oh, wait a minute, I see Aaron through the window coming up the walk. Can I talk with him for a few minutes, Anna? I'll join you very soon—promise."

"Sure, be careful, though."

"You're up and looking well-rested, sweetie."

"It's hard to believe, but I feel good. Why do you call me sweetie, Aaron? I mean, I like it a lot and hope it means something special."

"Um, I haven't thought much about it; I must have picked it up from your father. He loved calling you sweetie and sweetheart. I do too."

"Am I your sweetheart, Aaron?"

"I'm not sure I understand, Britta. You are a sweetheart; that's what I mean when I call you that. But, well, you know you're not *my* sweetheart. Ortrud is."

"No, Ortrud doesn't deserve your love, Aaron—I do."

"What, what are you saying, Britta? You know I cherish you, but it can't be like that."

"No! You don't know Ortrud. She turned us over to the Gestapo. She's the one responsible for us going to Ravensbruck—all the hell we went through!"

"I don't believe it. I know Ortrud is jealous at times, but she'd never do that."

"If I can't convince you, Aaron, talk to Anna; she can."

"Listen, Britta, I don't want to be cross. And I do care for you, but for now, let's drop it. I need to call Ortrud if the lines are working and tell her I'm coming home tonight."

"No, don't leave me; I want you to stay!"

"I can't, Britta. My place is at home with my wife and daughter. I've already spent too much time away looking for you. And now that I've found you, my responsibility to your father is fulfilled. I'll miss you, though, you know that."

"Will you do one thing for me before you leave?"

"What?"

"Take me to our hiding place at the Keller's house."

"Why, Britta? It's empty, and no one knows what happened to the Kellers."

"It's about father. I'll be able to say goodbye to him—close that chapter of my life, and move on to the next one. When we went there in January, I couldn't bring myself to go in; I wasn't ready to say goodbye."

"Okay, I'll take you there this afternoon."

1:52 p.m.

"The door's stuck, Britta"

"It wasn't locked before."

"It's not locked. Probably just swollen from moisture. Stand back; I'll give it a shoulder. Uh, okay, it's open. You sure you want to go in?"

"I need to face it, Aaron."

"Most of the furniture's gone. It stinks; what a mess! And look, people are living here."

"No surprise; many have no homes of their own. Ah, hope no one's here."

"It looks empty. Your hiding place is upstairs?"

"Yes, the concealed door in the closet of the bedroom on the left. Do you think the homeless discovered it?"

"Probably not—too desperate to be curious. Here it is, sure doesn't look like a door."

"It couldn't, Aaron. See, it opens here, like that. Ah, now I'm shaking, almost afraid to go in. I guess I shouldn't be surprised at the emotions rushing in. Oh, father, father."

"Here's my handkerchief, Britta. Wipe the tears away and pull yourself together—don't rush it."

Hmm, Aaron's arms around me are like heaven coming down. They bring the joy that's been missing. I feel his love for me; it's powerful! I could stay here all day and soak it up, but I have to go in and say goodbye to father. "Thanks, Aaron; I'm ready now."

"Be careful, there."

"Nothing's changed, Aaron; it's the same as the day we left. Oh, the mirror sends chills through my body. I don't know why. I think it's talking to me, but I don't know what it's saying."

"Your infamous mirror. I have to say it's beautiful with the ornately detailed edges, like something out of the French renaissance. It must be valuable."

"I'd like to take it to the orphanage if you can carry it. Or, maybe not; the idea of having it scares me."

"I can carry it, and it can't hurt you. It's only a lifeless mirror. What are you doing, Britta?"

"Getting up the nerve to touch it."

"Why? You're starting to worry me."

"I don't know. It's pulling me forward, and I need to touch it. Okay, slowly, Britta, gently. Ah, no, no, no!"

"Take your hand off, Britta! Quick, I've got you!"

"Thanks, Aaron; I'm woozy. It spoke to me. I'm confused and will never be able to explain it to you or anyone else. Please, Aaron, hold me until this passes."

"I've got you, sweetheart; lay back on the bed."

"Ah, that's better; hold me tighter."

"No, I shouldn't! The temptation, and you're starting to come out of it."

"No, stay close, Aaron!"

"Please, Britta, I can't. Don't kiss me like that; it's wrong. Don't do this to me!"

"I can't help it; I love you, darling. Kiss me with the same passion. No one will ever know. Kiss me like this."

"Ah, it's not right. We can't, Britta? Oh, I can't fight it anymore!"

June 10, 1946, 7:09 p.m.

"Sit and rest, Britta. The endless dishes every night gets old. I wish we could get a place of our own."

"Do you think it'll ever happen, Anna? We have no means and have to be thankful that Vera keeps us off the streets. But I hate the drudgery as much as you do. Now that I'm sick half the day, I don't know how much longer I can do it."

"What are you going to do, Britta? I know you think about it all the time."

"I don't know. How could I be that stupid—so selfish? I trapped him; it's my fault, Anna."

"Are you sure? You love Aaron, and though he can't admit it, he loves you too. He could have walked away that afternoon, but he didn't. Now we must find Aaron and tell him you're carrying his child."

"I thought we did, too, but when we had no way to find him, I felt differently. If he wanted me in his life, he would have given me his address or phone number. No, Anna, he'll never know. As hard as it is, that's my decision."

"Oh dear, are you sure, sweetie? We can't take care of ourselves; how can you support a little one?"

"I have no idea, Anna. But I won't ruin Aaron's and Ortrud's lives. It tempts me when it comes to Ortrud, but it would hurt Aaron, so I won't. I'm the one to blame, the only one who deserves punishment.

It's hard to make a final decision, but I'll probably give my baby to the orphanage for adoption."

"Don't think about it, Britta; it's too important to decide now. You have plenty of time."

"I'm thankful I have you and Vera to help me through this mess."

January 8, 1947, 8:04 p.m.

"Hmm, still looks good. I'm glad they restored the dining room to how it looked before the war. The fresh coat of white paint brightens everything."

"The new tables, with cheery tablecloths and new chairs, help too, Vera. It took a long time, though."

"It seemed like forever, Anna, but the orphanage depended on donations to do the work, and few people had the means to help. You're quiet tonight, Britta; it's been a long day. Marie loves looking after the baby, but you should go up so she can get to bed."

"In a few minutes, Vera, but I need to ask you something first."

"What is it, dear?"

"You didn't say anything about the lunch you planned with the American military couple; I thought you would. If you met them, what did they say?"

"Ah, I was thinking about it, Britta, waiting for you to bring it up. Until you make a final decision, it's hard for them to commit."

"Well, I've decided, and this time it's final. I won't change my mind again. The Americans can move forward with the adoption. It seems right to me, and I know my child will have the best chance for a good life in America. Can I meet them?"

"No, sweetie, it's not allowed. You'll never know who they are, and they'll never know your identity. The only thing they'll have is the birth certificate with the baby's name: Cara Schumann."

"I'm still surprised that you used the name of the girl in that crazy mirror."

"I am too, Anna, but it was a strong impression. Speaking of the mirror, Vera, did it come up as we talked about?"

"Yes, great news! She's been collecting antiques to take home and loved the picture of the mirror. They'll pay you fifty dollars, which is quite generous."

"Did you tell them why, Vera?"

"Of course. They're concerned about you, Britta, they care, though they'll never know you."

"When—how long to complete the adoption before I say good-bye to Cara?"

"If you're sure, I'll start the process tomorrow. They'll complete it by the end of the month, and Cara's new parents will return to America in April."

"Start it, Vera. I should protect myself and stay away from Cara, but I can't. So I'll say goodnight and go up to be with her."

Evening, December 24, 1947

It's Christmas Eve, and I'm sad, as low as the day I learned of father's death. For the first time in months, I've picked up my pen to enter tear-stained words. It should be a joyous occasion to celebrate our Lord's birth, but it's not, and I feel far from Him. Cara's first birthday was nineteen days ago, and it hurts not being with her. I think of her all the time: Is she happy and safe? Do her new parents love her as much as I do? How much has she grown? Is she still the beautiful child I love? I guess my heart will never heal, though I have to find a way to move on with my life.

In September, Anna and I moved to a recently renovated apartment building. Our apartment is small, with one bedroom and bath, a tiny kitchen, and a close but comfortable living room. In June, I found a job as a seamstress in a factory near the orphanage. Anna continues to work at the orphanage, receiving a salary instead of room and board. It's not easy, but we scrape by. Fortunately, we can walk to work. We're saving what we can to purchase an auto.

Anna got bad news in July; the Nazis murdered Rolf at the Chelmno death camp. She struggles with it on most days. However, we've each met a nice young man in our building; maybe our saving grace. I've had several dates but still find it difficult to get Aaron out of my mind; I doubt I ever will. I think of him and Ortrud often, wondering if I made a mistake not to track down Aaron. Maybe Thomas will make the thoughts of Aaron fade. Anna has mixed feelings about moving on and leaving Rolf behind.

Our country struggles to recover. The economy is in shambles, and fear, mistrust, selfishness, and hate darken the light that love brings. I don't know if life will ever be the same again.

Though gone for several months, my dreams are back. I think Cara in the mirror is real, not a dream. I feel close to her and know that's why I named my baby after her. No one understands, but I had to do it. I now have new dreams that are beyond my understanding. I see people, places, and things that are familiar to me. I don't know how, as they've never been part of my life. Trying to put it all together continually vexes me; I guess I'll never solve the mystery.

We'll spend Christmas Day at the orphanage with Vera and the children. I pray it'll lift my spirits and get my mind off myself.

—Britta S

19
A LIFE TO LIVE

June 23, 1952, 12:42 p.m.

"Wonderful meal, Anna."

"The French pastry's delicious, Britta. The location gave me pause, but Jutta's café recommendation was spot-on."

"Tell her thanks. It's been too long since we've had lunch together."

"Over two months. Talking on the phone is one thing, but I miss spending time together."

"Well, you're a busy woman now. A husband and little girl take most of a wife's time. And you're a good, dutiful wife, Anna. Marlene is precious, and you have a gem in Rudy; he beams with love for you."

"I'm blessed. I never thought I could care for, let alone love, another man the way I loved Rolf. But I feel sad in talking about it—sad for you, Britta. Will there ever be another man for you after John?"

"I guess not. I doubt I'll ever have the confidence to trust another man."

"I understand, sweetie. John seemed nice when he swept you off your feet. How could you know he was abusive? But it's been two years; someone is out there waiting for you."

"Ah, I don't think so, Anna. My mind always goes back to Aaron, though it's been six years since I've seen him. You know how much it hurt last year when I went to Nuremberg after discovering Aaron might be there."

"Hmm, when you learned he and his family was no longer there, and no one knew where they went. I wish I could help you, sweetie—comfort you. Maybe you should see someone that can work through it with you."

"A psychiatrist?"

"Well, someone to help you who has the training and skill."

"I've thought about it, Anna, but haven't had the nerve to do it. I keep thinking about the imaginations that concerned father when I was young. And then there's Cara and the mirror. I don't want to admit it, but I fear that I'm mentally off."

"It's not that bad. Listen, Britta, I know someone who might help if you want to try."

"I have to help myself. Please give me the name and telephone number."

"I'll call you later with it. You're doing the right thing, Britta. Oh, that's sad."

"What?"

"Behind you, don't stare, though. A woman with horrible scarring, probably from burns."

"Oh, yes, it's terrible—poor thing!"

"Ahh, I think she's coming over, Britta. She's crying."

"Excuse me, are you Britta and Anna?"

"Yes, dear. Do you know us?"

"Friedl, I'm Friedl Shantz."

"What! Dear God, Friedl! How, how could it be? Huh, huh, huh. Oh, Friedl let me hold you; I can't believe it!"

"We thought you were dead, Friedl. The Russians hit you so hard—all the blood. And they burned the house! How did you survive?"

"I don't remember anything after they hit me, Anna. I woke up several weeks later in a rundown hospital. The pain from the burns was unbearable, and they couldn't help me. Everyone thought I'd eventually die, and at the time, that was my desire."

"Praise be, you survived, dear one. But tell me something, Friedl, how is it that you can now speak?"

"No one knows, Britta. The doctor's best guess is the blow to my head loosened whatever prevented me from talking."

"Thank God for whatever it was. We're amazed, Friedl, so happy for you! I haven't felt such joy in years. Where do you live, dear?"

"Not far from here, Anna. Oh, I'm delighted to see both of you; I gave up looking years ago."

"We were never able to know you, Friedl; your family and friends, your likes and dislikes, who you were. But our love for you was great. And now we'll learn all about you; count you as a dearest friend. We're looking forward to it with joy."

~ ~ ~

November 14, 1957, 5:29 p.m.

"Thanks for staying late, Britta, but it's getting dark, and you should call it a day. Can I drive you home?"

"No, I'll walk, Claire. I know you're anxious to get home to your family. It's not your fault that my auto broke down again. They'll have it repaired tomorrow, and it's only four blocks."

"Are you sure?"

"Uh huh, thanks. See you tomorrow."

The damp cold goes right through me. Button your top button, Britta, that's better. Walk fast. Where is everyone? It's not late; just get home. Why can't I get a reliable auto, one that doesn't need repairs every month? Claire's the best employer I've ever had. Leftover stew, another boring supper alone. I'm so looking forward to Christmas with Anna. I miss you, dearest friend. It's been two years since your family moved to Hanover.

"Ha-ha, you're the last person I expected to see."

"Ah, who . . . who is it? Come out of the shadows."

"Someone you'd never dream of seeing again. I thought they ended your miserable existence."

"No—not you! Where'd you come from?"

"From the darkness. Ha-ha, from the darkest memories of your past, Britta. You always denied me. I thought there'd be no more chances; it looks like I was wrong."

"Stay away from me, Ernst Keller! I'll scream!"

"There's not a soul around—go ahead. Come with me quietly into the alley, or I won't hesitate to hurt you. You owe me!"

"No, I'm not going with you!" *Run, Britta! You can make it home— only two blocks.*

"Ha-ha, you thought you could outrun me—crazy bitch. Now get back in the alley!"

"Ow, that hurts; let me go!"

"Now, I will. Get back in the shadows. Don't make it hard on yourself, or I'll beat you half to death. Get your skirt off and lie down on that old mattress—do it now!"

Dear God, help! If I do it, he'll kill me after he finishes. You can't allow it; fight, Britta, fight!

"Bitch! You hit me; I'll show you! There, that's hitting."

Ah, oh, that hurt . . .

~ ~ ~

August 18, 1965, 2:19 p.m.

"Relax, dear. Give me a minute to review Doctor Lange's notes."

"Um, go ahead, doctor." *I hate losing Adde Lange. Why did her husband take her to Brunswick? Her kindness and insight got me through the last thirteen years. But now you have to move on, Britta; pull yourself together and give Doctor Sommer a chance. Adde said I could trust her, and she's an excellent psychiatrist. Oh, I hate it, the confusion—all the years. From the looks of her office it seems like she's doing well. Some make it big in life, and others don't make it at all. I guess I know which I am.*

"Okay. You know, Britta, that Adde Lange and I have worked closely together for years. She's a dear friend. I'm sure you miss her as I do, but I hope you'll trust me as you did her."

"I want to—I'll try."

"I see you were at Schumacher from late '57 to '59. Tell me what happened."

"Ernst Keller! He raped me or tried to."

"Tried to?"

"He pinned me down in a dark alley and took my clothes off. I was petrified, knowing I'd feel pain any second. Before I passed out I heard voices coming toward us. The next thing I remember is waking in the hospital five hours later."

"The aftermath sent you to Schumacher?"

"Physically, I had a black eye and scrape on my knee. It wasn't that; I was hysterical for three days. Seeing Doctor Lange didn't help. She knew I needed more help, so I went to Schumacher the next day and didn't come out for two years. Dear God, I never want to go there again."

"Um, they do good work, but no one wants to be in a sanatorium."

"I don't know if they helped or hurt me. They tried, but I couldn't get what Ernst did out of my mind. Then the imaginations came back, the ones I had when I was young. Drug therapies followed, spiraling me further down. They were close to giving up, and Doctor Lange was frustrated that she couldn't help me."

"But you finally came out of it. How did that happen, Britta?"

"My friends visited most days. The love and prayers of Anna, Vera, and Friedl played a big part. But something deep down inside made the difference in my recovery. I don't pretend to understand it, so I can't expect it from you or anyone else. Reasons unknown to me—out of the dim past—drive me toward something in the future. I don't know what it is, but I have to do it."

"The report says something about a mirror and Cara?"

"Aw, I guess Doctor Lange left nothing out. I think everything I do or have done since my father and I left the hiding place has to do with Cara and the mirror. I know things about her that I shouldn't—couldn't."

"Things? What are you talking about, dear?"

"Places, I see places that I recognize though I've never been there. They're foreign but real at the same time, if that makes sense. I see not only streets, houses, and rooms, but I also see people that are familiar but don't know who they are."

"I don't see it in the notes, but do you recall seeing Cara in the mirror?"

"For years, I had no memories of the mirror before the day we left. Then hazy snippets flashed before me. I didn't understand them."

"So, you saw her?"

"Saw and talked to Cara—I think."

"Well, your case is unique, Britta. I've never encountered a patient like you. Tell me, how's life been since leaving Schumacher?"

"It's up and down. I treasure my friends and Doctor Lange, but it isn't enough. I'll never have peace until I satisfy whatever's drawing me forward."

"Is it Cara from the mirror, or Cara, your girl?"

"Um, I don't know, Doctor Sommer—maybe both."

"You've never married. Is it due to Aaron?"

"I don't think so. Though I love him, and he's in my heart forever, he belongs to another—Ortrud. From what I know, he's happy, and I won't upset him. But I have ill-will toward Ortrud. I know it's wrong, but I can't get the bitterness out of my heart for what she did to Anna and me."

"It's all here in the notes, an awful thing she did. Tell me, Britta, why didn't you allow Doctor Lange to use hypnosis to get to the root of the mirror issues?"

"It scares me to death! I don't know why, but I couldn't do it. I can't give control of my mind to someone else. Maybe I'm afraid it'll remove the veil, and I won't be able to live with what's behind it. Do you understand, Doctor?"

"Oh, I do, dear. It tells me that we've got work to do. We'll do it, though, even without hypnosis. In our next session, we'll probe deeper into the mystery of Cara and the mirror."

~ ~ ~

July 15, 1976, 12:19 p.m.

"I'll have the Viennese salad."

"Thank you, Frau. Enjoy the sunshine after all the rainy days. Your orders will be out shortly."

"Thankfully, the sun's out again. It'll be good for you, Britta."

"The warmth feels good, Anna, but I'm also thankful for the shade of the umbrella. Munich is beautiful in the summer. But the blessing I needed most is seeing you and Vera again."

"Well, girls, according to my recollection, it's been over three years since we've been together. It sure beats writing and talking on the phone."

"It seems more like ten years, Vera. Dear God, it's wonderful to be with you again. And I can't express how I miss you, Anna. Time slips away quickly. It's hard to believe it's been thirty-one years since we left Ravensbruck. Most of them were difficult, and some I don't recall at all."

"I wish I could have stayed with you in Stuttgart, dear, but the opportunity here was too great to pass up. My adoption experience made me the perfect choice for the job. I love it and can't believe how it worked out. All the government contacts I have are amazing."

"Oh, I love this polka."

"He plays at this time every Thursday and Sunday, Britta. He's one of the best accordionists in Munich. Soak it all in, dear."

"You saw her here for lunch the past two Thursdays?"

"Um, yes, the last two Thursdays. I hope she shows today, but there's no guarantee, girls."

"You're sure it was her?"

"I am, Anna. It's the woman in the picture Britta showed me before I left Stuttgart, the one she said Aaron gave her many years ago. I could never forget that face."

"Okay, we sit and wait."

"I hope I didn't lead you and Anna astray by having you come to Munich. What are you going to say to Ortrud if she shows up?"

"I don't know; I'm still getting over the shock of it. Do either of you have any ideas?"

"Say what's in your heart, sweetie, let it lead you."

"Ah, I guess, Anna."

"Tell us more about Hans. We're hoping he's finally the man for you, Britta. More than anyone, you deserve the love and care of a good man."

"Thanks, Vera; keep praying that he is. He's kind and gentle; that's what attracted me to him. He understands how needy I am; most men wouldn't bother. Hans is also a man of means, which brings a sense of security."

"I so want you to be happy, Britta, precious Lord, please! Maybe then you can cease your weekly appointments with Doctor Sommer."

"Oh, I'm not sure about that, Anna. She's vital to me. I don't know what would happen without her support. I tried in 1972, and then Walter broke my heart, sending me back to Schumacher. No, I can't do that again."

"Look, girls, there she is!"

"Oh my God, it's her, Britta! She's aged, but it's Ortrud."

What should I do? Help, Lord! Should we sit here and see if she recognizes us? Then she'd initiate the reunion. No, Britta, you have to face this straight on; fear can't rule. "She seems to be looking our way. Do you think she sees us?"

"If she does, girls, she doesn't know who you are."

"I'm going over, Vera; maybe I'll invite her to our table."

"Good luck, sweetie."

"Do you recognize me?"

"Oh, it can't be! Is it you, Britta? You hardly look like the girl I remember."

"It is, Ortrud, and you don't look like the young woman I remember either. Would you join us? I'm sure you remember Anna."

"Vaguely, but I'm not sure I have anything to say to either of you."

"Please join us."

"Well, okay."

"This is my good friend Vera Vogel. Vera, this is Ortrud Gabel. And, of course, you know Anna."

"Sit here, Ortrud; glad to meet you."

"How is it that the three of you are here at this café? Have you been following me?"

"Only happenstance; I come here often, and apparently you do too. I let the girls know because they have unfinished business with you."

"What are you talking about? I have no business with them."

"No, Ortrud, you do! And you know it—don't lie to us. You ruined Anna's and my life. You worked with Ernst Keller to bring the Gestapo down on us, and we ended up in that hellish camp—Ravensbruck."

"No, no, no, you don't understand—don't know the circumstances!"

"What are you talking about, Ortrud. You can't lie your way out of this!"

"I know what you think, but you don't know what happened on that day. Yes, I was furious with you for kissing Aaron, but that wasn't it. I had no choice. I hated doing it."

"Get it out! What are you saying, Ortrud."

"Ernst approached me the week before, Britta, and said my father wasn't dead as everyone thought. I wanted to believe him, but I didn't. Then he took out my father's watch. He said he was injured badly when the Gestapo apprehended him but survived and went to Mauthausen. Ernst had assurances that the Gestapo would release father if I helped arrest other transport group members. I had to try. Don't you understand? I had to even though I wasn't sure!"

"But you got Katrin, Ida, and the others away from the house. Why?"

"Ernst was only interested in your capture, Britta; I'm sorry it was you and Anna. But I had to save my father and as many others as I could. Please believe me!"

"Well, did you?"

"Did I . . ."

"Did you save your father?"

"They released him two weeks later, Anna. He was in poor health and died within a month. I never saw him again."

"Oh, I'm sorry. But Katrin never mentioned what happened when she got to Ravensbruck."

"I don't know about that, Anna. Under the circumstances, was she in full possession of her senses?"

"Who knows, Ortrud, maybe not? I don't know, Anna, I want to believe her—it sounds possible."

"Oh crap, she could be leveling with us, Britta. We'll never know for sure. Can Aaron verify her story?"

"Um, where is Aaron? Does he ever join you for lunch, Ortrud?"

"Oh, Britta, of course, none of you know. Aaron was killed three years ago in an auto accident."

"Aw . . . oh." *Dizzy, gonna faint, hold . . . hold on, Britta.* "Hu hu, no, not that too! Tell me it's not true, Ortrud."

"It is; take my hanky. I cried for two years. The children and I miss him every day."

"Oh, how many children, Ortrud?"

"Two, Anna. John's twenty-seven, and Monika's thirty. They're both married with children and live far away. I'm here because I secured a position at the university last year."

"I'm sorry for you and your family, Ortrud. I think I believe you—want to, at least."

"Thanks, Britta. I know hearing about Aaron shocks you. I am telling you the truth, though."

"Speaking of truth, Britta, Ortrud needs to know."

"Shush, Anna, I can't!"

"Can't what, Britta? Is there something you don't want me to know?"

"Oh, Anna, she doesn't need to be hurt anymore."

"The truth will release you, Britta, so for your good, I'll tell her. Britta had Aaron's child. They came together once when Aaron found her in 1946. The times were crazy—things happened."

"A baby! I didn't expect that. I also didn't expect a confession, Britta, but Aaron told me about his betrayal twenty-five years ago. You know how honest he was, a man of good conscience. It hurt like hell, but eventually I forgave him. We had a happy life. He loved you in his own way, though he always regretted his transgression. Of course, he knew nothing about the baby. Your child must be close to thirty."

"Yes, wherever she is."

"Ah, you didn't keep her?"

"I couldn't, Ortrud. I had no means or will to do so. I wish I had more courage, but I didn't. I've regretted my decision ever since, thinking about what's become of Cara."

"I think I'll skip lunch; I'm not hungry anymore. I'm sorry you don't have your girl, Britta—sorry for the way everything turned out. I don't know if you and Anna want to see me again, but you can reach me through the university if you do. I hope you will. Goodbye."

20
REUNION

Tomorrow's the day; I'm excited and scared but have to know. Either way, I'm moving forward to satisfy the tugging of my heart. I pray she'll allow me to see her. I called her Cara, but Vera said her name is Sarah. I like the biblical name. Thank God Vera arranged for the adopting mother to intercede for me. So much has happened, and now I'm finally ready for this.

Hans Bergmann became the love of my life in 1976. It was unexpected at age forty-eight, but he pierced my heart with gentle kindness and caring that swept me off my feet. His love was a healing balm to my lingering sadness. Without Hans, the news of Aaron's death would have crushed me. Even so, I've never completely recovered from the shock of it.

Seeing Ortrud in 1976 was a blessing in disguise. We've seen each other many times since, rekindling a long-dead friendship. I came to trust she did her best in the horrible circumstances which sent Anna and me to Ravensbruck. If there was a chance, she had to save her father. I also held on to some sense of guilt regarding my transgression with Aaron and the result. Knowing he confessed it to Ortrud and they moved on to a happy life relieved my guilt.

But then the veil of sadness overcame me again. In October, the doctor told us that Hans had colon cancer—there was no hope. He suffered horribly. It hurt so much. I buried him in December. I fell apart, and by February, Doctor Sommer advised my return to Schumacher. I hated the idea but knew I had no choice. I was there for seven months. I'd completely lost my way, and Vera, Anna, and Ortrud couldn't break through the curtain of darkness surrounding me. It was there that I constantly thought of my girl. It was the only spark of life I had, the only hope for useful existence. I knew Cara was the key to either giving up and dying or getting up and fighting for a better life. Thank God I chose to fight.

My dreams of Cara and the mirror abruptly stopped five months ago. It puzzled me for weeks until I understood why. As Doctor Sommer said, my sub-conscience worked through my dreams to reveal something I needed to know. Though the doctor strongly disagrees with my conclusion, I now see the reason for these dreams. I also understand the mirror's role that day in 1942 when father and I escaped our hiding place. Or, at least, I hope I do. I pray it's not another deception in my overburdened mind—I don't think it is. This revelation spurred me to ask Vera to intensify her search for Cara.

It was the most joyous day when Vera said she contacted my girl's mother, and she was flying to Germany to meet with her. I held my breath until word came that she would assist in arranging a meeting with her daughter, another glorious day.

Tomorrow I'll fly to Chicago, Illinois, in America, to visit Anna and her family. Their move to America three years ago was more than hard for me—it hurt. Though we had lived in different cities, we talked weekly and traveled to see each other monthly. Now we only write. She's closer than words here could ever describe. I was grateful that her husband had a marvelous opportunity to advance his career and that Anna and the family were excited over the new adventure before them. But my joy for them was overwhelmed by deep sadness in knowing Anna would be far away. Now I know Anna is there, so I have a place to stay while waiting for Sarah's answer.

I'm eternally grateful for Vera. She arranged for my baby's well-being many years ago, and now she's done all she can to reunite us. That alone is beyond anything I could expect. But the truth is, she saved my life more than once in Ravensbruck and in the years that followed. I can never repay her, only show her my love for the rest of my life.

I look forward to my ongoing relationship with Ortrud. Some would say it's complicated; I guess it is. We started as friends, though I resisted it, being jealous of Aaron's love for her. Beyond that, I liked her and knew she liked me and tried to keep the peace between us. On that fateful day of perceived betrayal, I thought our friendship was permanently on the ash heap as hate welled up. But hatred is hard; it takes so much energy and serves no purpose. I'm glad we mended fences, and love has replaced hate.

I'm sorry to say that Friedl moved to Bonn in 1968, and we saw her infrequently over the years. We all tried to nurture the relationship but realized that Friedl was failing mentally and physically. She was vibrant and lucid in the beginning, and our hopes for her were high. We sadly learned of her passing in late 1979.

The scripture card I found years ago is now in my hand. I always keep it with me and read it several times a day. I call on God often, though I'm not close to Him. I hope I will be someday. I don't know why, but these words speak to something deep within me—I can't explain what it is. But I know the words are meaningful: "Greater love hath no man than this, that a man lay down his life for his friends."

Tomorrow my journey begins. I pray it leads to a glorious reunion, the day imprinted on my mind for years—

December 19, 1982, 12:21 p.m.

"You've hardly eaten a thing, Britta. Are you sure you don't want half a sandwich?"

"Thanks, Anna, but I could hardly get the bowl of soup down. The tension of waiting for the call has upset my stomach. I can't get my mind on anything else. I'm terrified she'll say no."

"I don't think so, sweetie. They wouldn't let you come this far to say no."

"Are you trying to make me feel better, Anna?"

"No, I think your daughter wants to meet you, out of curiosity, if for no other reason. You still have time to make reservations, and they said they'd call today—it's only half-past twelve."

"Ah, don't mind me, Anna, I'll be fretting until they call. But I'm thankful for you and Rudy's hospitality, inviting me into your home and showing me the sites in Chicago—keeping my mind occupied. I'm sorry that the kids aren't home, so I could see them again."

"They were too, but they're grown and have their own busy lives. We're blessed to have you, Britta; I missed you every day."

"Oh, there it is, dear God!"

"I'll get it. Be calm, sweetie—pray."

"Hello. Yes, Mrs. Shepherd, I'll get her. It's her, Britta, the woman who adopted your baby."

Dear Lord, help me; I can hardly breathe. Please, please let me hear the right answer. "Hello."

"Is this Ms. Schumann?"

"It is, Mrs. Shepherd."

"You can call me Barbara, dear. Did you receive the note we mailed with the return address?"

"We did. Does that mean—?"

"Yes, Sarah has consented to see you, and we want you to stay with us. When do you expect to be in Denver?"

Thank you, thank you, dear God! "On Tuesday, I'll call right away to book the flight arriving at 1:40 in the afternoon. I'll come to your address by 3:00. Are you sure it's alright for me to stay with you?"

"Yes, we're sure. Just one thing, Britta. Don't expect too much. It'll take time for Sarah to come around—be able to process your visit."

"I understand, Barbara. I'll see you Tuesday—goodbye. Oh my God, Anna, I'm going, going to see Sarah!"

"Praise be. I'm thrilled for you, Britta. Have you settled on what you'll say?"

"I'm still not sure. I hope my plan is right; that my conclusions aren't delusions."

December 21, 1982, 3:03 p.m.

Um, we turn west off Kipling here. What? No, no, it's not here. My memory is too fuzzy. Maybe it's the next street. Yes, here it is. Thankfully, the cab driver knows the way. Only a few minutes now, I think. Dear Lord, I doubted myself—never thought it would happen. But here I am; it's familiar, but the detail escapes me. Is this our corner, or is it the next one? Yes, the next one—going left. Which house? Why am I unsure? Yes, it's the driveway on the right. Oh, do I want to go through this? You have to close the circle; set everything in its place. "Stop here."

"Can I help you with the bags, Ma'am?"

"There's only two; I can manage, thanks, here."

"Thanks, have a good stay."

That's Danny's bike in the driveway like I remember. Help me, God, I'm shaking all over. Take a minute and settle yourself. Be calm; you'll be alright. Okay, ring the doorbell.

"Welcome, Britta, come in. You're right on time."

"Thank you, Barbara."

"Set your bags over here for now. I'll take your coat. Please, have a seat on the couch. How was your flight?"

"Not good. I fly infrequently, and it scares me. It must sound silly at my age."

"Not at all, dear. I noticed on the phone that your English is surprisingly good."

"It's slipped over the years, but I brushed up before coming. A lovely home, comfortable."

"Thanks, Britta, we think so. I need to tell you upfront that we're going through a rough patch. It's about what happened to your granddaughter, Cara, and its effect on Sarah."

"Oh, I'm sorry. What happened?"

"Well, the truth is, we're not sure what happened yesterday morning. We think that Cara was attacked in the basement by one of Danny's friends. Danny's Cara's brother."

"I know, but what happened to Cara?"

"You know about Danny? I don't recall mentioning him, Britta."

"Oh, don't mind me, I'm a little off; the stress of the trip. Is Cara okay?"

"We think so. Apparently, Luke knocked her out and set a fire in the storeroom. The fire burned Cara's hands, and she spent last night in the hospital. They're holding Luke at the police station. He admits to breaking into the house but said he found Cara unconscious and didn't set the fire. We're still sorting it out, and Cara's having a hard time remembering."

"Dear Lord, how awful!" *Thank God, this is the time.* "I guess Sarah's with Cara now."

"Mm-hmm, but she'll be down shortly. Did you have lunch on the flight?"

"They served it, but I could only get down a soft drink. I have to admit I'm nervous about meeting Sarah. It's hard for me to concentrate on anything else."

"I understand, dear. Sarah's every bit as nervous. It's a hard piece of ground to till. If it helps, I think it'll all work out if you're patient with each other. The incident with Cara complicates it, though; keep that in mind."

"Of course. Thanks for your expression of encouragement, Barbara. It helps put my mind at ease."

"Would you like a cup of tea? It always soothes my nerves. We like Christmas peppermint during the holidays."

"Yes, sounds good."

"Relax. I'll be back in a minute."

Relax? If I only could. What do I say to her—what to call her? Dear Lord, I'm scared and conflicted.

"Oh, I didn't hear anyone come in; are you—"

"Yes." *Get up, go to her. Oh, mom, mom! How do I untangle the impossible?* "I'm your mother, Sarah. I don't deserve to be, but I hope you'll find it in your heart to forgive me."

"I've thought about this moment all day and still don't know what to say. I don't know what I feel. To be honest, my daughter's condition is more important to me now."

"I'm sure it is. Barbara told me what happened. I'm sorry that I'm complicating everything."

"You had no way of knowing, but it's hard dealing with it all."

"Take my handkerchief. Can I hold you?"

"Hu hu, I wish you would. Oh, feels good. Thanks, your kiss reminds me of Cara's pecks, and your arms around me feel strangely familiar."

"Yes, familiar. Maybe time can't break mother and daughter bonds. Come sit by me on the couch." *What do I say now?*

"Tell me, why did you give me away?"

"Um, I loved you too much to keep you, Sarah. I know it's hard for you to understand, but I was in a dark place. My mind and body were recovering from Ravensbruck."

"Ravensbruck, what's that?"

"A Nazi prison camp for women. We were there from 1944 until the war ended. It took years to recover my strength and senses, so I had no ability or means to take care of you. I wanted to, but it would have been unfair to you. You never would have had the opportunities, the life, you've had here."

"I didn't know. It sounds awful—terribly hard on you."

"It was, but I thought of you every day, hoping you had everything I couldn't provide. It hurt, dear one, every day it hurt. I'm sorry for crying; I tried not to."

"Crying's healthy moth . . . what do I call you? Miss Schumann, Britta? I can't bring myself to call you mother, at least not yet."

"Britta, please, not Miss Schumann."

"I'm racking my brain; where have I heard that name? It's unexpected, but I feel close to you already—have peace about this."

Dear Lord, I can't tell her why. I can never explain it.

"Well, here's the peppermint tea. I made a cup for you too, Sarah. It's cooled some, but I heard you come down and didn't want to interrupt."

"Thanks, Mom, it's okay. Britta was telling me about herself. It's sad—very sad."

"Thanks for the tea, Barbara; it's tasty. I guess the travel and too much excitement have worn me out. If I could go to my room, I'd like to lie down for a while."

"I'll take your bags up and show you the guestroom."

"Don't bother, Sarah. I'll bring them up later. I know where the guest room is."

"You do?"

"Oh, didn't you tell me, Barbara? That it's next to Cara's bedroom?"

"Um, maybe, I don't remember. Get a good rest, Britta; we'll let you know when dinner's ready. Sarah's son, Danny, will be home by then. But her husband, Brent, is out of town on a business trip."

"Thanks for everything; I'll see you later."

6:07 p.m.

"Thanks for waking me, Barbara; surprisingly, I slept soundly."

"Sit here, Britta, next to Sarah. This is Sarah's son, Danny."

"Hi, do I call you Miss Schumann or Britta?"

Danny, Danny, I want to hold you! My God, is that your face? Time has erased it. "It's a pleasure to meet you, Danny, and please call me, Car, Britta."

"For a second, I thought you were about to say Cara."

"Ah, I must have her on my mind, Sarah. Is she coming down for dinner?"

"I took a tray up to her; she's still not feeling well. Cara's disappointed that she hasn't been able to meet you yet. But Doctor Symons thought she should stay in bed for now."

"Doctor Symons, Mom?"

"He's filling in for Reyna, Danny, until he gets back after the holidays. I hope you'll enjoy the fried chicken, Britta; it's my specialty."

"It's not common in Germany, but it's delicious. I can see that you're an excellent cook and mother." *I couldn't be a mother to you, special one. It would have ruined everything. Being your daughter's imprinted on my heart forever. If only I could go back.* "I wanted to ask you something, Barbara; it's about the mirror."

"The mirror? Oh, that's right, I almost forgot. We bought the antique mirror from you. Strange that you should ask, Britta. It's downstairs in the storeroom. But it's been a curse—certainly to Cara."

"Oh, I'm sorry. It meant a lot to me in the place where father and I hid. May I see it after dinner, Sarah?"

"Well, I don't understand why you want to, but sure."

7:08 p.m.

Dear Lord, should I go through the door? I have to. Breathe, control your fear; it was long ago. "There it is. Ah, it's broken; half the glass is on the floor. Some of it is scorched. Look at the burns on the jacket and blackened spots on the couch." *See your face in the mirror? No one will look back again. No, whatever happened is finished. Ahh, the old desk in the corner. Think, think, Cara. That's it; the diary's under papers in the bottom drawer. Did she tell you—I'm confused?* "Here it is. Take it upstairs; it'll help fill in the blanks." *Oh, I have to tell someone, release the tension! But how? If only Doctor Sommer could steady me. Maybe Doctor Symons? You could ask Sarah.*

December 22, 1982, 12:19 p.m.

"Thanks for arranging it, Sarah."

"Well, it just so happened, with the holidays, that Doctor Symons has no other appointments for the day. I'm still puzzled about it, though. He can meet with you after seeing Cara. He'll be here around one."

"It must seem odd to you. To be truthful, I've relied on therapy for most of my life."

"I can't imagine—I'm sorry."

"I feel your tenderness, Sarah; for that, I'm grateful. But I need to let it all spill out. No one here is ready to hear it; only someone not involved."

"We don't understand, but whatever you need, dear."

"Thanks, Barbara."

"Oh, there's Davey; he comes to see Cara every day. Davey, please come in. I'd like you to meet someone."

"Sure, Mrs. Corrigan, I didn't see you in the dining room."

"This is my birth mother from Germany, Britta Schumann. Britta, this is Davey Windly, Cara's boyfriend."

Davey, Davey, Davey, so long, it's been so long. Why don't I recognize your face? No, it's too much, Lord. Davey and Aaron will never be part of my life—it hurts too much—the cost, the price! "I'm blessed to meet you, Davey. Thanks for watching over Cara." *I burn to hold him but never will.*

"Nice to meet you too. I'll always watch over Cara. I'm sorry, but my mother is expecting me, so I have to get home."

4:56 p.m.

"Well, I must say, Miss Schumann, or whoever you are, it's been a most interesting afternoon. And you certainly are an enigma. I can't believe it's been over three hours. I'm sure they're curious, if not concerned, about me being in your room this long."

"I'm sorry for spewing it all out on you, Doctor Symons. I feel better, though, releasing the tension. I hope Sarah and Barbara aren't upset with me. I wanted to make things better, but I'm afraid I've made this impossible situation worse."

"Possibly. You've certainly spun quite a tale—kept me on the edge of my chair all afternoon. Remember, the keyword you mentioned is impossible. You do know that what you've told me could never happen. The implications are baffling, if not frightening. Your story would make a stirring novel but never make the medical journals."

"I never expected you to believe me or acknowledge my life's path. How could you when even I'm still unsure? But thanks for listening, Doctor. I know where I have to go, and it's frightening. I guess I was just looking for confirmation."

"Um, I do wish the best for you, Miss Schumann. And I strongly recommend you continue therapy when you get home. If I may, I have two parting questions. First, making the wild assumption your story is true, would you have sacrificed yourself if you knew the hell waiting for you—the high price?"

"That's what haunts me; I don't know and probably never will. I only hope I still would have had the courage to do it. What else do you want to know?"

"Do you have a plan, a reason for being here?"

"It's complicated, but I do. To accomplish it, though, everything needs to fall in place."

"I won't ask what, but for your sake, I hope it does, Britta."

December 23, 1982, 7:22 p.m.

"Thanks for helping me clean up, Britta. I'd like to call you Mom. Is it okay?"

What can I say? I only want to hold you, Mom, and never let go. It's impossible, totally impossible. Dear God, dear Lord, help! "Of course you can if you think I'm worthy—I've never been sure."

"I've thought about it. The sadness in your eyes breaks my heart. How could I ever blame you for wanting the best life for me? I can only think of the pain if I had to give Cara up and never see her again. Oh, I didn't mean to make you cry. Here, take my hanky this time."

Oh God, if she only knew what she said. I can't do it anymore—can't take it! "Thanks, Mom, hold me."

"What? You called me Mom!"

"Ah, don't mind what I say. I'm having trouble with it all. But I do know that you're a special mother."

"I wish I were, but I've made too many mistakes to qualify. I won't go into it now, but I've deeply hurt Cara and the rest of my family."

"Don't hold it anymore; they've forgiven you." *Oh, Mom, your arms make the sadness go away; I never want to leave them, but I have to.*

"Maybe, except for Brent. I don't know where we go from here, if he'll even be home for Christmas. Do you have to leave in the morning? We thought you'd stay through the holiday."

"It's best for all. I've made my reservation, and Anna expects me for Christmas."

"What's that on your hand, Mom? I've noticed you always keep your hands closed. Why?"

"It's hard to explain, so I try to avoid it by hiding my palms. See the old scarring on both hands. Many years ago, a fire burned them, a horrible experience that I'd like to forget."

"I'm sorry. It's strange—quite a coincidence—that Cara also burned the palms of her hands when Luke attacked her. Did we tell you that, Mom?"

"Ah, I think I heard someone mention it."

"Oh, now I'm crying. I don't want you to leave when we're getting to know each other. When will we see you again?"

"I don't know. Staying will only complicate everyone's lives, but you're always welcome to my home in Stuttgart. I need to go up now and pack—get ready for my early flight."

"Can I ask you something first? It's about my father, what kind of man he was, and why did he abandon you."

"It's not easy to explain, Sarah. But know this; he was a wonderful man that you would have adored. But Aaron had no choice; he had to leave me—fate was against us. It hurts too much to say anymore."

"It's enough, Mom, thanks. I'll see you in the morning."

"No, dear one, I've arranged for a cab to pick me up at six. Please don't get up for me, but let our goodbye be now. I have one request, though; can I see Cara before I leave? I expected to every day but think Doctor Symons is protecting her."

"We all are. I hoped she'd come down for meals, but she needs to stay in her room for now. But, yes, you can talk to her when you go up. I think she's on the phone now. We asked her best friend, Gracie, to call and lift her spirits."

"Thanks. I love you. One last hug?"

"Definitely! I love and forgive you, Mom—goodbye."

Oh Lord, it hurts more than the fires of Ravensbruck to turn my back on the woman I love with all my being, knowing it might be the last time I see her. I'm so conflicted about her; my mind's hazy—all over the place. But now, what do I say to the girl upstairs? Her door's open; she's talking—must be Gracie. Stand in the doorway, so she sees you.

"Oh, Gracie, I think my new grandma is at the door. Hold on a sec. You can come in. Are you Miss Schumann?"

"Grandma or Britta, please, not Miss Schumann."

"Okay. Britta. I've heard the name somewhere but don't remember when. I should—my mind's upside down since Luke attacked me."

Be aggressive now—do it! "Um, you might find it odd, but may I speak to your friend?"

"Ah, why do you want to speak to Gracie?"

"Please! Thanks. Hello, Gracie."

"Oh, is this Cara's grandma?"

You have to be strong, single-minded, with her, for Britta's sake. "Listen, Gee; I've only got a minute to talk."

"Gee! How do you know that? And why are you whispering?"

"I've pulled the phone as far away from her as I can so she can't hear. Just listen, please! I'm Cee, and you're the only one who can help her; the only person that can know."

"What are you saying? I thought Cara was losing it, but you're bonkers!"

"The eighty-sixers are no more. Bee's moved to California, and her beauty has taken Tee from us."

"Oh, my God! But how, how in the world can this be? Only Cee knows those things."

"Remember the scripture, the one from John that I couldn't shake? Greater love has no man."

"Of course I do! Cara thought she could never love like that—didn't have the courage. Ah, I'm struggling to believe it. You're Cee. Wait a minute; you found the courage! You—"

"Yes, I did, I did it, Gracie. And you're the only one who can help her now because I'm leaving tomorrow and don't know if I'll ever return."

"I want to believe you, but how do I know for sure? Remember in second grade when you dared to stand up to Ruth Conklin?"

"Ah, I'm afraid I don't. Are you testing me, Gracie? It's been a long time, and my memories are fading."

"No, I'm not testing you. But it's too much to get my head around, Cara, but I'll do it—help her if I can. So I was talking to Britta? And it was the mirror? Are you positive?"

Oh, Lord, if only I knew for sure. But I don't! My mind is jumping from one thing to the other. Is it tricking me? "Yes, the mirror was the only way, though I never understood how. Britta doesn't know it yet. It might take years for her to come out of the fog and realize who she is. It took me decades to understand. You need to be with her every step of the way and help her along—be her guide. Mom, Danny, or Davey wouldn't understand or believe what happened; it's all up to you, Gee."

"Why can't you stay, Cee?"

"It'll never work. She expected a mom, but my heart's as a daughter. You'll eventually understand."

"But you were only trying to help Britta. You weren't going away for good."

"I had no idea at the time. It's only been a few days for you, Gracie, but I've been gone forty years. I'm not the same, and nothing will be again. I've lived Britta's life, and now she'll live mine. My sacrifice will never end. Take care of her, Gracie. I love you—goodbye. Here's the phone, dear."

"Hold on for a minute, Gracie. Why were you whispering, grandma? What did you say to Gracie?"

"I thanked her for being your friend and taking care of you. Listen to her closely, Cara; she'll help you now and in the future."

"I will. She's my best friend, but what about Mom and Davey? They'll help me too."

"They'll try their best, dear, but Gracie will have the answers when you need them."

"Answers, what answers, grandma? I'm confused; it sounds like you have them already. If so, please tell me."

"Only in time, Cara, when you're ready. I won't be here to help you, though, but Gracie will."

"Why can't you stay?"

"It won't work for any of us. You'll learn one day that I had to go away. But I hope you, Danny, and your mother visit me in Germany. Oh, your hands, all wrapped up. Is the pain any better?"

"No, they hurt all the time!"

"I know, sweetie, see."

"Ah, your palms, they're scarred."

"Yes, from burns, like yours. So I know both the physical pain and the fog that's clouding your mind. It'll get better, though; give it time. Here's something to remember me by, Cara. I've carried it for many years. Someday, you'll know its power."

"Thanks, I know this scripture, the one about laying your life down for a friend. But can people like us do that? I'm confused about everything, Grandma. Can you tell me anything else before you go?"

"Yes, Cara, please listen carefully. I want you to make life an adventure every day. Be joyous, love your family and friends, and be charitable and kind to all. And above all else, live life to the fullest; it's been paid for."

July 9, 1992

I sense this is my last entry, then I'll have nothing else to say. As I reflect on the morning I left Colorado, Sarah's love comforts me. Of course, she got up early to have freshly baked cinnamon rolls and coffee waiting. She sent several with me for the trip to Chicago. We cried until the cab arrived, then hugged and expressed our love. It was such a special moment. Fortunately, my flight left Denver hours before a blizzard closed the airport.

Sarah and Cara came to Stuttgart for a week in 1986; Cara's graduation present. Though awkward at times, we all drew closer. I sensed our goodbyes were final. We correspond, but the letters are infrequent as the years' pass. They have their lives to live. Cara's hands healed, leaving familiar scarring. After the mirror incident, she saw Dr. Reyna for several months but never went to Elmwood. Cara stabilized and, as far as I can tell, has had none of the issues I struggled with for years—thank God.

Davey stayed by Cara's side for several years, but they drifted apart after his family's return to Colorado Springs. She said her feelings for him were never the same after the attack in the basement. Davey married last year. Cara says she's deeply in love with a young man she met last year. Gracie married several years ago and moved to Florida, though she talks to Cara weekly. I pray she'll have the answers for Cara when needed, though now it appears it won't be necessary. Danny's now an engineer working for a large corporation in California. He's still looking for the right woman. Brent never lived with the family again after that holiday season in 1982. He and Sarah divorced in 1983. Sarah struggled with guilt but met a remarkable man two years ago. It sounds like wedding bells are near. My heart breaks for her and Cara every day. Cara said that Luke, Andrea, and Albert served jail time for what they did to her and Davey. Their whereabouts are unknown—good riddance.

I had a long session with Doctor Sommer this afternoon. She soothes my mind, though I'm never sure who's right. I pray she'll never abandon me. I'll always need her. All my doctors have attributed my imaginations to my unusual disorder, admitting that I'm an enigma.

Loneliness haunts me; my nights are endless. Thankfully, Vera returned to Stuttgart after retiring. She works part-time at the orphanage but manages to visit me several times a week. Ortrud visits when she can and calls frequently. What would I do without them?

The cruelty of my perceived sacrifice is evident. I finally had the courage to step off the cliff into the darkness, thinking I would safely land. But I keep falling, knowing I'll never have the firm ground of knowing beneath me. It won't end, and I can't go back. And I'll never know for sure, but I think I did it, I guess I did.

—Britta S.

ABOUT THE AUTHOR

Born in Wray, Colorado, Greg Carson moved with his parents and brothers to Denver in 1953. He attended the University of Colorado before and after his three years in the Army. Greg served in Vietnam from 1966-67. He drifted through various jobs before working for the Colorado Department of Labor, which developed into a successful career. Greg retired in 2003. He enjoyed traveling with his wife, Vivian, fishing, and other outdoor activities. He surprisingly started his new writing career at age 71. Greg currently lives with Vivian in a vibrant Lakewood, Colorado, retirement community.

Other Novels:
Bridge to Somewhere
Bridge Across the Chasm
Bridge Home